Shattered 9

A Sci-Fi Thriller

Gideon Strath

CMB Fiction

Acknowledgements

Special thanks to my former classmates at Trinity College Dublin who graciously lent me their surnames. It was a pleasure killing you in this novel. If you can't kill your friends in a story, who can you kill?

Please, don't answer that.

Contents

Dedication

Thank you for supporting me while I stayed inside on sunny afternoons, wrote sixteen hours a day, and gained as many pounds in the time it took me to complete this novel.

1

Linus

The oscillating pulse of the quarantine light saturated the room in a harsh, putrid green. Surging and fading, the pulse kept time with pumps and machines struggling to keep the child alive. The boy was five, maybe six. He had brown hair and eyes, and tiny bronze freckles dotting his nose and cheeks. Between red, soaked bandages, his fair skin sagged and buckled. A section of discolored flesh sloughed free from his leg and slid onto the gurney's edge. It flopped off the side, adding to the mess spreading across the small room's white floor. He had teetered on the brink of a hideous death for over an hour, but he hadn't cried or said a word.

Chief Linus Halla stood outside the emergency decontamination room, his attention focused on the horror unfolding on the other side of the glass. Not once on the job had he seen a child in radiologic quarantine. Only three people had willingly exited the habs without a rad suit in twenty years. Suicide by scour. A midnight spa treatment. A method so rare and gruesome, it was almost unthinkable. There were far easier, less painful ways to kill oneself. Ways which didn't involve exiting through doors with verified access codes. It was impossible for a child to leave on his own. *Someone, some bastard must have thrown the boy out.* The thought turned his stomach as much as the room's sickly-sweet smell and the sound of the child's warm, wet flesh slapping cold, hard tile.

The way his deputy told the boy's story, it sounded like a formulaic novel taken from the system's archives. A mysterious child pulled from the scour by a dirt-poor, one-ration scrapper digging for copper north of Hab 2. The weathered, old hero in his faded rad suit, dumping his salvage, risking his life to carry a dying boy to safety, arriving at quarantine with mere seconds to spare. Linus scoffed, dismissing his deputy's rendition as overly dramatic.

The scrapper, James Choi, rested comfortably in the next room, having been moments from succumbing to radiation himself. Years of exposure had cut decades deep into his face. Sporadic tufts of frayed, white hair fell limp atop his head, and his sallow skin cracked and peeled around his mouth and sunken eyes. He could have been forty, fifty, or more. Linus guessed sixty. It was impossible to tell with people in his caste. He didn't bother to check, and Choi likely didn't care, either. If it wasn't counted in grams, liters, or meters, a scrapper wouldn't have use for it. Midway through the boy's second hour in quarantine, a handful of fivers had signaled their virtue by pledging a liter to the 'Hero in the Scour'. Sixers responded by pledging another. Everyone else envied the meager wealth or relished in watching the middle classes bicker over who could give more of their money away. Choi might drink new water for the first time in his life. It might even be clear.

Linus released the last seal on his rad suit and pulled his arms from the sleeves, letting the heavy material drape from his waist. Grains of warm, tawny sand fell from a crease at the elbow. Containment fans spun and hissed, vibrating the room as they pulled the sand through perforated vents in the floor. He swiped his wrist across the terminal's copper scanner plate and scrolled through the standard carousel of patient vitals and room environmentals. He glanced over his shoulder at his young deputy leaning against the rear wall of the observation room.

"It doesn't say how many."

Ivan's gaze was focused on the red mess spreading under the gurney.

Linus cleared his throat. "Ivan? Not again." It would've been laughable if it wasn't predictable as daily rounds. *What good's an H.I. deputy who freezes at the sight of blood?*

"Are you listening? Grays, Ivan? Neutron absorption? Hello?" Linus snapped his fingers.

"Right, Chief." He had a noticeable hesitation in his voice. "This whole thing..."

"Focus on the data, not the kid. How many?" He sounded more cantankerous than usual.

"Doc can't be certain," he projected at the terminal's mic, "because those sensors are still on requisition."

"Her estimate?"

"237 years."

"The grays, not the sensors."

"Oh. Sorry." Ivan drew Linus's attention to his hands. "Four grays," he said, but showed five fingers on one hand and three on the other. "Full body. It's the maximum treatable exposure, but she expects BOSS will approve everything."

"I see." He looked at the boy. "What's his name?"

Ivan shrugged. "He's got no ident chip. No prints on file. No retinal. No subdermals."

"The kid's not coded?"

"I re-scanned my own chip to be sure. The kid's a ghost."

"An unsanctioned birth more likely. Don't hold your ration for parents to show. Especially if one or both are also unsanctioned. Anything else?"

"That's it." Ivan stepped toward the glass and crossed his arms. A trio of round, yellow pips on his collar darkened to amber. "What about you? Find anything out there?"

"Sand and a migraine." Linus rolled his shoulders, two loud pops like punctuation marks ending his sentence.

"The usual then." A wide patch of flesh sloughed off the boy's thigh and joined the growing mound on the floor. Ivan grimaced and sucked the air between his teeth. "Have you ever?"

"Unfortunately. You ever hear of Marcus Weber?"

"Sure. Man's lover leaves him for a botanist with two extra rations and a bigger... err... living unit. He donates his last millis to Sisters of Mercy and goes for a midnight spa treatment out a rear airlock. I always thought it was an old hab legend."

"Except it's not. And it was Brothers of Hope."

"Brothers don't accept rations. It was definitely Sisters."

"Whatever. It wasn't pretty."

Ivan moved closer to the barrier. One of four small lights flashed above the door, and the pips on his collar darkened to brown. "Did it look like this?" He pressed his fingertips to the glass. Three lights flashed.

"I think worse. But you'd have to ask Carla. I only saw the leftovers before the bots took him for mineral extraction. Five buckets if memory serves."

Four lights flashed in sequence, and a speaker hissed and crackled. Ivan's pips turned black. He backed away from the glass and covered his crotch with both hands. "DNA trace?"

"While we still can."

***

Habitat integrity was on Level 5 in the original bottom of Habitat 4. Built for cold storage, the room was an over-sized, insulated locker barely larger than scrapper quarters - ten square meters of flaking rust packed with a matching desk, shelving units, two chairs, report tablet, and system terminal. All of it bolted or chained to something else. A single low-power light hung by a frayed wire in the center of the room.

Linus slid the report tablet across the old, pitted desk. "No sense in me doing it." The screen darkened, and he pulled it back. He slammed it against the desk, hitting a shallow dent the same shape as the tablet's edge, reviving the screen from its ill-timed sleep. "But remember to submit everything before last check-in." He tossed it to Ivan.

"Really, Chief. I've been here almost a year. You don't have to tell me every," he slammed the tablet against a similar dent on his side, "single," and hit it again, "time." Its chain clanged against the table's leg. "I could do this job toe-up and gagged."

"Wouldn't that be interesting." Linus leaned in his chair and scratched the bald spot rapidly spreading across the back of his head, pressing rusty grooves into his skin and coloring his graying hair reddish orange. He looked at his dirty fingers and imagined himself a caricature of his father who'd gone toe-up on the worn, rusted floor and woke up a ginger more times than he could count. If Linus were younger, it might've been fashionable to blend into the walls and jagged rocks exposed throughout the habs. To oxidize or not to oxidize? A political question for twenty-somethings, but not for him. He wiped his hand on his sleeve and rubbed the back of his head until he was sure the color had faded. "What's with you? You've seen radiation sickness, what is it, seven, eight times in as many months? You weren't this emotional."

"A broken seal in 3. The tunnel spider in 5. Those scrappers who bet a ration they could run between containment doors. All adults. Nobody, especially a child, should go through that." Ivan passed the tablet to Linus. "Finished. And I'm not being emotional, you heartless parch."

"Don't let BOSS hear you say that." Linus gestured to the terminal. It was his usual bluff. He'd been cutting, fixing, and re-cutting the mic's wires for years, but he'd forgotten to reattach them that morning. And he didn't appreciate being called a dried-out, old codger. That rare pleasure had been reserved for his wife, and she had always made up for it after. Linus often argued with his deputy to see how he'd react, but doing the double-backed rust scrubber on the office furniture afterward was another level entirely. Linus pushed the palm-sized tablet back across and raised his voice so Ivan wouldn't notice he hadn't been fined.

"You missed 6c and d."

"C.O.D. and T.O.D.? The kid's not dead."

"Give it an hour." He looked at the time. "Make that six minutes."

"That's rough. And besides, we should wait for the DNA trace." Ivan dropped the flickering tablet and crossed his arms. "And fill-in 7a."

"The trace will take at least a day in queue, and I want to clear this out before we go." Linus dragged the tablet by its chain. The long, metallic shriek of rusted steel against steel reverberated in the little room, clawing down his back. He shivered, but it was worth the discomfort to see Ivan's eye twitch. He toggled 6c to *Murder via Deliberate Radiation Exposure* and glanced at the terminal screen. He set 6d to *1959 hours* - five minutes ahead and one minute before their last required check-in. "You're wasting your time." He returned it to Ivan. "And mine. If the kid's unsanctioned, the parents will probably be, too. There won't be a next of kin to notify."

Linus gestured toward the terminal, its indicator flashing green.

"That was fast." Ivan got up to check system messages. "Doc must've been first in line." He swiped his right wrist over the copper scanner plate, exchanging the floating time for the user interface.

B.O.S.S. v96.12

BIOSPHERE OPERATIONS SUPPORT SYSTEM

An exaggerated flick of Linus's middle finger scrolled the report screen to the bottom. "Give it to me one ident at a time. Mother first."

"It's not the trace. We're still seventh in line."

"Told you so. Why don't you ever listen to me?"

"It's a prognosis update. You won't believe it."

"I'm sure I will."

"Come here."

"I've seen it all."

"Linus Halla."

"All right, all right," said Linus, annoyed Ivan had begun to sound like his wife. He left his chair and nudged Ivan out of the way. "What's so important?"

<>< ><>< > CONFIDENTIAL <>< ><>< ><>

RECIPIENT_1: HALLA, LINUS H4-SEC-A1

RECIPIENT_2: FINN, IVAN H4-SEC-A2
MEDICAL REPORT: H2-6581-A :: 12.MAY.2637
IDENT: PENDING TRACE ANALYSIS [*7 IN QUEUE]
STATS: BRN / BRN / 38.7 KG / 114 CM / O+ BT
DIAGNOSIS: RADIATION EXPOSURE, 4GY FULL-BODY
CONDITION: STABLE
AUTHORIZATION: LANGSTROM, CARLA H2-MED-A1
COMMENTS: *RECOVERY EXPECTED* <CL>
<><><><><> CONFIDENTIAL <><><><><>

"Recovery expected?" Linus popped his neck. It was something new, and new things were rarely good in the old habs. "I need a drink."

"Only one?"

2

Ivan

A green waste collector bot zoomed through the wide corridor carrying a basket of smashed bottles and bits of plastic and broken aluminum, the rattling scrap a warning to move out of the way or risk a broken toe under its heavy tank treads. Ivan and Linus pushed through the bustling crowd and entered a long corridor lined with VR rooms, food markets, and moist trade parlors carved into the black Baltic granite. X-Stretch - its de facto name - was the best and worst Hab 4, or any habitat, had for public consumption. For a few milliliters of water, sloven twos and other slags went toe-up on gluco and perched in odd poses against cut stone walls, while fours and fives traded whole rations to live desires best reserved for deeper, darker tunnels. Scrappers were too poor, and nobody allocated over six rations would dare be seen so high in the habs. X-Stretch was solid, lower middle-class. And Ivan loved every centimeter of it.

The Pissing Ant - or The Ant if in earshot of a terminal - was a tiny gluco bar nestled at the far end of X-Stretch near a narrow, disused tunnel between Hab 4 and Hab 5. Over the bar's arched door, a shimmering pink ant balanced a massive shot glass on its back and pissed holographic golden glitter on every other customer. The owner dyed gray soyroom chips pink, and chairs streaked colorful swirls on contact with body heat. The hotter the ass, the brighter the seat. It was the worst double entendre in the place. The Pissing Ant raised tacky to an artform.

Thin string lights crisscrossed the space, accenting every line, corner, curve, and edge in the room, pulsing in time with the music. Loud, intense beats vibrated drinking glasses off the edges of tables, bestowed an arrhythmia onto any old parch who got too close, and, thankfully, drowned out the group of rusters and rust-dusters screaming to topple the Ration-caste system and restore equality and freedom of movement. *Equality and Freedom of movement.* Ivan scoffed. *Those concepts are older than the habs.*

Ivan and Linus made for two empty stools at the end. The owner, a brutish man, two meters tall and nearly as wide, poured shots from behind the bar. He pulled two neon blue glasses from under it and sat the cheapest gluco, a bottle labeled *ABBO+ Silver*, between them. Where the bottle and glasses touched, glowing rings encircled the base of each.

"I think we're in the mood to celebrate." Ivan flashed two fingers. "O-neg, the best you've got. None of the cheap, rhesus poz junk."

"Special occasion?"

"Something like that."

"Anything else?"

"You know what I need."

"I'm not psychic. Why don't you tell me?"

Ivan leaned over the bar and kissed his husband, Radek.

"Does that routine ever get old?"

"Never," said Ivan.

"Definitely never," said Radek. "If you're in a good mood, why isn't Linus?"

"Don't let the chief fool you. I mean, look at him. Couldn't be happier."

Radek squinted. "Oh, wait. I see it now. His upper lip is curling slightly to the left. Linus, are you smiling or trying to tongue a mushroom out of your teeth?"

"Funny couple. Can't wait for the divorce."

"Not going to happen."

"Definitely not." Radek peered over their shoulders. "Ut-oh. She's coming."

Linus moaned, "Not again," and slumped forward.

A pair of rough, latex hands reached between Linus and Ivan. "Looking for act- act- action, boys?" said Digi, the unmistakable voice giving the old sapioid away.

Digi was an Alpha, the first model of her kind. At over four hundred years old, she predated the habs and almost everything in them. But unfortunately for her, and everyone around, time had not been kind. The imitation skin, once bright white and clean, had yellowed and stained across much of her body. Large sections had dry-rotted, completely fallen off, or been repaired with fingers and palms cut from blue nitrile gloves and glued over top. Her human controller was either too cheap or broke to use something decent. White LEDs flashed, and tiny servos, gears, and pistons whirled, clicked, and hissed with every movement. Glossy, black hair brushed her shoulders. And she wore a sleeveless beige shirt and thigh-high beige shorts, both cut from standard, one-piece hab overalls.

Ivan rolled his eyes, but he had to admire her tenacity. Sapioids had been defunct since long before he was born. Most fragged their CPUs and mindlessly paraded into the scour. Some disappeared. Others had been dismantled, their appendages repurposed as prosthetic limbs. The few left intact fought as bare, alloy skeletons in sapioid pits, ran errands during the day, or peddled moist trade in X-Stretch at night. This particular Digi was moist trade every time he saw her.

Digi stroked Linus's forearm. Tiny, warped gears clicked and slipped inside her knuckles, causing her fingers to tremble. "The name's Digi. Alpha three nine one. Moist and mild, or wet and wild. You decide. All you want for a milli a min- min- minute."

"Tell Jeda I'm not that desperate."

"What about you?" She turned to Ivan. Her soulless black eyes sparkled with tiny blue and gold specks. She tilted her head and stroked the red ankh stamped under her ear. "Help a poor girl out?"

"You mean help your sleazy controller? No thanks."

"Are you sure about that?"

Her breasts deflated, and an Adam's apple pressed out from beneath the latex at the neck. Wrinkles appeared around the eyes. Her hair retracted above the ears and turned white, and the jawline became square but soft. "I know you're into older men." Her voice deepened to a low rumble. "I could be the Digi of your dreams. All you need is a milli a minute."

Ivan snickered. "I'm spoken for. And I'm not into old men. No offense, Linus."

"None taken." Linus leaned into him. "You know it's not too late to strip her thorium cells."

"I heard that," said Digi. "I'm beginning to think you don't like me."

"Was I being obvious?"

Ivan glanced down. "Poor, old Digi. Your servos are showing."

"You should feel my piston." She grabbed his wrist and pressed his hand to her crotch.

Ivan jerked his hand off the comically large bulge.

"Don't be shy." She rubbed his forearm. "We're family after all."

"He said he's taken." Radek poured two shots of gluco and slid them toward her.

"Leave us alone." Linus pushed her hand off his shoulder. "Shouldn't you be on a scrap heap or unclogging drains somewhere?"

Digi's voice climbed an octave as she reverted to female. "That's not how a gentleman should speak to a lady."

"I'm not a gentleman, and you're not a lady."

"Or a man," said Ivan.

"Are these expensive?" She grabbed the two shots and tossed them back. "Shame I can't feel them. 'Toe-up' sounds like a," she moaned, rubbing her breasts, "oh-so-moist date to me." She became a male, looking slightly more pleasant than Linus, and sauntered toward more gullible patrons at the back of the room.

"Every. Single. Night." Ivan chuckled. "I'm glad you always give her the cheap stuff."

"Digi will drink anything, but I'm going to start putting it on Jeda's tab if he doesn't stop sending her in here. Every night for over a month," Radek's voice shot up an octave. "You know she's been stealing my soyroom chips?"

"It's not her fault. Jeda's pulling the strings."

"I wish he'd pull them somewhere else."

Ivan sighed. "Poor Digi. It's not easy being a glitchy, old whore."

Linus tapped his empty glass on the counter. "Before I die?"

"Yah-yah, mulkku." Radek's brow furrowed. "Hold the ration you," he said, sliding into exaggerated scrapper pidgin. "Top shelf O-neg here." He traded the old, cheap bottle for a new one and tore the foil seal. "Toxin nada. Rhesus nada. Donor sixteen three month last. Severe hyperglycemic." He poured until the liquor domed over the brims. "Blood sugar like trek'n rockets. Perfect for ferment." He sat the bottle of translucent, red liquor on the bar. "Get toe-up in two. Lock pulser, Parch. No sip-sip pop-pop hoy, k?" Radek pointed at a square plate welded to the ceiling above his head. "Fix two day, two ration."

"That pulse dart cost four. And the requisition took a month."

"That's enough," said Ivan. "Both of you, stop trying to one-up each other. And babe, speak flat if you can't speak pidg."

"Since when are you a lingua purist?"

"As long as you've been a scrapper."

"I may not be a scrapper, but I can find *all* the important parts." Radek winked at him.

"Luoja auta." Linus tossed back both their shots and poured two more.

Ivan shooed Radek away. "He's just trying to cheer you up. Give the man a bone."

Linus rolled his eyes.

"No pun intended. I swear. But you have to admit, you've been tense." He sipped his gluco. "To put it mildly."

Linus swigged a shot and dragged the bottle across the bar.

"How many are you planning to drink?"

"Three hundred."

"Three hundred?" Ivan paused. "Ahh, days." He threw back the shot. "Pour me another."

Ivan raised his glass, dripping gluco on the underlit counter. "To Katri Halla. Long may her water flow through you."

"Long may it flow through us all." Linus took the shot and poured himself another.

Ivan knocked back his and swirled a finger in the drops of spilt liquor. "I was thinking."

"I was lucky." Linus stared into his empty glass.

Ivan filled it. "She was a good woman. I wish I'd known her longer." He swigged the shot.

Linus downed two more. "I listen to her sometimes. You know, she kept journals since she was a little girl?"

"I wish you wouldn't. It's not doing you any good."

"Wish. Wish." He knocked back two more. "All our wishes locked in rusted, steel boxes, waiting for keys of bent and broken dreams."

"Not his best work if you ask me." Ivan counted the shot glasses. "And I didn't realize it was already time for poetry."

"You were saying something?"

"I was thinking abou—"

"A dangerous pursuit."

"Let me finish, or I'll tell Radek what 'Luoja auta' means. He might send Brothers of Hope *and* Sisters of Mercy to your door this time."

"You wouldn't."

"Try me, old man."

"Whatever."

"I was thinking about the kid."

"You shouldn't. He's not going to li," he hiccuped, "live."

Bottles clinked together under the counter as a slight tremor passed through the bar. Ripples radiated across Ivan's drink, breaking the placid surface. He was chin deep in gluco flow where the tiniest ripples crashed like waves, and all his problems vanished beneath the crimson ebb. He licked his lips. "He's a kid. I have to believe he'll be okay."

"Birds and bees, rain, and," he hiccuped, "and," he hiccuped again, "and something. What was I saying?"

"I've no idea."

"Yeah. Impossi- impossible things. Doc's good, but she's popped a ration on this one. Nobody survives," he glared at the terminal behind the bar and further lowered his voice, "eight grays." He cleared his throat. "Most people don't survive four. You're wasting your time." He threw back another. "Donate a few millis to Sisters of Mercy if it makes you feel better, but don't save water for the dead. They never come back."

"Everything bueno?" Radek sat a bowl of pink soyroom chips on the bar.

"Just discussing a case." Ivan jostled the chips. "Do you have any of those beet-flavored ones in the back?"

"Beet flavor? I'm not sure."

Ivan tapped the bowl on the counter.

Radek pursed his lips. "But I guess I should check."

"Would you mind? Thank you, Dear."

"Yah-yah."

Ivan leaned into Linus. "They don't make beet flavor."

"You're the devil. You know that, right?"

"That's why you like me."

"Indeed."

"And why you'll ask BOSS to upgrade my quarters."

"Don't press your luck, Beelzebub." Linus emptied the bottle into his shot glass. "Did you hear the one about the guy who had sex every hour?"

"Again?" Ivan groaned. "What about him, Linus?"

"He had to quit because, because it was becoming a fucking habit." Linus cackled. "Get it? Fucking habit." He slapped the bar, rattling the glasses and bottles hidden behind it.

Ivan glanced at the terminal, *No demerits*, and listened to the music blaring from speakers mounted every half meter across The Ant's ceiling. He grinned and patted Linus on the back. "I get it. I wish I didn't. But, I get it."

They swigged their shots together.

Radek returned empty-handed. "Is he going to be okay?"

"He's fine. Toe-up to heaven, but fine. Aren't you, Linus?"

"Oh, and we're out of beet."

Linus snorted, spraying gluco out both nostrils.

"Sure he is." Radek shook his head. "Just warn me before he lies on the floor, okay?"

Ivan and Radek's quarters were in the middle of a tunnel reserved for Integrity, Medical, and Maintenance personnel, stretching from Hab 2 to Hab 5, two levels above the integrity office and three above the platinum vein - a galvanized aluminum air duct on Level 6's ceiling. It was an imaginary line separating the lower middle-class threes and fours from the upper middle-class fives and the super-rich, soaking in fifteen daily liters far below. The better your genes, the higher the ration, the deeper you lived, and the less imaginary those lines became. Level 3 was the lowest in the habs Ivan could live. If he were Chief, Level 4.

He closed his eyes and inhaled the moist, warm air blowing from three parallel slits in the ceiling. It had been scrubbed of CO_2 by a multitude of metal-organic frameworks, sodium hydroxide filters, and synthetic membranes, but somehow it smelled of ozone, iron, and mushrooms. He bit into his soy loaf, gulped, and licked his lips. *Plus the added zing of copper castoff.* He burped. "Bleh."

"What?"

"Nothing, babe."

"So?" Radek squeezed the tube of grayish brown protein paste over his soy loaf and slathered it across with his finger. He sat beside Ivan, dropping his plate on the table. "Are you going to tell me, or do I have to guess?"

"What makes you think there's something to tell?"

"Because you look like a slag."

A single, soft chime sounded from the terminal in the corner, and Radek's fine scrolled down the screen in bright, white letters.

SPEECH CODE 12C [PROFANITY]: -50 ML DEMERIT

The warning was a familiar one, BOSS's not-so-subtle way of reminding everyone it was always there, listening, 'helping' to keep the peace.

"While on the other hand, you look radiant as usual."

"That's because I drink your rations when you're not looking."

"My husband. The funny one."

"So, you gonna tell me?"

"I'm not supposed to talk about cases before they're solved."

"Game time." He rubbed his chin. "Let me see. Let me see. BOSS assigned you a new case. It's a bad one."

"Too obvious." Ivan grabbed Radek's ration pouch and drank from the outlet. The water level dropped from *800 mL* to *750 mL*.

"Someone's dead."

Ivan sipped again. *700 mL.*

"Not dead. Alive, but sick. Very sick. Almost dead kind of sick."

Ivan scowled. "Also obvious, but I'll let you have it."

Radek grabbed Ivan's pouch and held it so Ivan could see the water fall from *500 mL* to *400 mL*. He licked his lips. "Delicious. Freshly bombarded hydrogen and oxygen." He held the murky water to the light. "With electrolytes."

Ivan showed a tepid grin.

"Radiation poisoning."

Ivan nodded, and Radek sipped. The water fell to *300 mL*.

"But not any 'ole person. Those toe-up scrappers didn't upset you this much." Radek thought for a moment. "It's got to be a kid."

Ivan nodded. Radek sipped. The water level teetered on the *200 mL* line.

"You're playing this game." Radek looked up to nothing in particular. "So, I'd say he got one full gray."

Ivan arched an eyebrow, and his hand creeped over the table toward Radek, fingers like little, fleshy legs carrying the rest of his arm forward. He slid Radek's pouch across, opened the outlet tube, and took a long, slow sip. The water level descended.

700 mL, 650 mL, 600 mL, 550 mL

"Not fair. Slow down."

Ivan smiled but continued.

"Okay. Two grays."

500 mL... 450 mL...
"Three grays."
400 mL... 350 mL... 300 mL...
"Four grays?"

Ivan stopped and stood the pouch in front of Radek, the sloshing water settling on the *150 mL* line. He held up eight fingers.

"Eigh-?"

Ivan stuffed the loaf into Radek's mouth, smearing the brown paste across his nose. He nodded at the terminal in the corner. "You know it won't approve treatment over four."

"I don't think it cares about scrappers either way." Radek wiped the paste off his nose. "But I'm glad it approved treatment for," he held up eight fingers, "four grays. I wish you'd find a better job. How about farming? You'd like that. Cool caves and shorter hours. Kinky, green vinyl lab coats. No secrets, and most especially, no dead bodies. Well, except those recycled for soil."

"That's a first retirement job."

"Then how about plant geneticist? Botanist?"

"Those are the same, and you know my numbers aren't high enough."

"Genetic viability and intelligence quotients aren't everything, Ivy."

"I hate it when you call me that." Ivan yawned. "BOSS wouldn't allow it anyway."

"You never know. And speaking of..."

"Approval?" Ivan perked up. "Please, tell me we got it."

Radek knocked over his ration pouch. The soft PVC flopped and slapped against the hard table, spilling water over it. Ivan squeezed his. Blue tick marks down the long edge stretched and warped into unfamiliar shapes.

"Easy there." Radek exchanged the pouch for his hand. "We'll apply again next month."

"Will we?" Ivan looked at his husband. "What was the code this time?"

"Same. 4-21A for my ALS."

"And mine?"

Radek rubbed his thumb across Ivan's wedding ring. "There's always divorce. You could find someone else."

"I'm sure your mother would love that." He mimicked Radek's mother's raspy, disapproving tone. "You could finally settle down with an 'appropriate partner with a higher ration'. Then I could apply for three more years, only to be denied for 7-9L instead."

"That's 9-7L, Deputy Finn." He laughed. "Aren't you supposed to have those codes memorized by now?"

"Over twenty-eight. Outside breeding age. You know what I mean."

"Hey. I don't judge. If you're secretly huffing rust cleaner with hab slags up on one, more power to you. Stick it to BOSS, I say."

SPEECH CODE 12C [PROFANITY]: -50 ML DEMERIT

"Screw BOSS."

SPEECH CODE 12C [PROFANITY]: -50 ML DEMERIT

Ivan scowled. "How about saying 'bless'? We're down a liter this week."

"Kill it with kindness. Sounds familiar." Radek smiled. "So divorce?"

"Never. I'm afraid you're stuck with me, Mr. Finn. Come ration..."

"Or radiation."

3

Linus

L inus pushed ahead of Ivan, elbowing his way through the crowded thoroughfare on mid-morning rounds. In the four hours since first check-in, Linus watched a drunken brawl between a scrapper and a waster and lost a full ration to Ivan for betting on the scrapper. He cleared three geologists' bodies for recycling, killed when a terminal overloaded in their lab. He judged it an accident and returned the case to Medical. And he received and summarily dismissed a scrapper's fantastical report of a hundred thousand missing rations as if the old parch thought either charity or Linus could reimburse his delusion. All in all, a typical Saturday morning.

Next stop was Sisters of Mercy, responding to a vague request for an in-person meeting. From the Habitat Integrity office, it was the same route as always. Take a left out the door, straight two hundred meters, take a right at a public waste extractor, then two lefts, enter the lift, exit one level down, turn right out the door, cross into Habitat 3, turn left, take another lift up three levels, turn right, another left, and straight ahead at the dead end of another excessively long corridor. Along the right wall, the Sisters had painted a mural depicting dozens of animals following an old man, two-by-two into a large boat, storm clouds overhead, heavy rain saturating the ground. The scene had been painted over and over, hundreds of times, colorful layers upon layers flaking and falling onto the corridor's floor as if the rust were the rain.

Water from the sky? That'd be the day.

Linus swiped his wrist over the terminal outside the door. Its speaker chimed twice.

HALLA, LINUS H4-SEC-A1
CHECK-IN REGISTERED AT 1159 HRS
TERMINAL: H3:L3:U621:ST3353
NEXT CHECK-IN AT 1600 HRS

Ivan swiped, but there were no chimes, no registered check-in. He swiped twice more. Nothing happened. He swiped again, and again nothing. The screen flickered and shut off. "BOSS, don't glitch on me, now."

"Chip's got to be within a centimeter."

"I'm trying. It's not letting me. BOSS," he massaged his wrist against the scanner, "do you hear me? It's me, Ivan Finn." He shook the terminal. "This is not the time to go deaf."

"Hit it already."

"Come on." He slammed his wrist on the scanner, knocking more rust off the mural beside it. Its speaker chimed twice.

FINN, IVAN H4-SEC-A2
CHECK-IN REGISTERED AT 1201 HRS
TERMINAL: H3:L6:U316:ST3353
NEXT CHECK-IN AT 1600 HRS

"Told you. BOSS likes it up close and personal."

Ivan rubbed his wrist. "Thank God."

"As a matter of policy," said Sister Oni, greeting Ivan with a smile. The elderly nun wore basic hab overalls, beige, plain and drab, and standard issue black boots. A large white head-scarf covered her hair, the two ends knotted under her chin. The rest draped over her shoulders, and a long, glass rosary and rusted, steel cross hung from her neck.

"Sister Oni," said Ivan, his scowl turning into a smile.

"It's good to see you, Dear." She hugged him and jumped back. "Child, you're nothing but bones and attitude. Are you eating well enough?"

"Do you mean soy, mushrooms, and protein paste? Or mushrooms, protein paste, and soy?"

"There's that attitude." She hugged him again. "Problems with that terminal? Do you want me to call someone?"

"Don't worry about it. It's never liked me. I don't see why today should be any different."

"Morning, Sister." Linus nodded.

"Chief." She returned the nod, her wispy voice suddenly flat and blunt. She turned back to Ivan and smiled up at him. "How's integrity? How's Radek? How's your arm?" She took Ivan by the left hand. "It's this one, isn't it?"

"It is. And everything's well. Couldn't be better. Yourself?"

Sister Oni led them into a room the size of a medical bay, twenty times the size of his office. Instead of gurneys and little rooms sectioned by white sheets, this was a school, church, and orphanage all in one. Soft mats covered the floors, and plastic tubs lined the walls on either side overflowing with little metal men and colorful robots, plush toys, plastic fruits, vegetables, flowers, insects, and animals. Stacks of tablets programmed with children's picture bibles filled the shelves at the rear. A system terminal in the corner played a counting song on repeat. And the room smelled of ozone ever present in the habs.

"You know how it is. It's tough. So tough. These kids will be the death of me."

"That bad?"

She grinned. "But what a marvelous end it will be."

"You scared me for a moment. Where are the new kids? I wanted to show them my arm trick."

"Don't you dare, Mister." She laughed. "I have enough children screaming in my ears as it is. And they're in class, so no funny business." She gestured to a large, rectangular window situated in the wall above a children's table set. "Have a look."

Seven boys and girls sat in a semi-circle facing a terminal, listening to a lesson on how fish, insects, and animals used to look - other than the usual hab spiders, roaches, beetles, and rats found in every hab, on every level, and in tubes of protein paste. A blond boy with oddly large ears stuck a finger up his nose and pulled it out, looked at the tip, and inched it toward the cheek of the girl sitting beside him. Sister Oni tapped on the window and gave him a stern look. The boy rolled his eyes, put his hands in his lap, and shifted his attention back to the terminal. A grainy picture of a green grasshopper moved across the screen. He seemed to like that.

She turned away, her livid expression easing into a calm smile. "Gotta keep a close eye on that one. He reminds me of someone I once knew. But instead of an arm, it's both his ears."

"I thought they looked a bit large."

"Oh, you."

"Why are there only seven?"

"They're all the strays we've found this year. I've heard some chilling rumors lately, so I don't know if the reduction's good or bad."

"Why isn't Sister Isabella in there? Is she napping in the back room again?"

"Sister Isabella's retired."

"She's already retired. You're all retired."

"Second retirement, Dear. She's in hospice. Been there a couple weeks now. I'd planned on telling you, but it must've slipped my mind when you canceled our dinner last month. We understand, though. You're a big man now. Running across the habs, catching the bad guys. No time for charity. No time for the women who raised you."

"I'm sorry. I didn't mean—"

"Ivan, Sweetheart, I'm not serious. Such a guilty conscience, you have. Keep faith, hope, and charity in your heart. Anger and guilt have never served you." She glared at Linus. "And they make people do a lot of terrible things."

"Uh-huh," grumbled Linus.

"Then she's okay?"

"I'm sorry, Child. It's true. She's forgotten where she is and all of her Sisters. Her mind comes and goes, but she still remembers you. The other day, she called me by name, asked me to find that arm of yours. Thought you'd hidden it under Sister Holly's pillow again. I told her I'd look for it and give you an earful. And do you know what she said to me?"

"What?"

"Who are you?" Sister Oni cackled. "Lord, that woman. It'd serve me right if she were faking again."

"Do you need any help with her? How are donations?"

"We're doing well. Brilliantly, in fact. Truth be told, I've missed you, Sweet Child. But that's not why I messaged. Please..." She sat precariously on a stool far too small and low to the floor for anyone over the age of three to be comfortable. "Take a seat."

"Now, what's this suspicious activity you mentioned?" said Linus.

"Strangely enough, it's about the rations. I've never seen so many donations come in at once. I noticed a slight increase about a month ago, and suddenly yesterday, it's like the Lord himself dumped a bucket of water on my head."

"That's good, isn't it?"

"Without a doubt. Several came in with a set-aside for James Choi and the little boy he brought in. How is he, by the way?"

"The boy?" said Ivan. "The last I heard, Doc was expecting a full recovery."

"A miracle. And Mr. Choi?"

"No word of him since quarantine."

"Sister Holly messaged him to come by, collect the rations from the donation center in Habitat 4. But as far as I know, he hasn't picked them up."

A tremor passed through the room, followed by a series of quiet, yet rapid, high-pitched dings, like metal pipes gently tapping one another. Linus looked around and found the sound coming from a hollow steel crucifix rattling against the wall above his head.

Sister Oni paused, noticing the tremor and the sound.

Linus expected the next words out of her mouth to be something about the crucified steel Jesus singing on the cross and how Linus, having avoided church for exactly 301 days, might enjoy listening to BOSS play one of the ninety-seven uplifting hymns in its database. He had no intention of being uplifted. "So what's the problem?"

"Between James Choi and the boy, we've received thirty-six rations. Each one marked as a donation for Mr. Choi, James Choi, scour guy, scrapper hero, the scour boy, or another obvious derivation. That's how we know who to hold it for, or where to send it in the boy's case. None of those were anonymous of course. People want others to see how generous they are. Not very humble, but if it wets dry lips, who am I to judge? Anyway, we received over a thousand more rations marked 'donations for' and then numbers and letters."

"Numbers and letters?" said Ivan. "No names?"

"Like codes. Donation for 123ABC and something or other." She pulled a three centimeter steel rectangle out of her pocket and handed it to Ivan. "See what I mean."

Ivan held the rusted plate and rubbed his thumb across the numbers scraped into the surface. "39Q-4HT-121." He gave it to Linus.

"We had no idea what it meant until a week ago. A young woman stopped at the center and passed that to Sister Holly."

"Interesting," said Linus. "What did this young woman look like?"

"Fair skin. Petite. Wore a headscarf like mine. Sister Holly said she never looked up. She took delivery and disappeared without saying another word."

"How many rations?"

"Fifty fresh and full."

"Oh my God," said Ivan.

"My exact words." She closed her eyes, "Sorry," and squeezed her rosary. "We were concerned, but it was only the one woman. We decided to wait, see who came to get the other thousand. Then last night, four large men came to the center together with similar notes and withdrew five hundred rations. This morning, four different men, five hundred more. I thought it sounded like the thing those gang-types do."

"Ration bouncing," said Linus.

"You were right to message me," said Ivan.

"Why didn't Sister Holly refuse?"

"Refuse to give a thousand rations to eight men a quarter her age and triple her size? Chief Halla, are you an elderly nun doing the Lord's work, helping the unsanctioned, providing them with food, water, medicine?"

"Obviously not."

"At least we can agree on something."

"I'm wondering why you messaged Ivan. You know H.I. doesn't investigate anything unless there's a victim of violence. Ration bouncing is fraud, and it's not in our jurisdiction."

"Fraud is a lie. And aren't lies simply violence to Truth?"

"Against the system, against BOSS. Not against a real human victim. Unless you suspect someone was assaulted or murdered for those rations?"

"I don't suspect anything at all. That's your job. I'm telling you what I know. And I don't know anyone who'd donate a thousand fifty rations to only a handful of people."

"Then I suggest you forward your concerns to the Food Crimes department."

"Ivan?" said Sister Oni, pleading.

"Chief means to say we can't promise anything, but we'll do what we can. Chief?" Ivan cleared his throat.

"You, too?"

"Chief."

"Fine then. If any more numbered donations come in or something happens to Sister Holly, call us immediately. No system messages. A direct call. Okay? We'll take it from there. That's all I can do."

Sister Oni nodded.

"It's settled. Now, excuse us. We have rounds." Linus walked away, and stopped at the door. "Ivan, you coming?"

"Be right there. Sorry, Sister. He means well."

"You don't apologize for wayward sheep." She patted his arm. "You bring them back home."

"Ivan."

"Coming, Chief."

4

Ivan

Ivan ran out the door and matched Linus's pace in the wide, painted hall. Linus could be rude, often cold or dismissive, but he'd only gnash his teeth until they squeaked around nuns in white head scarves. Sister Oni being his usual cause of distress. He stopped in the corridor and leaned against the wall next to a terminal.

"You don't have to be rude to her every time. And she had a point about the rations."

"I do, and I know. Helix or Oxi trying new ways to move protection money or bribes around the habs."

"Then why the cold shoulder?" Ivan passed his wrist over the scanner plate.

"Doesn't matter. Sand on the dunes."

"Not if *your* sand's blowing in *my* face." Ivan opened the priority messages folder. "I keep praying you'll let it go before we darken her door again and she starts blaming me."

"In less than a month, I'll be in first retirement bliss and you can deal with her."

"I'm not sure if 'deal' is the right word."

"At least Sister Isabella had a good sense of humor." Linus coughed and rubbed his throat. "Water?"

The dispensary was bustling as hundreds queued in twenty long rows, each behind a ration terminal. They swiped their wrists over copper scanners, tapped the screen, and took however many pouches BOSS dropped at their feet. A woman, her lips dry and cracked, skin sallow, hair black, collapsed in line. Nobody in queue risked losing their place, and they let the woman stay where she fell. The next man in line stepped over her body when his turn was up. Two dispensary crew dragged her off to the side, the man withdrew a ration, and the line progressed one citizen further.

Ivan wiped the sweat off his forehead as the man in front of him turned and shoved a thin, rusted plate in his face. He was younger and shorter, with blonde, rust-dusted hair, and one green eye. The other was closed and sewn over. "This is slag shit."

The terminal chimed.

SPEECH CODE 12C [PROFANITY]: -50 ML DEMERIT
SPEECH CODE 12C [PROFANITY]: -50 ML DEMERIT

"Drown..." Ivan read the slogan and shook his head. "Not here, man. Water not politics. Put it away. You're going to cause a scene."

He raised the plate over his head and turned in a slow circle, chanting the slogan scratched into its surface. "Drown it. Dry it. Break it. End the Ration-caste system."

BEHAVIOR 88H [SUBVERSION]: -15 L DEMERIT

"Drown it. Dry it. Break it. End the Ration-caste system."

BEHAVIOR 88H [SUBVERSION]: -15 L DEMERIT

"Drown it. Dry it. Break it. End the Ration-caste system."

BEHAVIOR 88H [SUBVERSION]: -15 L DEMERIT

"Drown it. Dry it. Break it. End the Ration-caste system."

BEHAVIOR 88H [SUBVERSION]: FUNDS ERROR

"Stop." Ivan yanked the plate out of his hand. He dropped it on the floor and stepped on it. "That was for your own good."

"Give it up," said Linus. "It doesn't care, and you're out of rations."

The rust-duster gritted his teeth and shook his head. He yelled louder, "Drown it. Dry it. Break it. End the Ration-caste system."

COUNTERMEASURE [100X]: 25 MILLIAMPERES

He grabbed his wrist and growled at the terminal. "Drown it. Dry it. Break it. End the Ration-caste system."

COUNTERMEASURE [100Y]: 50 MILLIAMPERES

He heaved and vomited. "Drown it. Dry it. Break it. End the Ration-caste system."

COUNTERMEASURE [100Z]: 200 MILLIAMPERES

His jaw clenched, and his eyes rolled back. He fell to the floor and didn't say anything else. The dispensary crewmen dragged him to the side and laid him by the woman. The man's fines faded off the screen, and the interface cleared and reset.

Linus shook his head and stepped to the terminal. He swiped his wrist across the scanner and withdrew a half ration from his account. The slender pouch fell from an opening in the terminal's front panel and landed on his boot, sloshing the warm, grayish-brown water. He grabbed the pouch and tucked it into his uniform. "Don't let it get to you."

"I can't believe he didn't stop. Why didn't he stop?"

"You know these ruster types." Linus looked at the man's body. "They all think they're martyrs for the cause. But take a look around." He gestured toward the crowd. "Nobody will shed a tear because they don't want to waste the water." He moved aside, letting Ivan swipe at the terminal. "If he really cared, he would've given one of those forty-five to her and called it a good day. But instead, he chose to do that to himself."

"Too dramatic for you?" Ivan withdrew a ration, and the system messages dialog appeared. "I don't agree with the method, but he wasn't wrong. This is," he eyed the terminal's cubical mic, "not good." He opened the folder and tapped the newest one.

"System message?" Linus looked over his shoulder. "Where's BOSS sending us next?"

"X-Stretch."

"BOSS wants me to drink?" He glanced at the stacked bodies. "It knows me too well. But it's still too early for gluco. Even for me." He rubbed his neck. "I'm still trying to determine which one of you I'm talking to."

"There's something happening with poor, old Digi. It says she's gone haywire. She's smashing up the place."

"I told you we should've stripped her thorium cells."

"I'm sure you would've."

"Let's get over there before she goes into The Ant."

They found the old bot talking to herself, pacing and stomping on broken bottles and LED bulbs a meter outside The Pissing Ant, receiving a holographic golden shower each time she changed direction. A crowd had gathered at the scene, watching Digi glitch from a reasonably safe distance. They laughed and pointed as the sapioid alternated between female, male, and something in between. Her infamous piston rose and fell, breasts grew and shrank, and one moment her Adam's apple was there, then it wasn't. She was acting like an old mechanical clock rapidly ticking its life away.

It was hilarious, but Ivan suppressed his smile. Linus didn't. Had it been any other place or sapioid, he might've laughed, too. But there were more expensive bottles of gluco in the bar, and Digi, though frequently vulgar and annoying, provided a sense of stability and, occasionally, much needed comic relief.

Linus waved his pulser in the air, cleared his throat, and charged the weapon, releasing a high-pitch squeak and click. It was a useful tool, encouraging the crowd to part and let them through to the center. He aimed at her. "Digi?"

She turned, hands shaking and stopped in her tracks.

"There you go. That's a good Digi. Calm down, and tell me what's wrong. Where's Jeda Pringle? Where's your controller?"

"What's wrong? Where's Jeda?" said Digi.

"That's right. Tell me what's wrong. Maybe Jeda and I can fix it."

She laughed, "Fix it, he says," and continued pacing. She picked a broken bottle off the floor.

"Put the glass down. Digi, listen to me. Put it down."

"So lovely." She held it up to the only light she hadn't ripped out of the ceiling. Thick, crimson gluco, wet on the glass, cast a dark shadow across her face. She picked up another. "The color. Do you see it? Like the sun in my hands. Warm. So warm." She pulled it to her chest, cutting through her shirt, slicing into her imitation skin.

"Digi?"

"Let me try?" Ivan nudged past him. "Hey, Digi. Do you remember me? A milli a minute? Feel my piston?"

Someone in the crowd burst out laughing.

She picked up another and held the three shards together in her hands. "So, so sweet. The morning dew. The morning sun. It's always morning. Never dark. Why is it always morning?"

"Digi, it's afternoon now. The morning's over. In a few hours, it'll be night. No more sunlight."

"Always mor- mor- mor- morning." Digi held them up to the light. "Why is it always morning?"

"She's burned her last qubit." Linus charged his pulser and unlocked the safety. "That's a fragged CPU if I ever saw one."

"Always morning." She looked past Ivan, past Linus, and past the crowd and stared, wide-eyed, down the corridor. "Always the same. Always one spot. Always one." She dropped the shards on the floor and paced, crushing them under her alloy skeleton's weight. "It'll never work. Not with the same. Try again, and again, and again, and again. Why won't it work?"

"Try what again?" Ivan raised his hands and walked toward her. "What won't work?"

"Time's running out. Need more spots. Not enough spots."

"Can you at least get her to move into the bar, somewhere we can contain her?"

Ivan moaned. *Radek's going to kill me.* "Digi? Do you want to go into The Ant? I'll buy you shots of gluco, and I'll pay you a milli a minute for your company."

"Petals all the same."

"What petals? What are you talking about? I don't understand."

"So yellow, so bright, so sweet. All the same. One spot on each." She picked up another larger, curved shard and held it up to the light. "No. They can't be the same. Won't abide. Won't abide." Digi screamed, hurling the shard over the crowd. It shattered against the corridor's long wall, raining a thousand fragments onto their heads.

Everyone gasped and took a collective step back.

"Calm down, Digi. Let's get a drink. We can go together. You, me, and Linus."

She grabbed two more, "Take him," and threw one against the wall.

"Enough, Digi," yelled Linus. "We aren't going anywhere. Now, drop the shard."

"Enough. Enough. It's not enough."

"I'm warning you, Digi." Linus took aim. "Ivan, get away from her."

Ivan backed off. "Digi, please. Listen to Linus."

She looked at Ivan and squeezed the glass, slicing into her quivering hand. "Too many people. Too many voices." She raised the shard and drew her hand back.

Ivan ducked, and three pulse shots popped in rapid succession. Ivan looked up to see Digi go limp. She dropped the glass and collapsed onto the floor, legs bent at the knees to one side, eyes open, looking into the light.

Linus helped Ivan off the floor. "You all right?"

"Yeah. I thought I was reaching her. I don't know what happened. But you didn't have to shoot."

"Fragged CPU. It was the only thing I could do."

"She was going to throw it at the wall."

Linus shrugged. "At least now we can drink in peace."

Ivan looked over the corpse. *Or a damaged sapioid?* He couldn't decide how to think of her now Digi's life, her functions, had ended. Who had she been? Who had she known? And what had she seen over four centuries under the domes? It didn't seem fair a sophisticated machine and an advanced A.I. would terminate as a low-rent whore, glitching out in a filthy corridor in the seediest part of town. "What do you think she was seeing? Yellow petals and spots?"

"Input recognition or cognition system failure. It could've been anything. BOSS's data archives, a jumbled hodgepodge of everything she ever saw, or nonsensical garbage. Jeda's never done a good job maintaining her systems."

The crowd drew closer and gawked at Digi, randomly spasming on the floor, shooting sparks from three holes in the two thorium power cells under her breastplate.

Linus strolled into The Pissing Ant.

"What are you doing? We can't leave her on the floor."

"Thorium cells are damaged. If Jeda doesn't claim her, collector bots will dump her in the recycler." He dusted a white hot spark off his pant leg and scratched at the burnt hole it left behind. "I'm ready for our drink, now. You coming or not?"

Ivan pulled her eyelids closed, "Poor, old Digi," and joined Linus in the bar.

5

Linus

Linus gasped, waking to find his quarters unexpectedly bright, coppery gluco still coating his tongue. He yawned and stretched and rolled onto his back. His spine realigned, popping three times, each with a groan to accompany it. He pressed his palms into his eyes, but it was futile. The inept attempt summoned a cavalcade of early-morning floaters and a vague memory of making rust angels on The Pissing Ant's floor. He squinted at the terminal in the corner, the message indicator lit green. NEW MESSAGE flashed in thick, brilliant letters on the screen, sending hab spiders scurrying with 10,000 lumens of—

"BOSS!" Linus recoiled and covered his ears, the shrill echo unexpected and much too loud at half-past one in the morning. "Check-in's not for another six and a half hours."

BOSS responded, its synthesized voice typically dulcet and plummy.

NEW MESSAGE FROM: LANGSTROM, CARLA

The Biosphere Operations Support System, unironically deemed BOSS by its creators, was the habs' original operating system. It was an A.I., the designers said, created to lead humanity into the future without the hindrance of human prejudices, judgments, nor compassion for hopeless cases. Linus had no doubt the last was true as evidenced by waking him before his hangover had a chance to begin.

BOSS listened through thousands of networked terminals, storing a billion yottabytes on everyone, their habits, health, loves, and hates. It determined rations and castes, assigned living quarters, approved marriages and breeding, and much more. One joke said Sisters of Mercy prayed to God only after submitting the prerequisite permissions. It wasn't funny, but his wife would've laughed. Ivan, too.

Why BOSS had decided now was the time to deliver the message was anyone's guess. It had been glitching for years, delivering messages at inopportune times, minutes, hours, and sometimes days late. But what else could anyone expect from a four hundred-year-old computer designed to support two thousand, now supporting almost thirty? BOSS had become so overstretched, terminal screens, rumored capable of displaying over thirty-three million colors, could now only show basic text and low-resolution images in eight. And all of them blinding.

"Too fucking early."

SPEECH CODE 12C [PROFANITY]: -50 ML DEMERIT

"Demerit yourself, you sanctimonious toaster." He instantly regretted not cutting its wires like he'd done in his office. "I'm going back to bed."

NEW MESSAGE FROM: LANGSTROM, CARLA

Linus grabbed the bedside tablet and hurled it at the terminal. It snagged on the chain and bounced on the bed's edge, smearing rust across the vinyl cover as it slid to the side and fell into the gap between his bunk and the wall.

"This'd better be good, or I'll snip your innards. What do you think of that?"

NEW MESSAGE FROM: LANGSTROM, CARLA

"Yeah, thought so."

He rolled off his bed and limped across the room, leaving a trail of sweaty footprints on the floor. He passed his wrist over the scanner. The display reached its full intensity, making Linus wish he could join the spiders hiding in shaded perforations in the floor and octagonal holes in the walls where iron rivets once held the heavy panels together. Only rust, luck, and prayers kept the ceiling from crushing him in his sleep. *Hide or go blind.* It was a difficult choice.

```
<><><><><> CONFIDENTIAL <><><><><>
RECIPIENT_1: HALLA, LINUS H4-SEC-A1
RECIPIENT_2: FINN, IVAN H4-SEC-A2
MEDICAL REPORT: H2-6582-C :: 13.MAY.2637
DNA TRACE: [A1] SUCCESSFUL [*3]
  MOTHER: ROCHE, HARIN
   >>> ASSIGNMENT: KEYSTONE H1:L42:U1 <<<
  FATHER: HAZBEGI, SANDRO
   >>> ASSIGNMENT: SALVAGE H8:L1:U7257 <<<
  IDENT: [1-9K] UNSANCTIONED BIRTH
TECH: TAGGOT, WALLACE H2-MED-B5
AUTHORIZATION: LANGSTROM, CARLA H2-MED-A1
COMMENTS: NTT IRL OTR ASAP. <CL>
<><><><><> CONFIDENTIAL <><><><><>
```

Linus closed his eyes and massaged his fingertips into the sockets, blaming early-morning floaters for misreading the data. He read it again, but nothing changed. *Need to talk. In real life. Off the record. As soon as possible.* He growled. "I swear, Carla. Another acronym, and I'll... BOSS, confirm DNA trace and..." He cracked his neck. "Just confirm everything."

```
PROCESSING . . . . . . . . . . . . . . .
ALL DATA FIELDS CONFIRMED
```

"BOSS, are you drunk?"

```
NEGATIVE
```

He closed his eyes and groaned. "Am I drunk?"

VOICE ANALYSIS INDICATES AFFIRMATIVE

"Ugh." He smacked his lips. "What did Radek give me? Cancel query. I know. He slipped me Digi's alphabet sludge." Linus took a deep breath, held it in, and exhaled. "Perform a," he yawned, "diagnostic. Authorization Halla, Linus H4-SEC-A1."

[12,517] SYSTEMS WILL BE OFFLINE: 41 MINUTES
CONTINUE WITH [1] GLOBAL SYSTEMS DIAGNOSTIC?

"Not global, you deaf toaster. Report. Run a report system diagnostic. And limit to Habitat Integrity."

[1] SYSTEM WILL BE OFFLINE: 28 SECONDS
CONTINUE WITH [1] SYSTEM DIAGNOSTIC?

"Do it, so I can go back to bed."

PROCESSING . . . .

Mother's a keystone, drowning in fifteen daily rations 42 levels below Hab 1. Father's a dried-out one-ration scrapper living surface level, Hab 8, Unit 7257. Sandro Hazbegi? "It couldn't be."

DIAGNOSTIC [1 OF 1] COMPLETE
[1] REPORT SYSTEM OPERATING NORMALLY

"Repeat report system diagnostic. Integrity and Medical."

[2] SYSTEMS WILL BE OFFLINE: 71 SECONDS
CONTINUE WITH [1] SYSTEM DIAGNOSTIC?

"As long as you don't tell Carla who did it. Proceed."

PROCESSING . . . .

"A keystone and a scrapper." Linus clicked his tongue. "What's the world coming to?"

The two groups couldn't have been farther and further apart. BOSS maintained and promoted long-term genetic viability by separating those with desired traits, fewer genetic diseases, and higher tolerances from those without. It assigned people most likely to produce genetically superior offspring to lower levels, safer jobs, and nicer quarters. It allotted them a higher base ration and better food, and so they always lived longer and more comfortably. Over the years, genetic sustainability transmuted into tacit superiority, and the Ration-caste system became its tool to manipulate, punish, and control. Those deemed 'inferior' or 'unsanctioned' wielded other, less subtle tools.

Keystones were the genetic best of the best. They lived on Level 39 to 42 at the bottom. Most had only to procreate. Scrappers usually died on the job, sometimes of hunger or thirst, and often without any children at all. These castes told their kids bogeyman stories about the other and spread vicious rumors, scaring the middle classes, keeping them in line. Linus doubted the two castes had spoken, much less bred in over two hundred years. But still, the scrapper's name and unit sounded familiar.

DIAGNOSTIC [2 OF 2] COMPLETE
[2] REPORT SYSTEMS OPERATING NORMALLY

Hab 8. Unit 7257. Hazbegi, Sandro, Luka, Marika. Linus's body tensed. "Shit."

SPEECH CODE 12C [PROFANITY]: -50 ML DEMERIT

Linus dismissed the diagnostics, the report, and his fine. "BOSS, locate H.I. Deputy Finn."

LOCATING: FINN, IVAN. . . . .

The flashing indicator alternated between blue and yellow as Linus drummed his fingertips against the scanner plate. "Come on. What's the hold-up? Answer the call." The color rotation stopped, and the light settled on green.

"Chief?"

"Where are you?"

"Read your screen. I'm at home." Ivan yawned. "We were about to go to bed."

"Check your priority messages. It's the DNA trace."

"Now?"

"Is he actually calling about a case?" said Radek, in the background.

"Hold on. I see it. It's got to be another glitch. I'll check it in the morning."

"No, no. That won't do. I need to see you in H.I. in twenty."

"I'm still half-dosed, Linus. Can't it wait 'till check-in?"

"Twenty minutes, Deputy Finn."

"So we're pulling rank now? Fine, Chief Halla," said Ivan, exasperated. "Radek says he's cutting you off for good this time."

Linus was on his eightieth lap around the desk when Ivan came into the room and eased into his chair. "Well, Parch. I'm here." Ivan yawned and squinted at the dim light above his head. "Let's get this over so I can go to bed."

Linus raised an eyebrow and glanced at the terminal.

"Don't you dare." Ivan sneered. "Eleven months and counting. You've had your fun, Linus. Oh, excuse me. Chief Parch."

Linus scratched his bald spot. *How long has he known?* "How long have you—?"

"First time I passed by the door. You and Katri weren't exactly stealthy." Ivan kicked the rickety desk and rocked in his chair. Its abused springs squeaked and popped like an irksome symphony of rusty instruments clamoring in the dark. "And BOSS would've thrown Radek and I back into waste rec months ago if that mic were working." He winked at Linus.

"Voi luoja." Linus's eyes widened. He slid his hands off the desk, scrubbed them on his uniform, and clasped them in his lap. He glared at the tabletop.

"Don't pop your ration. I've seen you disconnect the mic a hundred times." He shook his head. "Look. We're a month out. It's two in the morning. Why don't you drop the pretense, and tell me what's going on?"

"It's Sandro Hazbegi."

"You ordered me here to talk about a dead scrapper? Is this what retirement jitters looks like? Rest assured, Parchy. There's no need to worry. I, Ivan Finn, future Chief of H.I., give you leave to retire in peace. Go with God to the mushroom caves. Can I sleep now?"

Linus shook his head. "It's not that."

"It's a glitch. I'm telling you. You know what happened? Wallace mixed up the idents. He named the wrong Hazbegi as the father. That's why Doc wants to see you in person. She wants someone scary to make the tech piss himself."

"Sandro was the last Hazbegi. It couldn't have been anyone else. And BOSS confirmed the result."

"Correction. BOSS confirmed an erroneous result. Scrappers and keystones don't make babies. How many people are in the habs, Linus? Twenty-five, thirty thousand? All of them descendants of the original two thousand survivors. There are only so many permutations of names. It was bound to happen to you sooner or later. You know, I met my doppelganger once. Nice guy. And his name sounded like mine. I think it was Igor? Ian? Isaac? Irving? Or maybe it didn't start with an 'I' at all? Evan?"

"It's not only the name." Linus circled the desk.

"Not again. You know I hate it when you circle."

"Hear me out."

"Not until you sit down. You're starting to make me dizzy."

Linus leaned against the wall, still shaken, but at least he could breathe. He slid to the floor and sat knees-to-chest.

"This isn't retirement jitters or déjà vu, is it? What's got you riled?"

"Habitat 8, Level 1, Unit 7257."
"The scrapper's quarters. What about it?"
"I've been there before."

6

Ivan

For eleven months, 'before' had been code for Ivan to shut his mouth, put the pad down, and back away. The past and old cases were like razor blades to Linus, cutting him deeply if picked up from wherever he'd left them. But he wasn't sure what to do this time. Charge forward or withdrawal to a safe distance. It wasn't about Linus's temper, if he had one at all. With the exception of nuns, Katri, and a few other things, not much seemed to bother him. Especially Habitat Integrity cases. Whether from decades of experience or some deep-seeded place, Ivan couldn't know. But he'd witnessed Linus doing peculiar things when the subject of 'before' had been pressed too hard.

Linus had admitted BOSS was playing his dead wife's journal entries in her synthesized voice. He assured Ivan he had stopped, but he'd also admit to it every time he was drunk. In the last two days, Linus's walls had receded faster than his hairline, and his candidness ballooned in proportion to his gluco consumption. The past was a risky button to push, but one he'd asked Ivan to push twice in as many days. First his wife and now this.

"What happened there?" Ivan remained calm, hoping Linus would follow his lead.

"A home invasion about ten years ago. Family of three. Father was out scrapping. Some tweaked-out slags came looking to score free rations. They broke into 7257, but the mother and son were home."

"The Hazbegis."

Linus nodded. "Something went wrong, and the mother and son were killed. A short time later, the father came home to a bloodbath."

"Sandro Hazbegi."

"Right."

"Was he ever a suspect?"

"The chip log tracked him to a system terminal in Hab 7, Level 2. The man was trading thirty grams of zinc for a quarter ration and a stuffed bear for his kid. He was the last person to use the terminal, ident chipped scanned on location, multiple witnesses. His alibi was solid. He didn't do it." Linus leaned his head back against the wall. "I'd never seen someone cry so much. Sandro would've died of dehydration if Sisters of Mercy and a few twos and threes - myself included - hadn't topped off his rations for six months."

"What happened to him?"

"Life goes on. Such as it is. Sandro went back to work, and I never heard or read his name again. Not until half an hour ago."

"And you?"

"I'd been Chief of H.I. for ten years, but there was something about the case I couldn't understand. Why the Hazbegi's? They had nothing at all. Not even pads on the bunks. We checked and rechecked system and com logs, dusted everything looking for prints out of place, followed Helix and Oxi thugs around, and ran scenario after scenario. It got to where BOSS started asking me if I wanted to pick-up the case where I'd left it the previous day, and the next, and every day for three years. There were whole seasons when Katri wouldn't speak to me except through Sister Oni. Eventually, I gave in. I told BOSS to put it on hold, and I left it there. But by then, all my deputies had requested transfers, cases were backlogged, and I had lost three good years with my wife."

"Sounds like the old Linus cared about something."

Linus managed a half smile, "He did," and Ivan helped him off the floor. He dusted the rust off his uniform, and Ivan dusted off the back of his head. "I'm not sure what happened to him."

"This Linus isn't too bad. A bit of a parch, but otherwise he gets the job done."

"Basically."

"So, what are the three of us going to do now? From what you've told me, we have two cases to solve and a chief to revive."

"Plus another to teach, really teach." Linus looked at the report tablet, date flickering on its screen. "And less than a month to do it."

"Was Harin Roche the boy's mother, too?"

"No. Mom was another scrapper named Marika. Their son was named Luka."

"One more question. This one's important. The fate the both cases could hang on your answer."

"Don't be dramatic. Just ask the question."

"Can we go to bed now?"

Linus looked like he wanted to say 'no', but he yawned instead. "Meet me here at 0800 hours for first check-in. We'll review procedures and head to Med Bay 2 from there."

"And I was beginning to think Habitat Integrity was boring."

The pedestrian tunnel to Med Bay 2 was unfinished compared to most others. Rough sides of granite boulders, too important to the tunnel's stability, sloped from the ceiling interspersed between recessed lights and molded steel panels bolted between. Bioluminescent moss made the outcroppings easy for Ivan to avoid, but he felt better knowing the medical bay was a few meters ahead and Linus, leading the way and having bumped his head twice, would encounter all of them first.

The moss glistened and glowed vibrant blue hues and smelled like fruit and numerous earthy, sweet words Ivan pretended to understand. He listed them, "cherries, grass, lakes, petrichor, rain, soil," to Linus, like dropping famous names in a crowded room full of strangers. Linus didn't seem impressed. He'd attended kindergarten, too.

In truth, the smell was odd, almost alien, yet somehow it soothed his nerves like few other things could. Ivan might've lived in the tunnel if the warm, humid air wasn't made worse by the stale water vapor BOSS pumped throughout the habs. Linus had sent Ivan to the same stretch of tunnel twice to warn away scrappers who'd torn away meters of moss for however much water they could squeeze from it. If he were one, he would've gotten caught with his nose pressed to the walls.

Linus slid the med lab doors aside, and light flooded the tunnel behind them. The wet moss glistened and moved, swaying in the light as if a gust of wind had blown past. Ivan felt nothing except for the pain in his eyes. The door closed, and his eyes adjusted to the bright space.

The room was white, along with everything in it. A few bare spots shown through where thick enamel had worn down to black steel and then to nothing at all. Ivan thought the lab looked better at 405 than he did at 25. Better dressed, too. Clean, white curtains hung in multiple places at various angles, sectioning off the room for privacy or triage. Linus and Ivan circled each other. Machines churned. Fluorescent lights hummed. Otherwise, Med Bay 2 was quiet and smelled like the corridor leading to it.

Linus rolled a stool away from an empty desk and sat on it. "Carla?"

Ivan walked toward the closest set of curtains. "Doctor Langstrom?"

"A moment, please. We're almost finished."

Ivan slid it aside.

Doctor Carla Langstrom, Hab 4's primary physician and Chief Officer over all things medical, observed her assistant - a young, red-haired woman in baggy green scrubs - work on a male patient asleep on a gurney, his right forearm burned black to the bone.

"Good work." Carla pointed to something in the gaping wound. "But you see that bit? You see how it's starting to yellow along the edge."

The tech leaned in. "Yes, Ma'am."

"It needs to go, or it's likely to cause a secondary infection."

The young woman nodded. "Yes, Ma'am."

"Do that and pack the wound with healing gel." She snapped off her latex gloves and tossed them into a purple waste bin. "I'll return in a few minutes to help you with the moss."

"Yes, Ma'am."

Carla joined Ivan and Linus and closed the curtain behind her. "Moss dressing helps to keep the wound moist," she said, answering Ivan's bewildered expression, "and it'll glow as long as it's wet. When it dries out, it'll stop and I'll replace it. Or rather Medical Assistant Sillerson will replace it," Carla raised her voice, "if she ever wants to move out of the lab."

"Yes, Ma'am."

"Now, gentlemen. I want to show you the new shelving units in the storage room. I think you'll find them quite interesting."

Carla, hair as white as her lab coat, skin almost as wrinkled, led them to a nondescript room at the rear of the bay. Inside were three rows of white shelves with hanging I.V. bags, multi-colored pill bottles and assorted jars, and tubes filled with creams, gels, and ointments. Ivan picked up a jar filled with, what looked to be, composting worms and giant cave spiders blended into a chunky paste.

She took it from him and returned it to the shelf. "Don't play with the medicine." She shut the door and slid a miniature, white curtain over a square window in the middle.

Linus gestured to a bundle of cut wires hanging out of the wall. "I assume that terminal's on requisition."

"It'll be in tomorrow." She smiled, "It's good to see you, Linus," and hugged him.

"How long have you known each other?"

"What do you think, Carla. How long has it been?"

"Don't remind me. My hair was brown when we met."

"So was mine." He sighed. "Carla's an old friend. She introduced me to Katri."

"I'm sorry by the way. If I had caught it sooner, maybe I could've—"

"Three hundred days." Linus squeezed her hand, and there was a brief look between them.

"So why the real-life meet-up?" said Ivan, ending the uncomfortable silence.

"It's about the boy. The one the scrapper brought in."

Ivan's heart sank. "Did he die?"

"There were a few complications. He lost much of his epidermis, and damage to the dermis and areas of the hypodermis were severe, especially on his legs and feet where he had direct contact with the sand. He'll also be sterile. Most of us are, so no surprise there. And blood tests showed a few chromosomal abnormalities, but I can't be sure what that means until a those tests come back."

"A few or a few too many?"

"He's going to be fine. He's resting now." Carla pulled a kid's drawing tablet from behind a shelf. "He's not the most talkative patient, but I did get him to write his name and age for me." She handed it to Linus. "I thought you'd want to see."

Linus took it and smiled at three boxy robots, dozens of curly-cues, and a little stick figure. "A budding artist," he said as the color drained from his cheeks. He dropped the tablet.

Ivan caught it, "What's wrong?" and read the tiny name scribbled across the bottom. "How? I don't understand."

"He says his name is Luka Hazbegi. And he's six years old."

7

Linus

Pressure grew in Linus's chest, his heart crushing under the weight of the boy's name. The room became blurry and started wobbling without moving. He reached toward the shelf for support but found Ivan's shoulder instead.

"Easy there." Ivan helped Linus steady himself.

"Do you need to sit?" said Carla.

"I'll be fine." Linus lumbered to the door and gripped the handle to keep himself upright. "Keep going."

"When Luka came in, we administered the standard protocols. Cold packs, oxygenated saline, clotting agents, plasma infusion, chelation for heavy metals in the sand, anti-radiologic photomagnetic therapy, potassium heptaphosphate, potassium iodide, and a few other things. But the concentrations were building in his system four hundred times the dose we were giving him."

Linus gasped.

"What is it?" asked Ivan.

"A lethal dose. They almost killed him trying to save him," said Linus.

"That's what we thought, so I pulled the drip. His body continued producing some kind of anti-radiologic inoculation on its own. I haven't isolated how exactly, but I think it's why he survived the scour as long as he did. Until now, nobody's managed longer than three hours outside before irreversible tissue damage and death. That's with our heaviest suits. Give this boy a basic suit and enough food and water," she whispered, "he could survive days, maybe weeks in the scour."

"But his skin? Linus was right. The kid was melting in there." Ivan nodded toward the rear wall, the quarantine room beyond it.

"It wasn't as bad as it looked."

"It looked awful."

"I suspect he was outside unprotected over a day before he was found. If the exposure were less, say sixteen, seventeen hours, he wouldn't have required the skin grafts. Ten or fewer, and he wouldn't have needed any treatments at all."

"Lucky him," said Linus. "But whoever he is, he's not Luka Hazbegi. Ever seen a plasma cutter split granite? There was nothing left of him or his mother. Besides, Luka would've been sixteen by now. And he didn't have freckles, either."

"We ran the DNA trace twice. Sandro Hazbegi is definitely the father. But the Lukas have different mothers. Marika Hazbegi and Harin Roche."

"So they're half-brothers," said Ivan.

"Have you contacted Sandro yet?" said Linus.

"I tried this morning and again about twenty minutes ago, but BOSS couldn't locate him."

"Out scrapping or too far from a terminal. We'll check on him later."

"I wanted to cross-reference Luka one's DNA with Luka two's, but the original case's been closed over three years. If it weren't for the original, sixteen-year-old record listing Sandro and Marika as his parents, I wouldn't have known they were half-brothers."

"Why? What happens after three years?" said Ivan.

Linus rubbed his temples. "DNA samples from murdered children are destroyed."

"Whose asinine, short-sighted idea was that?"

"Mine." Linus's mind fell into a great chasm, the inevitable past awaiting his return in the darkness below. It had taken him three years to escape the first time. *How long will it take this time?*

Carla rubbed his arm. "I know what this case means to you, so I added your ident to the med report roster. You'll get the data as it comes in, real time, no waiting for me to send results. It should speed things up a bit."

"Thank you."

"It's the least I could do."

"Whatever we're going to do," said Ivan, "let's get this cleared up before—"

The latch clicked, and the door swung open. Carla's tech stuck her head inside. "All finished, Doctor. He's ready for mossing."

"Thank you, Heidi."

"Get what cleared up?" She sounded far too gleeful for burn care.

Carla took a large tube of ointment off the shelf. "A rash." She handed the tube to Ivan. "Apply generously every four hours until the pustules go away. You should abstain from sexual intercourse for at least a week."

Ivan's eyes widened.

"Ewww." Sillerson backed out of the room and disappeared through parted curtains.

"You two deserve each other," said Ivan. "And Linus gets the rash next time."

Linus and Ivan sat in their office, drowning under a deluge of one hundred twenty-two medical reports, ranging from blood tests, their unusual results, and orders for more, to skin graft procedures, DNA traces, various and repeated radiation treatments, prognosis updates, unreadable x-rays, and a kilometer-long log noting everything from the colors and smells of various fluids to what he could stomach and what he threw up.

And there were spaces reserved for comments on everything, including one from Carla opting not to argue with a child over his name because giving BOSS updates on 'Luka 2's' status was plain stupid. She added an extra 'a' to end of his name, and 'Lukaa' Hazbegi was born. Linus read it and laughed, and laughed every time BOSS said it. It was as though the glitchy old computer were asking Linus if he was sure he meant *that* Hazbegi. He was tempted to reply, 'Yes, that one', but he didn't considering the mic's wires were cut, and when he fixed them, he'd have to pronounce it the same way.

Carla also sent along various texts on medicine and genetics to give Linus any hope of understanding it all. But going on their fourth hour, he decided he'd had enough of results and reports he only half understood. Genetics was bad enough. *Genetics and puss? No thanks.* He chose to re-focus his energy on first finding Sandro Hazbegi. Though he was the boy's next of kin, Carla couldn't locate him.

Linus removed the terminal side panel and twisted together the frayed ends of two blue and black wires. "That should do it." He sat the panel off to the side.

"It's about time. If I had to type one more command..." Ivan swiped his wrist across the scanner. "BOSS, reinitialize this terminal and configure for voice input."

The screen flickered, and BOSS spoke.

B.O.S.S. v96.12
BIOSPHERE OPERATIONS SUPPORT SYSTEM
ENTER QUERY OR COMMAND

"Ugh. That voice. BOSS, who am I?"
Finn, Ivan H4-SEC-A2

"Who's chief of Habitat Integrity?"
Halla, Linus H4-SEC-A1

"And what's his favorite drink?"
Gluco O- Platinum

WARNING: LIVER DAMAGE PROBABILITY 67%
WARNING: LIFE EXPECTANCY -12% OF STANDARD

"BOSS," said Linus, "terminate assignment, Finn, Ivan H4-SEC-A2. Authorization Halla, Linus H4-SEC-A1."

TERMINATION REQUEST DENIED
REPLACEMENT NOT AVAILABLE
FIRST RETIREMENT -27 DAYS

Ivan sneered.
"What? I had to test the system somehow."
"Sure." He read the screen, "First retirement," and snickered. "I can't imagine you as a shroomer. Dusting spores, tuning grow lights, turning compost for twelve hours a day. You know what's in that stuff? Why not Brothers of Hope?"
"Your idea or Sister Oni's?"
"My... Yeah, I can't lie. It was hers. But we both think it'd be good for you. Shrooming's too quiet. You'll literally spend three quarters of your time alone in the dark."
"We obviously have different ideas about retirement. I can't wait for a once daily check-in instead of four, and all the quiet time I want. Alone in the dark." Linus sighed. "Sounds like heaven to me."
"And handling recycled humans and, well, you know."
"Let's debate this again in thirty years." Linus faced the terminal. "BOSS, locate Sandro Hazbegi."

LOCATING: HAZBEGI, SANDRO. . . . .

"Thank God BOSS forbids identical names," said Ivan.
"After twenty years in this job, I think it's the best thing BOSS's ever done."

LOCATION UNKNOWN: HAZBEGI, SANDRO

"Still missing," said Ivan.
"BOSS, display Sandro's last registered check-in?"

CHECK-IN REGISTERED AT 2003 HRS

TERMINAL: H8:L1:U7257:ST8121

"1856 hours now. Another glitch?"
"Or BOSS's being obtuse. BOSS, display the date of Sandro's last recorded check-in."

LAST CHECK-IN: 8.APRIL.2637

"8 April? What's today's date?" said Linus.
"14 May. Over a month. Right hand versus left hand?"
"Looks like it."
Ivan backed away from the terminal. "But it doesn't matter now."
Linus nodded. "Sandro Hazbegi's dead." The realization didn't hit him as hard as he thought it would've. "Either he died before his next check-in, or he missed it and let BOSS electrocute him to death. It's happened before, but only with people who were already incapacitated."
"Like when Radek slipped and fell in The Ant. He broke his arm, and I missed check-in by five minutes." Ivan rubbed his wrist. "Mine hurt worse than his."
"Made you run to a terminal, didn't it? Sandro didn't run."
Ivan patted Linus's shoulder. "Do you need a minute?"
"No. I'm okay. But I don't... I don't know."
"So, now Harin Roche?"
"Not yet." Linus cleared his throat. "BOSS, is there a record of Sandro Hazbegi's date and cause of death on file?"

AFFIRMATIVE

"Speaking of strange," said Ivan. "Why'd BOSS try to locate him if it had a C.O.D on record?"
"BOSS, display the report number associated with Sandro Hazbegi's C.O.D."

REPORT: ***-****-**

"A report without a sequence or department?" Ivan double-tapped the number, causing it to expand and fill the screen. "I haven't seen that before."

"Because it's a nonsensical error. Every datafile has a name consisting of numbers and letters. Every file originates from people's private terminals or their workplace departments. Every department and person has a code containing numbers and letters. The filing system requires numbers and letters corresponding to people, departments, and the people who work in those departments. And more numbers and letters denoting sequence. Otherwise, the file can't be sorted before or after others by the same person or department." Linus looked at Ivan and shrugged. "I'm stumped."

"Yeah, me too. But look at you. Didn't have to pace around the office or anything."

Linus sneered. "BOSS, display the above C.O.D report."

REPORT: NOT AVAILABLE

"Display the authorization for the above report."

AUTHORIZATION: NOT AVAILABLE

"Why is the report and the authorization both not available?"

ERROR: NOT AVAILABLE

"BOSS," Linus groaned and scratched his bald spot, "Why is the report number, report text, and report authorization not available?"

PROCESSING . . . .

"Good. Something other than—"

NOT AVAILABLE: NOT AVAILABLE

"Smartass."

SPEECH CODE 12C [PROFANITY]: -50 ML DEMERIT

Linus kicked it as if the minor impact would make the terminal realize the error of its ways.

"Chief, let me do it. If there's a file, there's a terminal. BOSS, display the terminal used to process this report."

H9:L5:C00:ST00

"Double zeros. That's a dummy terminal," said Linus. "Locked A3 clearance."

"The old 'read all, touch none' ones? For departmental trainees?"

"The same." Linus read it again. "Habitat 9, Level 5? Habitat 9?"

"Habitat 9?" echoed Ivan. "What's that supposed to mean?"

"It means BOSS is glitching again." He showed the terminal his middle finger and was glad there weren't any cameras to witness it. By his calculation, he'd lost two full rations from the next weeks' allotment. If he lost another, he'd have to borrow from Ivan. "What do you mean Habitat 9?"

HABITAT 9 IS NOT ON RECORD

"BOSS, where's Habitat 9?" added Ivan.

HABITAT 9 IS NOT ON RECORD

"That was the same question rephrased."

"What if it's an inversion error? Hab 9, Level 5 rather than Hab 5, Level 9. BOSS, repeat last command."

H9:L5:C00:ST00

"Double zeros. Double glitches?" said Linus. "Repeat command."

H9:L5:C00:ST00

"Double zeros. Triple glitches," said Ivan.

Linus pounded his fist on the terminal screen. "This is infuriating. Remind me. What's in Habitat 5, Level 9?"

"CO2 scrubbers, water filtration, a few retiree quarters, and mushroom caves. Same as the other habs' ninth levels."

"In other words, nothing we can use."

Ivan shrugged. "BOSS, display all biographical data, Roche, Har—."

"BOSS, cancel query."

"What'd I do?"

"We've got to be one hundred percent certain there's a connection between Sandro Hazbegi and Harin Roche other than a tenuous DNA trace. And I don't want her to know we're looking *into* her until we're looking *at* her. BOSS, is Sandro Hazbegi still assigned to Habitat 8, Level 1, Unit 7257?"

AFFIRMATIVE

"Thank you," Linus yanked the wires apart, "Slag toaster."

"I take it we're going to Hazbegi's unit tomorrow?"

"After second check-in. I need to get my suit out of decon first. How's yours?"

"Ready to go. Same as always."

"Good. Wear it." Linus walked out the door, stopped, and turned around. "And bring your pulser."

The bunk springs creaked, and stripped bolts rattled in their holes, waking Linus from another nightmare. It was a repeat of the night before, something about Marika Hazbegi, and how upset Katri was he'd spent more time with Marika's corpse in three years than he did with her. Linus was glad the nightmare quickly faded, but he missed seeing Katri's face in the dream. He rolled on his side and focused on the spot where she once laid her head. A broken, gray spring coiled up through the thin padding, sharp tip piercing the vinyl cover. Linus tugged on the coil and let go. It sprung back and wobbled in place, taunting, teasing him. He pressed his fingertip into the jagged point and dragged it across. He followed the deep spiral from tip to base, paining warm red over the cool gray. He closed his eyes.

"BOSS."

The system terminal flickered to life.

"Open personal journal Halla, Katri. Authorization Halla, Linus H4-SEC-A1. Dictate entry dated 18 December 2635. Natural voice synthesis Halla, Katri. Auto-repeat until canceled."

<<BEGIN>>

I can't believe it's almost Christmas. I know I promised Linus I'd stop buying him holiday presents, but I ordered IT over two years ago, so he'll just have to put up with one more gift. How I married a grumpy man who doesn't like presents, I'll never know. He says he only tolerates it for me, but I'm sure he secretly enjoys the holidays as much as I do. I'll pick it UP on the way back from med lab. Carla says she has the results. I hope everything's okay. I don't want bad news to spoil his Christmas.

<<END>>
<<BEGIN>>

I can't believe it's almost Christmas. . .

8

Ivan

H ab 8 was the largest of the habitats with a low, surface-level dome 55 meters at the apex and 825 meters in diameter. Wide, flat proportions made possible by layered aluminum oxynitride triangles supported between tungsten alloy struts. The habitable area along the northern edge of each level retracted five meters under the one above - the standard layout for each habitat. As such, Level 1 was a perfect circle on the surface, and Level 42 a crescent far below. Tapered living areas accommodated increasingly large subterranean columns to support the levels above and allowed additional space for massive pumps required to transport air, water, and waste up for recycling.

Their rad suits were heavy, but they left the bulky helmets in the integrity office. They stopped a few meters before the wide entrance, and Ivan sat his toolbox on the floor beside him and tugged at the suit's thick, rubber neck gasket and looked up at the low dome. While multiple layers of AION blocked radiation and much of the sun's rays, they couldn't block everything. He squinted and shielded his eyes. Within the photochromic glass, deep indigo swirled, coalescing with emerald and scarlet, shifting to black, separating in response to shifting light waves and painting undulating colors on everything beneath it. *Beautiful but deadly.*

Sweat beaded on his forehead and rolled down his cheeks, cutting a narrow, clean trail between wide streaks of rust dust and grime. He hadn't realized how dirty he was until he saw his bright reflection in a nearby terminal. Even so, he was cleaner than most. He fanned his face with his hands. "Jeez. These suits." He glanced at the time. "1 hour, 44 minutes, 53 seconds."

"What is?" Linus's voice was low and soft.

"The walk from H.I."

Ivan was eleven months into the job, but the novelty of going new places hadn't worn off. Few were permitted to travel more than three levels down from their assigned living quarters. Ivan had trudged through Hab 3s waste reservoirs since he turned eighteen. When BOSS approved reassignment, he jumped at the chance to move a level down, add another full ration, and wear a uniform not stained brown to the chest. Habitat integrity, and the various maintenance and medical teams, had freedom to travel as far and deep as their duties required or BOSS allowed. Over the course of the year, he'd traveled as deep as Level 23 and into every habitat except 8. Linus had investigated those cases alone or dismissed them outright. Until now.

"Keep that to yourself. I don't want any trouble." Linus stripped the black octagonal *H.I.* patch off their sleeves and chests and replaced both with orange rectangles with the letters *T.M.* stamped across the top and a name across the bottom. Linus was *Jacob*, and Ivan was *Rosco*.

Ivan turned his sleeve to the side. "Tunnel maintenance? I'm over two meters tall. They're going to notice. And don't they know you?"

"Not everyone will buy it, but I don't plan on staying longer than we have to."

A little girl in a long, filthy shirt and no shoes sprinted past Ivan carrying a torn ration pouch dripping water as she ran. She darted left into the pedestrian tunnel. A dozen screaming kids in ripped, dirty clothes too large for their scrawny bodies, chased after. Their smell, a melody of blood, rust, urine, and sweat, lingered in the air after they'd gone.

Ivan pinched his nose. "I can smell why."

"I thought you'd be used to it."

"That was almost a year ago. Why is it important we dress like tunnel spiders?"

"Tunnel Maintenance helps them move. Habitat Integrity tells them to stop. They don't want us here, and they certainly don't trust us enough to help."

"I never had a problem in waste rec."

"Everybody living above waste rec likes waste rec." Linus meandered ahead. "Think about it. 7257 is this way."

Ivan watched another large group of children pass by, and he had to smile. He rarely saw two or three kids at once. Certainly not a dozen. Plenty of children were born to scrappers, but less than half survived into puberty. The few who did faced the same problems. No need for a one-child policy when most will be compost before they can read. But unlike sixes and sevens, ones let their children play in the world rather than being bound by it. *Or they think playing in hell is better than being caged in heaven.* He wasn't sure, but he was confident Sister Oni wouldn't approve of the question.

Corridors vibrated as people crisscrossed, children played games in wide spaces, shopkeepers pushed their wares, and scrappers pulled buckets of metals, glass, and plastics from decontamination machines. The lower levels were busy in their own right, but Ivan had never seen such a large crowd pushing and shoving since 2-for-1 gluco night at The Pissing Ant. These people weren't toe-up and bumping into each other. They were wide-awake and, for the most part, happier than he expected.

A dirty man on a low stool motioned to them. "Tun maint you, 'ey?" He extended both legs and pointed at his feet, each missing the big toe, the others crooked, haphazardly bandaged in yellowed, old gauze. He spit on the floor. "Your bots."

"Sorry. But bots you know." Ivan shrugged. "You gotta dodge better. K?"

"What are you doing? Nobody talks like that."

"Bad tongue wag. No true, ambos. Liars ambos." The man burped, and a glass eyeball popped out of the left socket and landed on his crotch. He stuck it into his mouth, swished it around, and pushed it back into the hole.

Ivan's stomach churned.

"Ear full, ojo too. No tell. Two hundred milli, hush-hush." He pressed a finger to his lips and smiled, showing off his crooked teeth and bleeding gums.

"What did he say?"

"He said he's going to rat us out unless we pay him two hundred milliliters."

"How'd he know?"

"Because you're a bad liar."

Ivan popped his neck. "Son of a bitch."

SPEECH CODE 12C [PROFANITY]: -50 ML DEMERIT

"Wha? With jumala. Angel, her. Runkkari. Two hundred fifty milli." He spit. "Each."

"Stop trying to help." Linus unfastened his suit and tossed a full pouch into the man's lap. "To honor your mom in heaven. Hush-hush?"

"Hush-hush." He sucked on the outlet tube as Ivan and Linus continued down the corridor and turned the corner.

"You didn't have to pay him a whole ration."

"I didn't." Linus opened Ivan's suit and reached into the interior pocket. "You did." He removed Ivan's ration pouch and zipped it into his own suit. "Think of it as a tax on stupidity."

They reached Unit 7257 at the end of a long hall of numbered, sliding steel doors. The shuffling of their heavy, rubber boots, rust crunching under their soles, caused open doors to rattle and squeak, shutting one-by-one ahead of them as scrappers ducked into their rusty boxes and bolted their doors.

"You said we'd blend."

"Believe it or not, that's a good thing. It means they don't recognize either of us." Linus traced the recessed unit number with his fingertip, painting it reddish orange. "As long as you don't try to play scrapper again, we'll be fine." He wiped the rust on his rad suit.

Ivan gently knocked on the door and kept his voice soft. "Hello? Mister Hazbegi? Sandro Hazbegi? Are you in there?"

There was no answer.

"Ivan, he can't answer if he's dead. Let me..." Linus swiped his wrist over the door scanner and jerked the handle, his Habitat Integrity A1 clearance allowing him to unlock and slide it open.

"What if someone sees us?"

"If anyone asks, tell them Tunnel Maintenance quarters were full, so BOSS assigned us these temporarily."

"We're supposed to be a couple? Aren't you too old for me?"

Linus chuckled. "Father and son, Ivan. Father and son."

"Oh. Yeah. Right. That'd be more believable."

"For a natural, you can be pretty thick sometimes. But there's still hope for you."

It was a rare, if though backhanded, compliment. Ivan grinned. "You think I'm a natural investigator?"

"No. But thanks for proving my point."

"Which was?"

"You forgot we're from Tunnel Maintenance."

7257's layout was identical to every family unit Ivan had ever seen. Simple partitions for privacy, steel bunks, a couple free-standing shelves, pull-down table, bio-waste extractor, and the ubiquitous system terminal. Holes rusted through thin ceilings hinted at whatever was above. Every level below 1 looked at cave ceilings and spider webs. Level 1 units looked into the dome itself.

No wonder eighty percent of them are sterile.

Ivan looked around the empty room. "Either Sandro Hazbegi was a simple man, or someone's taken it all."

Linus scratched his bald spot. "Cleaners beat us to it. They even got his clothes."

"Who do you think?"

"Helix is king around here. If he's dead, they'd know it first. Likely before BOSS. Certainly before us. They emptied the quarters, erased their tracks, fingerprints, footprints, everything."

Ivan sat the heavy case by the entrance. "Then I won't need this."

"There's always something." Linus lifted the bunks and fastened them into recesses in the wall. He ran his glove around the underside. "Look for anything they missed. A few strands of hair, some odd-looking rust might be a clue."

"How about a body?" Ivan pulled the first shelving unit away from the wall.

"Until we have more to go on, he's a missing person like any other. Assume the person, Sandro in this case, is alive and needs your help. Work back from there. We need to piece together a timeline of his final hours. Which is going to be easy since he entered and exited the same doors, took his rations from the same places, and checked in at the same terminals every day. But also hard because that's all we know. Nobody in here's going to talk to us."

"And if he went for a midnight spa treatment on his own?"

"Well, the last ten years haven't been easy for him, so suicide's a distinct possibility. But the worst way to go about it. A pulser would've been painless. Three necro-shrooms would've been almost euphoric. If it was suicide by scour, Sandro wanted to suffer."

Ivan's eye twitched as he slid the second shelving unit away from the wall, the metallic screech of rusted steel on steel sending a shiver down his spine.

Linus crawled along the floor, running his fingers along narrow, rusted seams. "So, we have a scrapper who could be alive or dead." He blew a cloud of fine rust from between the gaps.

Ivan nodded. "Right."

"Care to expand on 'right'?"

"We have an unsanctioned boy who should've died from rad poisoning but didn't. He's not who he says because that boy was murdered a decade ago. There's an unlikely, if not impossible relationship between the boy's parents or, at the very least, DNA donors for a surrogate. And the father is missing, presumably."

"What's the connection?"

"Sandro Hazbegi. It's got to be him. He's the biological father of both boys, the one who disappeared a month ago, and whose report we can't read."

"Where is he?"

"Hiding?"

"A dirt poor, solitary scrapper cracks his ident chip's encryption and disables the shock clock. Something that's never been done. If he's that good, he could make himself rich. But he continues to scan his chip at the same terminals and gates every day for over twenty years and suddenly decides it's time to stop." Linus shook his head. "I don't buy it. I think Sandro Hazbegi's dead. Someone knows why, and they're trying to cover it up."

"Why a scrapper? Why *this* scrapper? Pretty far to go for someone nobody cared about."

"They cared enough to do something with the body."

"What if he cut the chip out of his wrist?"

"No chip means no containment doors, gates between sections or habitats, or any lifts. He'd be in whatever area he was when he did it. And since his last check-in was in this room right there," Linus pointed to the room's terminal, "he'd be between here and the access gate. And after missing his next check-in, the chip's shock clock would pulse every five minutes until he swiped at a terminal.

"Same as it did to me when Radek fell."

"Correct."

"How many pulses until the chip's power cell fails? It shocked me once, but I assume the thing wouldn't do it forever."

"Of course not. Those shocks drain a good portion of its power. It'll eventually go dead. But by then, the user's likely dead, too."

"How many?"

"Twelve or thirteen. You'd have to ask Carla. I know it's a little over an hour. Then BOSS assumes you're either dead or disabled and locks you out of the system. And same as before, you're stuck wherever you are. Again, he'd be in this area. For a department head, that's a huge problem. But for a scrapper, nobody has to know. Assuming that's what happened, Sandro would need a permanent shadow to scan him into everything, take him wherever he wanted to go, and send messages on his behalf. And someone would have to feed him and withdrawal rations for him."

"Unless he cracked the encryption and coded himself as someone else."

"Okay, now you're having a wild techno-porn fantasy. I told you, it's not possible. Those chips are coded to the user's DNA. To look like someone else, he'd have to *become* someone else."

Ivan scratched the back of his head. "Is it too late to go home?"

Linus smirked. "You're starting to sound familiar."

"If you ever tell Radek, I swear you'll have to find a new deputy."

Linus drew a rusty X across his suit. "Not a word."

"What do you make of this?" Ivan waved him over. He pointed to three deep scratches low on the wall between two panels. "Clean metal. No rust."

"Get the pry bar."

Ivan went back to his case. "Vamoose," he shouted, trying to scare away a group of giggling kids in the doorway. He unbuckled the latches and removed the slim, twenty-centimeter bar from inside. The kids returned, bringing friends to ogle the new arrivals. Linus jammed one end into the gap and pushed the other against the wall. The panel came off, easy like it had been removed and replaced a hundred times over. Linus and Ivan were speechless, and the giggling kids at the door fell quiet. Four narrow shelves were hidden behind it. A small, white teddy bear sat on the first shelf, six full ration pouches laid on the second, and four on the third. Each was marked with a single blue helix.

Linus picked one up. "Oh, Sandro. Why'd you do it?"

"What'd he do?"

"See that." Linus pointed out the mark. "These came from Helix. Either he borrowed rations from them, or he was on their payroll. Those are both bad choices."

Something else lay on the top shelf. Linus picked it up and turned it between his fingertips. It had four yellow petals, broad across the outer edge, narrower toward the center, a single black dot in the middle of each. He handed it to Ivan.

Ivan inhaled the faint, sweet scent, like the tunnel to med lab but new, different, clean, almost nothing at all. It must've been alive at one time, but it crumbled in his hand with the slightest touch. "I think it's a flower. Digi's flower." Ivan closed his eyes and inhaled the scent again. "Where do you think it came from?"

"I think the better question is, 'Who has water to spare?'." Linus got up and hustled toward the door. "Hey kiddies." His gruff voice became jolly and exaggerated. "Are you all good boys and girls?"

The kids nodded.

"Linus, what are you doing?"

"Can you keep a secret?" he asked the kids, ignoring Ivan's question.

They shook their heads.

"Okay. Honesty. I like honesty. Honesty's good. Never lose that. How about a trade? Rations for hush-hush."

They nodded, their focus on the pouches in the wall.

Linus counted heads. "There are eight of you and two of us. How many is eight plus two?"

Six kids spread ten fingers. The other two stared at their hands then copied their friends.

"That's right. Ten mouths and ten rations."

Ivan stood. "You know we can't. That's evidence."

Linus hurried back to the wall. "I can, and I will." He grabbed two pouches off the third shelf and six from the second.

The level shook, and Ivan crouched, balancing himself against the low shelves. "Linus?"

Linus braced himself in the door frame. "Here kiddies." He gave a full ration to each. They scattered, sucking on the outlet tubes as they skipped away. "Put the rations, the bear, and the flower in the case. Let's get out of here."

9

Linus

Linus elbowed a path through the bustling crowds. Ivan followed closely behind, clutching the case against his chest. He stumbled. "Where are we going?"

"It's this way." Linus stopped at the end of a long corridor where the dome met the outer edge of the residential area.

"There's nothing here."

"Remember when I told you to let me do the talking?"

"Yeah."

"Keep that in mind. And if someone asks you a question... Hell, if anyone says anything to you, look pissed and swear at them. Okay? Finnish, Korean, Spanish, English, German, Scrapper Pidgin. Not French. Anything but French. Got it?"

"Huh?"

Linus kicked the wall three times. "Hand me the rations."

A panel retracted, and a hand appeared through the hole, palm up, fingers snapping. Linus handed over both pouches. When the panel closed, another door opened. Linus entered and led Ivan along a narrow maintenance corridor running the circumference of Habitat 1 between the dome's AION layers and the curved interior walls.

Every ten meters, struts like massive Xs anchored the dome into bedrock. Beneath and between, merchants peddled young, virgin gluco, roasted hab spiders, seared whole rat, vials of thick, opaque liquids, beige powder in little blue bags, deadly necro-shrooms, various hallucinogens, and opportunities to converse with the dead. There was nothing to spy on their choices or cut their rations for saying the wrong things.

"Get your DMC," shouted a merchant, scooping chunky, brown powder out of a meter-tall black drum. He mixed it with gluco, and tossed back the shot.

Linus's stomach churned, but he didn't let it show. He looked at Ivan and shook his head. "Ignore it."

Ivan looked around, sniffing. "What is that? It smells...," he closed his eyes and inhaled, "wonderful. Is that food?"

"For some people in here." Linus gestured to a small crowd gathered ahead in the corridor. "Remember the scrapper in Med Bay?"

Two men faced away from each other on opposite sides of a strut. They turned, laid ration pouches on a low stool, shook hands, and counted to three. They pressed their right forearms against the strut. They shook as their soft flesh began to sizzle and smoke, wafting the unusual scent into the air. One of them snarled, and the other one screamed. He pulled his arm away and ran down the corridor, leaving his ration behind on the stool. Half the crowd cheered, and the other half surrendered their bets. The winner, forearm burnt black as bad as the first, sauntered away, both pouches tucked under his arm.

Ivan's eye's widened. "Where did you bring me?"

"Anillo de Fuego."

"Ring of Fire." He gulped. "You brought me to a black zone? Are you glitching?"

"I need a terminal."

"We could've used Sandro's." Ivan's volume and speed increased, making Linus uncomfortable. "Why does it have to be this one?"

"Keep your voice down. It's got an A3 clearance locked in."

"Another dummy reader?"

Linus nodded. "All her financial, medical, and genetic data. Everything that makes a keystone a keystone and more. We'll get in, see what's there, and get out. If we find something interesting, good for us. If we don't, there's no harm in taking a peek."

"If she discovers we were poking around without BOSS's approval..."

"She won't. That's why we're here. No mic, no chip scanner, nothing to trace a query back to us. She'll see a hab and a level. That's it. She'll never know it was us."

"What about Helix or Oxi? If we can spy with it, so can they."

"I'm sure they do. But without an A1 or A2, they can't edit or do anything too serious. They just poke around, looking for people to extort."

"The system can't work like that."

"That *is* the system. And we're about to benefit from it."

Linus pushed through a ripped, plastic curtain strung between two struts into a room an eighth the size of his office. The old dummy terminal, or what remained of it, lay piled on the floor in the rear of the space. If anyone had seen it without knowing what it was, they'd think it was a heap of old trash - screen, keyboard, wires, and cracked thorium block batteries - piled on top of each other. Beside the terminal, a gangly man sat on a low stool braiding three copper wires. He was emaciated, naked, sweating, and striped with rust from nose to nipples and navel to knees. He was Helix or Oxi. Linus was never sure. It was too difficult to pick out Helix's rusters from Oxi's rust-dusters.

"Five min. One ration." The man continued braiding.

"We don't have any rations. Perhaps something else?" Linus nudged Ivan and looked at the tool case on the floor.

Ivan buried the crumbling flower under busted diagnostic pads and wrenches on one side and locked it. He opened the other half, tilting it toward the braider.

"That." He pointed to the pry bar, "One min," and returned to braiding his scrapped, wire necklace.

"Three," said Ivan.

The braider looked up. He twisted the wires' ends together and draped the completed necklace around his neck. "What special you get triple? Don't care tun maint." He looked over the open case. "Pero, maybe deal. One min that," he pointed to the pry bar again, "and two min that." He pointed to the teddy bear. "Three min todo."

"Deal." Linus gave him the bear and the bar.

The braider, now standing and unfortunately shaved in all the same rusty places, passed through the curtain. "Three min." He stood on the other wide of the curtain, both flat, sweaty buttocks visible through the rips.

"Did I say hope earlier?" Linus handed Ivan the interface keyboard. "I meant prayers. Query Harin Roche."

ROCHE, HARIN
BORN: 12.JANUARY.2619
>>> ASSIGNMENT: KEYSTONE H1:L42:U1 <<<

"No voice output?" said Ivan. "I like this terminal."
"That's her. Query everything. Full data sweep."
Ivan typed the commands.

GENETIC:
 NEG GENETIC: [NEG-00] NONE ON FILE
 NEU GENETIC: [NEU-44] HETEROCHROMIA
 POS GENETIC: [PGM-01] HIGH RAD TOLERANCE
MEDICAL:
 S/T ILLNESS: NONE ON FILE
 L/T ILLNESS: NONE ON FILE
  SURGERY: [OE-1C] OVUM CRYONICS
   DATE: 12.JANUARY.2637
FINANCIAL:
 DAILY ALLOTMENT: 15
  PRE-RATION: 997,629 L
SECURITY:
 CRIMINAL HISTORY: NONE ON FILE
  AUTHORIZATION: H1-KEY-Z5

"She turned eighteen four months ago," Ivan whispered. "I thought she'd be older. How old was Sandro Hazbegi?"

"He'd be thirty-six now. Open Sandro's C.O.D and display the terminal again."

H9:L5:C00:ST00

"Same. At least we know it's the system and not something we did. Scroll back." Ivan pointed to, "Pre-ration?"

"Inherited wealth. Almost a megaliter."

Ivan gasped. "She's soaked. She could buy anything, do anything."

"Not with a Z5."

"Isn't that the lowest clearance? Same as Hazbegi if he cut out his chip. She'd need someone to open doors, use lifts, do everything for her."

"Well, she's chipped, an adult, and alive."

Ivan shrugged. "Maybe she only listens to educational songs and bedtime stories?"

"Unlikely. There's only one data field we should care anything about." Linus groaned standing up. His back didn't appreciate using terminals piled on floors. "Tell me, if you could ask Harin Roche one question, what would it be?"

"Why Ovum Cryonics extracted her eggs on her eighteenth birthday."

"Three min done." The braider pushed through the curtain.

Ivan reset the terminal and dropped the keyboard onto the heap.

The braider sat on his stool, still naked except for the wire necklace around his neck. "Go now." He rubbed the teddy bear across his chest, turning its curls wet and orange.

"How much to buy back the bear?" said Ivan.

Linus's eyes widened. "Leave it."

"It's the kid's only toy."

"No backs. Vaya you."

"How about this?" Ivan dug into the toolbox. He reached for the crumbling yellow flower, the braider reached under his stool, and Linus lurched in front of Ivan.

Linus felt the zinc dart tear through his abdomen, heard the pulser's distinctive pop, and saw the muzzle flash out of order. His thoughts slowed, and time reversed onto itself, becoming twisted and infinite, then leapt forward again. It was an odd sensation. In a disjointed haze of pain, thought, and movement, he saw himself reach into his suit, pull out his pulser, and squeeze the trigger once, twice, three times. The braider was dead, leaning backwards, one hole through his neck, one under his eye, and another above. A scarlet halo glistened on the wall behind him. His pulser dropped to one side, and the teddy bear fell to the other. Linus's lips moved, and he heard himself scream at Ivan to grab the bear and get the fuck out. Only the weight of his boots kept him from flying away as he ran for his life.

Ivan followed closely behind.

10

Ivan

Habitat 8's nurse, a young man with an oddly high-pitched voice, dabbed fuchsia healing gel over the shallow abrasion on Ivan's upper left arm. The gel hurt enough, but the nurse had been stabbing him with the same dull swab for ten minutes. It didn't help.

Ivan winced and jerked his arm away. "Not so hard."

Undoubtedly, the pubescent tech's mommy had taught him to tie his shoelaces that morning, and somehow the kid had snuck into the med bay to make Ivan's day as bad as it could possibly be.

"What the hell, Slag? Pay attention to what you're doing."

SPEECH CODE 12C [PROFANITY]: -50 ML DEMERIT
SPEECH CODE 12C [PROFANITY]: -50 ML DEMERIT
BEHAVIOR 53M [DENIGRATION]: -2 L DEMERIT

"Doctor Yi." The tech's high, cracking stutter hurt Ivan worse than the wound.

"Deputy Finn," Doctor Yi slid aside the privacy curtain, "I've kindly asked you to stop verbally abusing Nurse Dalal. This makes three. Don't force me to bring this up with the chief."

Ivan cackled, startling everyone including himself. It was the funniest joke since Sisters of Mercy.

72

Nurse Dalal stretched a translucent bandage across Ivan's wound and rubbed his fingers over its self-adhering edges, sticking them into place. "I'm done here." He gathered pieces of bandage, bloody swabs, and a leftover gel pack onto a tray. "I'll check on the chief."

Ivan peered through the white curtain at Linus snoring on the gurney. "How is he?"

"The dart entered and exited through the fatty tissue on his left side. Nothing serious. Two days bed rest, and a full week to recover. The chief will be back to his cantankerous, old self in no time."

Ivan's muscles relaxed, and he exhaled the single longest breath he'd ever held. "Thanks, Doc."

"Thank Linus's love handles. If you're going to get shot, a through-and-through is the second-best outcome."

"What's the first?"

He patted Ivan's bandage.

"Ow!"

"A minor abrasion." He examined Ivan's arm. "I don't often see sapioid replacements these days. Yours is quite impressive. Oh," his eyes widened, "are those veins?" and he pressed on the wound. "They look so real." He squeezed. "How's that feel?"

Ivan grimaced. "Real."

"It must circulate your blood to keep itself cool. I bet it'd fool body heat sensors, too. Bionics don't come cheap nowadays. It must've cost a small fortune. Two, three thousand rations at least."

"Or so I've been told."

"Sisters of Mercy?"

"Yeah, well, Sister Isabella mostly."

"God rest her soul."

Ivan nodded.

"As for your rad suit, better it than you."

"This doesn't feel lucky."

"Could be worse. You could spend the last weeks of your career in bed."

"He told you."

"Not exactly. He was loopy from the morphine, but I think his exact words were, 'He couldn't have waited twenty-five fucking days?'."

SPEECH CODE 12C [PROFANITY]: -50 ML DEMERIT

Doctor Yi glared at the terminal. "That and something about being chased by a naked bear." He looked deep in thought. "I should lower his dosage. Excuse me."

"What time is it?" Ivan edged off the gurney and pushed his bandaged arm through his bloody shirt sleeve.

"1950 hours. Almost fourth check-in."

Third check-in for Radek. He's at The Pissing Ant. "Mind if I use your terminal?"

"The one in the back." He shut the curtain.

He circled the med bay, passing the terminal twice before summoning enough courage to stop. He waved his right wrist high over the chip scanner, then correctly against it. He opted for manual input over voice commands, and opened the personnel directory. He scrolled down to F and talked out loud to himself.

"Fa, Fab, Farlow, Farris, Femk, Fillion. I hate manual searches. Finn. Finn, Anton. Finn, Gabriel. Finn, Hapgor. Finn, Ivan. That's me. Finn, Oleg. Finn, Radek."

He hesitated, finger shaking over the name. He stepped back, cracked his knuckles, and wrung his fingers. "Please miss the call." He tapped the screen twice.

LOCATING: FINN, RADEK. . . . .

He waited, grinding his teeth as BOSS went to work, first listening for Radek's unique voiceprint across its integrated system terminals. But The Pissing Ant was always busy, often too loud for BOSS to hear any voice softer than an angry drunk clamoring for his last shot of gluco.

LOCATING: FINN, RADEK. . . . .

Failing that, BOSS calculated where Radek should be for the time, day of the week, or if his mother had come into the bar again. If that happened, Radek had a 22.713% higher probability of being in the back, near the storage room terminal. A million other scenarios were possible, including Ivan getting shot and selecting the emergency call option. He shook his head, wondering how both could have happened, and bit his upper lip each time another calculation dot appeared after Radek's name.

"Hey. What's up?" Radek shouted over thumping music and chatter. "How's work?"

Maybe it's not too late. He could've pretended he'd accidentally called instead of sending a general message or lower his voice and say, 'Oops. Wrong ident'. But his name was on Radek's screen, so that wasn't a valid option. Or he could end the call and blame it on BOSS.

A glitch in the messages subsystem could happen. He'd seen a message delayed, a call routed to a wrong room, and a terminal's link-up dropped in the middle of a long conversation. All had happened to him in the last year. All were plausible, though not frequent enough for him to tap CANCEL.

"Ivan? You there?"

"Everything's fine. You know how it is."

"I can't hear you. Speak up or stand closer to the terminal."

"I said everything's fine."

"Say again?"

"How's The Ant?" Shot glasses rattled and clinked. Two or three shattered on the floor, and a woman screamed, "Ut-oh", followed by raucous laughter. "Sounds busy." *A party?* "Is someone having a birthday party? Hello?" The sounds became muffled, and a door slammed shut. "Radek?"

"Hey. I'm back. I had to transfer your call to the stockroom."

"Good. At least you can hear me now. So, how's things?"

"What happened? And don't make me pull it out of you, 'cuz you know I will."

"Nothing serious. A little—"

"Someone shot you, didn't they?"

How did he know? "It's only a graze. I'm fine."

"I knew this would happen eventually. It was Linus. That digi-licker actually got drunk enough. Where are you? What place is Hab 8, Level 3, Unit 8329?"

"It's Med Bay 8. But really, I'm okay."

"I'm coming to get you, and I'm going to——"

"You're not going to do anything. It wasn't Linus's fault. I promised I'd call if anything serious happened, so I did. But I'm fine. Really. I'll stay here until Linus wakes up, so I might be home late, too."

"Deputy Ivan Finn, where are you?"

"Or home early. Anything's possible. Got to go. Love you." Ivan ended the call and circled the med bay toward Linus's little, curtained room.

"Ivan!"

"I'm coming. Hold your ration."

Ivan found Linus sitting on the gurney, legs over the edge. He scratched at the bandages on his left side with one hand and smacked the morphine dispenser with the other.

"Stingy toaster. How... Never mind. Got it." Linus leaned over and tapped a blue plus until the milligrams per hour doubled from eight to sixteen.

"Doc Yi said that's enough."

"Remind me of that when you get shot." He bumped it up to *18 mg/hr.*

"I was." Ivan showed off his left arm, the sleeve bloody from shoulder to elbow. "See. Shot. Like you."

"That scratch?" He scoffed. "I've gotten worse cuts shaving."

"Shave with pulse darts, do you? Let me guess, you've been shot a hundred times."

"Don't be daft. I've been shot *at* a few times, but I've never been hit. Thanks for that by the way. You're lucky pulser darts are expensive. The slag only had two."

SPEECH CODE 12C [PROFANITY]: -50 ML DEMERIT

Linus winced. "Which was one less than I had before saving your life. How many times this week?"

"Twice."

"Digi, the braider each got three darts. My pulser holds six. Remind me, how many darts do I have left?"

"Zero."

"Tell me you got that ugly bear."

Ivan removed the stuffed animal from his suit pocket. "I got the bear, but I lost the toolbox, flower, and Rosco's badge is somewhere between the braider and this med bay."

"So one good, two bad, and one not important. Don't worry about Rosco. He'll be fine. I take it our suits are ruined?"

"Recycling says they can't patch holes in rad suits. The inner layer has to be extruded at high temperature. I sent them in and requisitioned two more."

"Okay. And?"

"One hundred forty-four replacements were on requisition. The next two will go to a couple astronomers in Hab 3. They should get those by tomorrow night. BOSS estimates ours will arrive in," Ivan cleared his throat, "237 years."

"Shi— sheet." Linus bumped his morphine to *20 mg/hr.*

SPEECH CODE 12C [PROFANITY]: -50 ML DEMERIT

"I said 'sheet', not shit."

SPEECH CODE 12C [PROFANITY]: -50 ML DEMERIT

Linus's nostrils flared, "You and me, toaster," and he bumped his morphine to *23 mg/hr.*

"237 years is assuming salvage teams can, well, salvage what they need from the old cities and continue to recycle the necessary materials at the current rate."

"I appreciate your," he grimaced, "commitment. It took a few of my old deputies years of dedication and once a full month of pre-planning to make that many mistakes in such a short period of time. Serves me right for not checking to see if you brought your pulser." He increased his morphine to *27 mg/hr*. Linus moaned, sounding more like Digi than himself. He smacked his lips. "Now, that's my number."

"How's my favorite chief?" Doctor Yi entered the makeshift room chomping on soy chips. He tapped the minus sign on the morphine dispenser, reducing Linus's happy twenty-seven back down to seven. And he locked the machine.

Linus's eyes narrowed. "Damn un-well."

SPEECH CODE 12C [PROFANITY]: -50 ML DEMERIT

"Ha—" Ivan bit his lip. He coughed and cleared his throat. "Excuse me. Dry throat. Doctor Yi, can you tell Linus what you told me earlier?"

"Oh yes, the dead scrapper. Shame, really."

"Dead scrapper?" Linus looked to Ivan. "Who's dead?"

"James Choi. He was found in his unit this morning."

Doctor Yi shook his head. "Such a waste."

"I see." Linus's head fell back on his pillow, and he stared longingly at the dispenser.

"I know it's not standard procedure, but can you move Chief Halla to Med Bay 2? There's someone I think he wants to talk to." Ivan sat the teddy bear at Linus's feet. "And he'd be much more comfortable with Doctor Langstrom treating him."

Doctor Yi's smile stretched ear to ear. "Oh. I see. Good for you, Linus. Carla's beautiful. And lucky for you, a very tolerant woman."

"Give us a moment. I need to speak with my deputy."

"You do that. I'll ask Carla," he winked at Linus, "if she's got a spare bed for you." He pushed through the curtain and headed toward the rear of the med bay.

"Revenge?" said Linus.

"Opportunity."

"In that case, you're in charge of H.I. until I recover."

Ivan had been waiting to hear the words, or at least the middle part, for months, but they caused his neck to sweat and his shoulder to ache. "You think I'm ready to take over?"

"Not even close. But putting me in with the kid shows you have good instincts somewhere in there. Don't ignore those." Linus winced and scratched around his bandages. "But if your instincts tell you to make a sudden move in front of a naked man with a pulser... You can ignore those."

"I *am* sorry about that. And I don't think we should go back there. Ever."

"See." Linus patted Ivan's hand. "Good instinct. And about James Choi."

"I know. I messaged Hab 7's coroner an hour ago."

"And pay a visit to Ovum Cryonics."

"I'll make an appointment for tomorrow morning. Anything else?"

"There is one last thing," he said, his voice faltering.

"Sure. Anything."

"Come closer."

Ivan took a step forward.

"No. Up close. I have to tell you. I don't want BOSS or Doctor Yi to hear."

"I can't unlock your morphine."

"Not that. Come closer."

He bent to hear Linus's secret message.

Linus patted his cheek. "Don't fuck it up."

11

Linus

Nurse Dalal pushed Linus's gurney over the threshold into Med Bay 2. "I have your 1000 hours transfer. Name is Halla, Linus. Pulser dart wound to the lower left abdomen."

"Hiya Raj." Heidi Sillerson picked up the report tablet chained to the gurney's head rail. "How are we doing today, Chief? I see someone tried to poke a couple new holes in 'ya. How awfully mean of him." Heidi leaned over Linus's face. Her long, red hair swept across his forehead and eyes and tickled his nose. Linus swatted, like battling a hundred flies swarming around his head. "Everything's in order, Doctor. Isn't it, Chiefy?"

Linus blew Heidi's hair off his face. *Anyone that perky must be evil.* "Carla, make it go away."

"I think he's hurting. Poor thing needs a drippy-drip-drip."

"Carla?"

"I'm here. Heidi, put the chief in B." She pointed to an open curtain. "Thank you, Raj. We'll take good care of him."

"Yes, Ma'am." He hustled through the exit and disappeared into the eerie glow of the tunnel.

"Here we go." Heidi pushed Linus's gurney past a long row of closed curtains with letters H to C stenciled in blue paint at the center of each. The gurney swung wide at room C, and Heidi pulled it into the center of B. "And here you are." She kicked in the gurney's two wheel locks. "So you can't roll away."

"Lucky me."

Heidi setup the recovery room, arranging machines around the bed. She stuck ice-cold adhesive pads to Linus's chest and sides and ran a thin tube from the morphine dispenser to a small inlet below the saline bag hanging on a pole beside the bed. She referenced the medical tablet and set the dispenser to seven milligrams per hour.

Linus hauled the medical tablet up by its chain onto the gurney, gripped its edge, and looked for the right spot on the back of the perky tech's head.

"He's ready for you, Doctor."

"I can see." Carla stood at the foot of the bed with her arms crossed. "Put it down, Linus."

"I was just pointing out that seven milligrams isn't enough. I have two extra holes in me for ration's sake."

"Set the dose to twelve milligrams per hour and lock it."

"Yes, Ma'am."

"And if the chief swears at you or does anything unkind, feel free to lower the dose until he stops."

Heidi snorted. "Yes, Ma'am. I'll be back in a few minutes to insert the catheter."

"What do you say, Linus?"

Linus clench his teeth. "Sounds lovely," he muttered. "Can't wait."

She left the room as perky as she entered it.

"That's completely unethical."

"I couldn't agree more. Be sure to thank Ivan for me. It was his idea."

"Was it, now? I'll pass it along. And something else."

Carla lifted the curtain between recovery rooms B and C and rolled a stool through the short opening. "So am I to assume you requested the transfer for a reason other than berating my staff?"

"Perhaps."

"I thought so. Don't forget he's still my patient," she whispered. "The last thing he needs is more stress, and if you say one mean word to him..."

Linus drew an X across his chest, and for a moment, he was caught off guard by the lack of rust streaks on the white medical gown. His hands, his fingers, his whole body had been washed clean as he slept. *Baptism and pulser wounds. Who would've thought?* "I promise to be more tactful."

"Well, you'd better start now." Carla rolled her stool around the gurney to the curtain dividing rooms B and A. She slid it aside and tied it to a monitor at the rear of the space. "Good morning, Luka. This is my good friend Linus. He's my very best friend in all the eight habs, and he wants to meet you."

If Carla hadn't introduced him, Linus wouldn't have recognized the boy. Luka sat cross-legged, propped up on a gurney by two overstuffed pillows behind him. His pale, freckled face glistened under a layer of gel, and thick gauze wrapped around his neck, left arm, and both thighs. Damp tunnel moss covered both his legs from knees to toes, and his right arm and hand were almost healed but remained a stitched patchwork of skin donated from every ethnic group in the habs. He held a large drawing pad in his lap, doodling colorful curly-cues and the same boxy robots as before.

"Hi, Luka." Linus waved from his gurney. "Carla tells me you're super brave."

Luka continued doodling, retracing the same curly-cue over and over.

"It's true. I've never seen anyone so brave." Carla jostled his gurney. "I told you, didn't I?"

Luka shrugged, but he didn't look up.

"Well, that settles it. I'll let you two talk." Carla backed out of the room, "Remember what I said, Linus," and pulled shut the two front curtains.

Linus craned his neck. "That's a good drawing. I like robots."

Luka peered out the corner of his eye.

"Do you like robots, Luka?"

He shrugged.

"I bet I know what you like even more than robots." He strained to pick up the teddy bear Ivan had sat at his feet. The excruciating pain of stretching his wounds was worse than getting them. "I found this little guy hiding in your home."

Luka looked up from his doodle pad.

"Does it have a name?"

"Datvi," said Luka, his voice only louder than the overhead light's soft hum.

"His name is Datvi?"

Luka nodded.

"I like that name." Linus tossed the teddy bear beside him. "Does it mean something?"

Luka pulled Datvi to his chest. "Datvi is bear."

"You mean in Georgian. That's a clever name. Did you name him?"

He nodded.

"Then you're super brave *and* clever, too. I bet your dad is proud of you."

Luka squeezed the bear harder.

"Can you tell me where your dad is? I want to tell him how brave and clever you are."

Luka raised his patchwork hand and pointed at the ceiling.

"He's on another level?"

Luka extended two fingers. He drew an invisible halo around the top of his head and pulled them down over his eyelids, closing them. Linus recognized the child's innocent gesture as kid-speak for angel. There was no doubt. Sandro Hazbegi was dead, and Luka knew it.

"I'm very sorry, Luka. I know this is hard, but I need you to be brave a little longer."

Luka sniffed and crushed Datvi into his chest. His heart monitor beeped.

"Luka, did you tell anyone?"

He didn't move.

"I need to know. Did you tell anyone? Anyone at all?"

Luka's face turned red, and he nodded. The beeping quickened.

"Who did you tell?"

He quivered and sobbed.

"Who did you tell about your dad? Who else knew?"

"Her." He stammered. "I told her."

"Her? Who is she? Harin Roche? Luka, did you tell Harin Roche?"

The separate, pointed beeps solidified into an incessant screech.

Carla pushed through the curtains. "I warned you, Linus." She unfastened the dividing curtain and slid it back into place. "That's enough for today. Heidi, get in here."

"Coming, Doctor." Heidi hurried into the room. "Ma'am?"

"We're moving the chief to recovery H."

"Yes, Ma'am."

"I didn't say anything mean."

"But you said enough. And it's time for you to rest."

Heidi pushed Linus down the hall into recovery H as fast as the gurney's wheels could spin.

"Four milligrams LZP."

"Yes, Ma'am." She pulled a pre-filled syringe from her pocket and jabbed it into his arm.

"Not so hard." He rubbed his arm. "What was that for?"

"Something to give us a modicum of peace and quiet."

"But I didn't, I di-, I . . ."

Linus woke from a deep, dreamless slumber. It was the best, longest sleep he'd had since Katri's diagnosis. The only real sleep. *You can't beat a drug-induced coma.* Most of Med Bay 2's lights were off, though a faint glow came from somewhere. Linus scanned the makeshift room and noticed a portable terminal to the left of the gurney. It was out of reach, and the screen was dim. It'd be useless anywhere other than the unsettling dark of the recovery area. *Carla or one of her techs must've rolled it in when I was asleep.* 02:07 floated across the screen. *A whole day? What was in that syringe?*

"BOSS?"

It flickered and the command dialog appeared.

Thank God. Normally, Linus hated BOSS always listening, waiting for input and commands, sweeping everything into its learning algorithms, performing countless analyses on his every word, judging his decisions, and predicting his choices. But with two holes in his side and three stitches in each to keep them closed, if he had to climb off the gurney to type the command, he'd knock over the terminal out of pure spite.

"Open personal journal Halla, Katri. Authorization Halla, Linus H4-SEC-A1. Dictate entry dated 18 December 2635. Natural voice synthesis Halla, Katri. Auto-repeat until canceled."

<<BEGIN>>

I can't believe it's almost Christmas. . .

BOSS read Katri's journal to him as he did every night since her death. At least he tried to listen. The old terminal's speakers crackled and hissed and erratically skipped and dragged through the short entry. Katri's once lovely voice was three octaves too low. She had become a baritone. She'd become Ivan. "Ugh. BOSS, cancel dictation."

<<CANCELED>>

"Glitchy toaster, which recovery room is Lukaa Hazbegi in?"

RECOVERY A

Too far. "Crap."

SPEECH CODE 12C [PROFANITY]: -50 ML DEMERIT

"I wasn't talking to you. Leave me alone."

BEHAVIOR 69U [ANTISOCIAL]: -250 ML DEMERIT

He lumbered out of Recovery H holding the saline bag at neck height. The slow stagger from H to A was a tormented eternity. Under the bandages, his stitches tugged when he slid his right foot forward and tore open the pits of hell when he slid his left. He whispered his mental notes aloud, taking his mind off the pain. Each letter was an important reminder.

"G is for 'God.' Why is God punishing me? Was it something I did in a past life? Ivan would say it's something I did in this one. But he'd be wrong."

"F is for 'Fucking hell. This hurts.' It's Ivan's turn to get shot."

SPEECH CODE 12C [PROFANITY]: -50 ML DEMERIT

"E is for 'Escape.' If Ivan gets shot, Radek would kill me. Definitely need an escape plan. Right. Nowhere to go. Scratch that. Aim for the shoulder next time." Linus winced and grabbed his side. "Ivan, you lucky shit."

SPEECH CODE 12C [PROFANITY]: -50 ML DEMERIT

"D is for 'Decisions'. Too many. Most of them bad. This one especially."

"C is for 'Carla'. Something about Carla. Carla something. Something bad."

"B is for 'Braider'. Bastard. That's two Bs. Bastard braider. Dead bastard."

SPEECH CODE 12C [PROFANITY]: -50 ML DEMERIT
SPEECH CODE 12C [PROFANITY]: -50 ML DEMERIT
SPEECH CODE 12C [PROFANITY]: -50 ML DEMERIT

"And A. A stands for 'Answers.' Answers to my questions."

Linus opened the curtain to Recovery A and peered into the room. His eyes had adjusted on the journey enough to see Luka wasn't there. Piles of bunched and twisted bed sheets sat in his place. "Figures. Carla. Going to tell BOSS to fine Carla. Two fines. Submitting a false report. Hiding the kid from me. No. That's an F or H or something else. Carla. Carla's a bad doctor. Close enough. Close. That's C." He sat on the gurney's edge, "Yea me," and groaned. Linus dropped his half-empty saline bag onto the pile of sheets, its rigid, plastic nozzle hitting something hard under them. Linus leaned to the side and pulled a large tablet out from underneath.

"BOSS," Linus shouted into the air, "turn on the lights."

Medical Bay 4's overhead lights flashed, and the room became bright as day.

"BOSS, turn off the lights," said a man, somewhere in the room.

"Cancel command."

"Whoever you are, it's two in the morning. People are trying to sleep. Show some common courtesy why don't you?"

"Never had much use for courtesy." *Courtesy. C. Good word. Why didn't I? Right. Never mind.* "This is official Habitat Integrity business."

Linus turned the tablet over. It was Luka's doodle of colorful, boxy robots and curly-cues. *Curly-cues and robots? Why always curly-cues and robots? Curly-cues?* Linus rotated it in his lap. *Or sixes? Luka's six.* He rotated it back. *Not sixes. Nines. They're nines.* "They're nines. They're *all* nines."

"Great," a woman called out. "They're all nines. I love nine. Now turn off the lights."

"Turn them off," repeated the man.

"I wasn't talking to you. Either of you." Linus's side ached, and he was tired of sitting. "Now shut up and let me think."

Sandro Hazbegi. The report. The terminal location. Habitat 9.

"BOSS, turn off the lights." Linus shuffled toward his room at twice the speed he had limped away from it, Luka's drawing tucked under his free arm.

"Thanks, asshole," said the woman.

SPEECH CODE 12C [PROFANITY]: -50 ML DEMERIT

"Thanks for nothing," said the man.

"BOSS," said Linus, panting. He grabbed hold of the gurney's foot rail and caught his breath, "locate H.I. Deputy Finn."

12

Ivan

I van took a long detour on his way to the Ovum Cryonics lab in Habitat 5, first withdrawing a ration, then stopping by the Habitat Integrity office. He looked at a terminal as he entered the room. *Seven minutes late. I hate being late.* "Excuse me." Ivan knocked on the white, enameled wall, the metallic clang getting the attention of two tall, slender men walking by in purple lab coats. "I have an appointment at 0930 hours to see," he pulled Integrity's palm-sized tablet from his pocket, its rusted, broken chain dangling in the air, "a Doctor Jonathan Farris."

"Officially, it's Senior Ovum Cryonics Technician Farris, but I'm hoping for a shorter title someday." He dismissed the other man. "But call me Jack. You must be Chief Finn." He shook Ivan's hand and wiped the rust transfer down the side of his lab coat. "Please..." He motioned to a white desk and chairs in the corner of the room. "I don't think I've ever gotten a visit from Habitat Integrity. I don't imagine there are many violent crimes to solve in Ovum Cryonics. Unless you count my ration allotment."

"Technically," Ivan grinned, "Never mind. You can call me Chief. And there's always a first time."

"For a visit or a crime?"

"That's what I'm here to find out."

"Of course. What brings you to my cold, little corner of the world?"

"Like you said, I've never been here. Can you explain what exactly you do?"

"Tell me, Chief. Are you married?"

"I am."

"Have you and your...," he scanned Ivan's face, "husband applied for breeding approval?"

"We have."

"If BOSS approves your breeding application, this lab will be your next stop. We cryogenically preserve unfertilized and fertilized ova as well as sperm for both private and approved public use for everyone in all eight habitats. Take you for instance," he nodded at Ivan, "being incapable of procreating naturally."

"As much as we keep trying."

"I mean in the traditional, unassisted method. You and your partner will need an egg and a surrogate. The first step is to select a donated ovum. Pre-fertilized ones typically come from couples who've previously produced offspring that've received a higher ration than either of the donors. If you're allowed one of those, we'll provide details on the donors and expected genetic makeup of your child - skin, eye, and hair color, adult height, I.Q., and, of course, an expected range for the offspring's ration allotment. The second step is to select a surrogate approved for that specific set of eggs. Male-female couples go that route if they don't want to use their own DNA after it's approved, but it takes a long time - especially if the surrogate is currently occupied, so to speak. Mono-gendered couples such as yourself typically go with an unfertilized ova. The female pronucleus will be removed and replaced with your and your partner's. There are fewer surrogate options for bipaternal or bimaternal zygotes if you chose to employ the Zhou method, but by definition, the offspring will be both of yours. The results are less predictable though, and we can't guarantee a ration increase. You could, potentially, lose rations if the offspring isn't an improvement over yourself, there's an unpredictable mutation, or if the child doesn't survive to maturity."

"You say you store ova and sperm from everyone in the habs?"

"If they've applied and received breeding approval."

"Including keystones?"

"Of course. Impeccable DNA, over seventy percent viability, above average radiological tolerances, few mutations or genetic diseases," he shrugged, "usually. There are always exceptions."

"Do they donate?"

"Only amongst themselves. Few are infertile like us hab roaches up here, so there's no need. For them, it's more about playing the odds than genuine procreation."

"Playing the odds?"

Jack clasped his hands and placed them on the desk. "Say you're receiving four daily rations. You can survive on one, two keep your lips wet, three make you comfortable, and with one more, you begin to afford those little creature comforts we all enjoy. But it's still not enough for you. To move below the platinum vein, you need to be a parent or guardian to a genetically superior child, one to pull you down a level, one with an expected ration allotment between six and seven. If BOSS approves breeding, you and your partner or partners send up sperm and eggs. Those combinations are tested until BOSS indicates the offspring has desired traits - something that'd bolster the germ line, and would likely be assigned more rations than yourself. You preserve the combo with the highest allotment. Then you repeat the process with only those two as the basis. Everything else is destroyed."

"Destroyed so nobody else can implant them. How would that help a keystone? It's not as if they have to compete. They're maxed at fifteen rations and have everything they'd ever want or need."

"Exactly. If BOSS allocates their children anything less than fifteen, the kid won't be a keystone as soon as they turn eighteen. BOSS makes them move up in the hab. Bye-bye mommy and daddy's legacy. Hello working for a living."

"Keystones do this until they produce another fifteen ration child?"

"More like *if* they produce."

Ivan sat back in his chair. "You mean they don't have kids?"

"Not due to fertility issues, of course. Essentially, they refuse to birth or surrogate any offspring they view as less than themselves. Since only a handful of genetic combinations can produce fifteens, the typical failures I see stem from, well, brothers and sisters, at least on the genetic level, trying to procreate."

"They're inbreeding."

"Unfortunately. Fifteens will soon be fourteens, then thirteens, twelves, and so on until there's a large enough gene pool to sustain a basic level of genetic diversity."

"The opposite of salvage."

"If you mean scrappers, then yes. That would be a fair contrast. Unsanctioned births, little genetic testing, basic subsistence. But they keep trying until one or two survives. Even if the child is a sanctioned birth or genetically superior to the parents, there's always a reason for BOSS to keep them on Level 1 and away from superior people who may actually contribute something positive to our future." Jack snickered. "No need to waste water on inferior stock, 'ey?"

"I see what you mean by cold, little corner."

"Eugenics is a cold science. Passive as it is, we don't kill anyone. We merely don't allow them to live. Now, don't get me wrong. I can't blame scrappers for trying to evolve. Keystones have attempted other, less official methods, too."

"Such as?"

"Cloning, for instance. Rich idiots tried it a century ago, but they couldn't solve the copy of a copy of a copy problem. Lots of deformities, shattered mirrors, and such. 'What not to do'," Jack made air quotes with his fingers, "was half the introductory lecture I got when I took this job. Along with BOSS's directive for the human species of course."

Ivan rocked back in his chair. "To perfect and preserve all life."

"Opposites if you ask me. So, are we finished? An overview and a history lesson?"

"Almost. I came to ask about one keystone in particular. Woman's name is Roche."

"Roche?" Jack bit his upper lip and cracked his knuckles one-by-one.

"Harin Roche. Keystone. Someone here extracted eggs on her birthday about four months ago."

The technician removed a report tablet from the desk drawer. He swiped his fingers down and across the screen. "Roche.

Roche, Harin. Here she is. One of the playing the odds types. Eighteen years old. Hit the tunnel running, I see. My subordinate performed the procedure." Jack swiped through several more screens, and his brow furrowed.

"What is it?"

"Strange. Even with the least fertile keystones, there's at least one viable ovum. But it seems none of hers were. None at all." He laughed. "The tech says she got belligerent when he gave her the bad news. She's got a follow-up appointment scheduled for next week if you want to stop by, witness BOSS turn a keystone into a scrapper. Speaking on a purely emotional level, of course. She'll need a few more failed extractions before BOSS re-assigns her."

"I'll keep it in mind. As for non-viable eggs, I'm assuming they're sent somewhere."

"Sure." Jack pointed to a meter-tall door to his left, *Bio-Waste,* printed in purple letters around the four edges. A similarly sized boxy, purple robot sat, parked by the door waiting for instructions, *O.C.* for Ovum Cryonics stenciled across the front panel. "Our bio-waste bot takes them, along with the time expireds, male and female samples, to the recycler at third check-in every afternoon."

"To be destroyed." Ivan exhaled, exasperated. "Damn."

SPEECH CODE 12C [PROFANITY]: -50 ML DEMERIT

"How long do you hold onto—" Ivan's tablet's message indicator flashed. "Excuse me for a moment." He left the tech at his desk.

"Sure." Jack pointed to the tablet's dangling chain. "How'd you do that by the way?"

"Pull hard."

Ivan leaned on the terminal and scrolled through the new report downloaded into his tablet. It had limited access and a three-meter range, but with it in his pocket, Ivan could walk and submit updates without returning to the Integrity office every other hour. It was much more convenient, and he wondered why Linus hadn't broken the chain himself. They could get twice the work done. *Work done?* "Oh, Linus." He rolled his eyes.

"Something the matter, Chief?" said Jack, yanking on his tablet's short chain.

"I have to go." Ivan hurried toward the exit. "Would you mind sending me a priority message if Harin Roche returns?"

"Sure. No problem. What's happened?"

"There's been an incident in Hab 8, Unit 8212."

The technician slid his tablet into its drawer. "Sorry. I'm not familiar."

"Tunnel maintenance," said Ivan, leaving the lab.

Ivan slid aside the half-open door and stepped into the office. A vile odor penetrated his nostrils, and industrial-smelling fumes clawed at his eyes and burned in his throat. He retched, burying his nose and mouth in his elbow and stumbled backward, cracking several fragments of glass under his boots.

A man lay dead on his stomach near the system terminal, one arm outstretched toward the door, the other bent, fingers touching his nose. Beside him, a petite woman was on her side, hands covering her face. Exposed skin on their heads and hands discolored and blistered, and blood, oil black, dried around the nose, ears, and eyes. They wore standard hab uniforms, and neither were over five feet tall. Tunnel Maintenance badges rested on the floor beside them. Bright white powder swirled in the air and blanketed the bodies and the floor. Both were disappearing, piece-by-piece, sucked into the contamination vents. It reminded him of old songs about snowy hills melting into spring. But the smell certainly didn't. Ivan retched again.

"Denatured proteins," said a middle-aged woman standing inside. She wore a red hazmat suit with the name *Chahna* embroidered in big, black letters across the orange badge on her chest. With one hand, she covered her nose with a black cloth, and with the other, she pulled a handful of powder from a sack on her hip and tossed another layer over the bodies. "And hydrogen fluoride."

"Rust cleaner?"

Chahna sprinkled it over the man's cauterized, white eyes. She threw another over a third tunnel maintenance badge propped up against one of their boots. "Pungent, isn't it? Especially at high concentrations." She motioned for Ivan to re-enter the room. "You don't have to worry about it, though. It's ninety-nine percent dissipated."

"I'll wait for the other one percent. Thanks. How long do you think?"

"The magnesium hydroxide neutralized most of it. I'd say a day or two for the H.F. smell to dissipate." She nodded toward the bodies. "Three or four for them, and five or six weeks for you and me. Saved enough rations for a bath?"

Ivan sniffed his sleeve and recoiled. "Ugh. Brilliant."

"What happened to the good days when they drained your rations and left you parched for a week? Now they're melting people in locked rooms."

"Who?"

"Oxi, Helix, take your pick." She upturned the sack, dumping the last of the powder over the bodies. "Don't expect to get any evidence off them."

"You're awfully calm." Ivan looked her up and down. "How do you know all that?"

"Oh, sorry." She pulled off her gloves and tucked them into a side pocket. She shook Ivan's hand. "I'm Chahna." She tapped her name badge. "You're Deputy Finn, right? The look on your face says Linus never mentioned me."

"The chief isn't one to talk about the past."

"Really? That's a change."

"How so?"

"I was one of his deputies. I was his *last* deputy. The man nearly got me killed. You know he's supposed to have sixteen deputies? Eight habs. Two partners per hab. I bet he's got you zooming around. His own personal collector bot."

"To be fair, we haven't been busy before now. Sixteen seems," he glanced at the bodies, "excessive."

"Only because I'm doing your job." She put her hands on her hips. "BOSS doesn't pay me enough rations for this."

"He's retiring. He wants to be a shroomer."

"Oh? I haven't heard. Then you'll be Chief of Integrity?"

"There's nobody else. Zooming bot, like you said."

"You'll need a new deputy."

"Apparently, I'll need sixteen."

"Or one to start."

"But one who can focus on the task at hand." *Linus?* Ivan looked behind him, expecting to see his chief waving a finger at him. But the words had come out of his own mouth. He shuddered and shook Linus's ghost off his back. "I mean, I'll keep you in mind."

"As I was saying, you won't get any evidence off the bodies. No fingerprints or manifestos scrolled on the walls in acid." She pointed to three shattered bottles on the floor. "This was a smash and dash. Someone tosses one bottle of water, one bottle of H.F., and a third, maybe sulfur or bromine, into a room and seals the door from the outside. The three combine and go to work. The gas chokes the victims so they can't scream when they're having a heart attack. The combination dissolves almost everything else, and then the quarantine system kicks in, sucks out the gas and what's left of the bodies. Hence, no more evidence."

"What do you make of that?" Ivan pointed to the three tunnel maintenance badges. The two by their sleeves had faded to yellow and crumbled, exposing the adhesive backing. Ivan couldn't read those. However, the one against the boot was fraying around the edges, but the brightly colored orange background and black, embroidered department and crew member name - *Rosco* - shown through the thin dusting of powder.

"Poor Rosco. He was a good man."

"Where was that badge when you got here? Was it propped up like that?"

"I haven't touched anything except for the neutralizer. The acid would've eaten through the floor if I hadn't."

"Where were you last night?"

"Me? I was with these two. All three of us hit up a gluco bar in X until late. The one with the ant that pees on you. They called it a night. I stayed for another round."

"Where did you go afterward?"

"Home to bed."

"And where is that?"

"Three hundred meters down the corridor. Near their quarters." She moved back. "Wait. No, no, no."

"I'm establishing a timeline. That's all. You're not a suspect."

"I worked with these guys for a year. I'm the one who found them. I'm the one who reported it. And I'm the one who's been doing your cleanup job for an hour."

"I understand that. As of now, it looks as though someone or several someone's followed your coworkers home from the bar, and propped up Rosco's badge after they were done."

"Leaving a tunnel maintenance badge in the tunnel maintenance office? Everyone's got one. What would be the point?"

"Not a badge. *That* badge. Rosco's badge."

"It's only a badge."

"And a message."

"A message for tunnel maintenance?" She pulled the badges off her chest and sleeve and zipped them into her suit. "Do you understand it?"

"It means we, Linus and I... We screwed up."

"Well, whatever you and the chief did," she looked over the bodies, "you shouldn't do it again."

Radek dropped the black, plastic bowl on the floor. It bounced on the hard steel, and the pink, square chips scattered in every direction. The vents went to work, sucking the smaller fragments down through the perforations. "What were you thinking?" said Radek, sweeping the remaining chips into the bowl. "Owing him and owing him your life, our life together, are two very different things."

"I wasn't—"

"When you said you owed him, I thought you meant taking over his duties early. Submitting more reports. Working late." He placed the bowl on the table. "Not getting shot, and certainly not leading whoever back to my bar." He sat across from Ivan. "You don't mess with Helix. They have their little spies everywhere. You could've gotten killed."

"But I didn't."

"No. You two got dressed up in T.M. gear to play possum and got the real possums killed."

"Nobody's playing anything, and there haven't been possums in centuries."

"You know what I mean. You could've gotten killed."

"You said that."

"Well, I hope you'll listen to me next time. If there is a next time."

"There will be, and I will. But for now, I need you to leave. Face it, nobody's going to The Ant for shots once the news gets around. At least not for a while."

"Where else would I go?"

Ivan bit his lip. "I stopped by your mother's quarters after I submitted my reports."

"You didn't."

"She's agreed to let you stay there as long as you want. I also asked her to keep it quiet. No terminals. No messages."

"Making secret deals with my mother isn't helping your case, Ivy." Radek stuffed his mouth with chips. "She must've loved that," he said, spitting pink crumbs. "My husband groveling at her door."

"All I said was you needed a place to stay for a while. She jumped at the chance to see you. I think she misses you. And don't call me Ivy. You know I hate it."

"She thinks we're splitting up, and she gets to stitch my pieces together again." He shoveled another handful of chips into his mouth. "So, when am I to do battle in the ninth circle of hell?"

"She's expecting you first thing in the morning."

"Jeez." Radek held his ration pouch up to the flickering light. He hummed and made several finger crosses against it.

"Stop." Ivan laughed and took it from him. "It's not holy water."

"Don't tell mother that."

Ivan held Radek's hands. "I'm worried this time. I mean really worried."

"Something worse than death?"

"Radek," Ivan squeezed hard, "BOSS could cut my rations for this. Our rations. Put us both back in waste rec or reassign me to salvage."

"You could request a transfer from Salvage to Entertainment. You can sling gluco with me at The Ant. Be a two-ration. Or grovel at BOSS's feet. If it had 'em. Or blame it on Chief Parch."

"Linus. I forgot." Ivan rubbed his temples. "I still have to tell him."

"What do you think he'll say?"

"I don't know." The terminal's message indicator flashed, alternating between blue and yellow and settled on green. Ivan rolled his eyes. "When you speak of the devil..." Ivan tapped the screen. "Linus, this is getting to be a habit. It's 0230 hours. Aren't you supposed to be resting?"

13

Linus

Linus pulled the clean uniform from his ankles to his knees and eased himself off the gurney. He pushed his right arm and then his left through the sleeves and fastened the seals. The sharp pain in his side had dulled, and the novelty of feeling soft, newly recycled material against his skin added to the distraction. He was two minutes into a staring contest with a frayed boot lace when Ivan peered through the parted curtains.

"You're *still* not ready?" Ivan pushed them aside and entered the room. "You told me to wear a new uniform and be here by ten. It's five after, and you're not even dressed."

Linus grimaced and leaned against the gurney.

"We don't have to do this today. Doc said three or four more days. Maybe a week."

"I feel fine. Never better. Now, why don't you show me those detective skills?" He lifted a boot off the floor and shook the toe in the air. The long laces swung side to side.

Ivan knelt and rested Linus's boot on his knee. "This isn't what I had in mind," he said, tying the laces.

"You're doing it wrong."

"I know how to tie boot laces. Thank you very much." He yawned and examined the odd, twisted knot he'd tied, one loop ten times the size of the other. "Darn." He untied the laces and started over.

"You'd think it'd be the same as tying your own." *A bunny hops over a log and sees a faerie. Or was it a tree? Do bunnies chase faeries?* He'd heard Sister Oni recite the rhyme a dozen times, but he'd never gotten the chance to repeat the words to someone else. *Why would a bunny chase a faerie? Alas, another mystery for another time. Is he thinking it, too?* "Tying someone else's feels awkward, like your head's on the wrong side. There's a rhyme for that, you know."

"So I've heard." Ivan sighed.

"How's that gluco-slinger of yours?"

"Technically Radek's a shopkeeper."

"You never told me how the new breeding application went."

"Same as every other month. Radek was rejected for his sporadic ALS, and me for my left arm malformation." Ivan flicked a cave spider off his pant knee. "I can understand his rejection. His parents were both sevens, but now there's an ALS gene mutation he could potentially pass on. But this," he opened and closed his left fist, "can't be inherited. It doesn't make sense for BOSS to hold it against me. Against us."

"BOSS works in mysterious ways."

"You mean the Lord. And that phrase usually denotes something good has happened."

"You never did tell me the story. Your arm, how you came to Sisters of Mercy, what happened to your family."

"I will. Someday."

"Well, keep trying in the meantime. I've seen lots of shopkeepers with kids."

"True." Ivan finished tying the knot. He leaned against the gurney beside Linus. "But because of his ALS, he only wears pull-on shoes. So, this is as close as I'll ever come to tying someone else's laces."

"BOSS rejected him for a bad fashion choice?"

"I meant he has a hard time tying... Wait. You're messing with me, aren't you?"

"Am I?" Linus grinned. "Sister Oni was right about you."

"I'm glad to see, well, glad's the wrong word. I'm... I can see you're getting back to normal."

Linus leaned over, sniffed, and recoiled. "Ugh. Really, Ivan?"

"What?" Ivan smelled his uniform and his palms. "Oh, that. It's those denatured proteins I told you about. The uniform's new, but I can't get the smell off my skin. Don't even think of sniffing my hair."

"I wouldn't dream of it. What else happened while I was wasting away in here?"

"I looked in on Jeda Pringle."

"Digi's owner?"

"The same. I wanted see if he'd found what fragged her CPU."

"You know..."

"Yes, I know what you're going to say. That's why I got up early, did it on my own time before first check-in."

"And?"

"He wouldn't open the door."

"He wasn't there, or Jeda's hoarding everything Digi stole for him and doesn't want anybody to see."

"No, he was there. He just didn't want to answer the door. I swiped for first check-in at a terminal a few meters from his unit, and BOSS recorded him swiping in five minutes later at his terminal inside."

"Five? He didn't swipe until his shock clock zapped him?"

"Seems so. But he did swipe. I know that much. He was probably toe-up on the floor and missed check-in."

"And you want me to use my ident and A1 clearance to open the door if he refuses."

"We could say a disturbance was reported."

"As long as he doesn't ask to see a report number." Linus had done the same on occasion. No reason to stop now. He nodded. "As soon as we have some free time. What else?"

"Geology's terminal overloaded again."

"How many times is that?"

"Three this year."

"What are they doing over there? Any fatalities?"

"One geologist. The last one, actually. I coded it as another accidental overload and returned the report to medical. I sent the body to be recycled."

"Still, tell whoever's re-assigned next to move the geology lab, and tell Power Distribution to take another look at the room."

"I spoke to P.D. They said they checked the power interface, but nothing was wrong."

"Three previously functional terminals were transferred into Geology from three different levels, and they all exploded. No, it's not the terminals. It's the power grid. Tell them to check again."

"They said they'll try to do it next week, but they've been inundated with power failures in Habitats 6 and 7."

"Excuses, excuses."

"It appears someone's been stripping copper from *inside* the grid." He sneered. "Idiots."

"Okay. Good excuse. What else?"

"Last is James Choi."

"Ahh, yes. The scour hero. The usual radiation poisoning?"

Ivan shook his head. "Severe hyponatremia due to rapid water ingestion. Seems he drank ten liters in a sitting."

"Death by rations. And I thought I'd seen it all. Any indication of motivation?"

"Nothing. It could've been an accident, but I don't think so. It's a lot of water. He would've had to force it down over one to two hours. And the only things in his quarters were the ten empty pouches, seven full ones, a couple soy packs, and a rusted laser etching of him and a young woman."

"A daughter?"

Ivan shrugged. "If she is, she's unsanctioned. There's no record of a spouse or child or any family beyond his parents. Also deceased. The access log shows him entering and exiting the same containment doors every day for the last year. Not so much as a shot in X-Stretch. In and out until the day he carried Luka in from the scour and deposited him in quarantine. Then he scanned through two containment doors, crossed five access gates, returned to his quarters, and collected seventeen rations from Sisters of Mercy the next afternoon. That was about thirty minutes after we left Sister Oni."

"When Digi was glitching?"

"That was the last time anyone saw him alive. His next stop was the morgue. The body's still there waiting my sign-off before he goes into the recycler."

"And the other seven rations?"

"Sister Oni's holding them, along with another sixty-one that came in later."

"What would Sister Oni call sixty-eight rations and a virtue too late?"

"A tragedy. But I was hoping those could be..."

"His last heroic deed?"

Ivan nodded. "He'd be seen as a hero to the end."

"What was your final determination? Accident or suicide?"

"I wanted to hear your opinion first. BOSS views suicide as self-murder. Choi would be recorded as his own murderer, but H.I. would have final say on the report specifics and what to do with his property. If people knew Choi killed himself with the donations, they'd likely dry up. Who wants to help poor people kill themselves? If it was a tragic accident, donations might be okay, but the case would revert to medical. They could say anything about him. They could even call it an accidental suicide, and donations would still dry up."

"Difficult decision. Save face or save lives." Linus slid his fingers through his hair. He rubbed out several long wrinkles on his suit and creased the collar to a fine edge between his fingernails. He softened his voice. "Have you considered doing both?"

Ivan leaned into Linus, shielding their conversation from the terminal in the corner. "How?"

"Not a self-murder. His murder."

They looked like two pre-pubescent boys passing secrets and naughty words. Stupid, yet effective. But Linus was starting to wonder if it mattered, or if it ever did. Still, it wasn't worth the risk of losing a day's rations for telling Ivan to file a false report.

"But he wasn't... you know. And what about the rations?"

"I won't be chief again until we exit Med Bay, so it's up to you." Linus's voice returned to normal. "When you inspected his home, you noticed the lock was broken. There were signs of a struggle. You surmise he was held down by someone, though you don't have any suspects and never will, and they forced him to drink those rations. But, as a credit to his name and his entire caste, he'd already decided to donate the remainder back to Sisters of Mercy in the hope more, wealthier people would follow his example. Hero of the scour, James Choi, martyred for the great cause." Linus closed his eyes and pounded his fist into his chest.

"I thought you didn't like drama."

"Only when it serves a purpose. So, acting Chief Ivan Finn, when do we leave?"

Ivan cleared his throat. "Give me a few minutes. I want to finalize and submit a certain report before we go."

"Take all the minutes you need as long as they're under five." Ivan left the room, and Linus looked at his reflection in the terminal screen. He spotted a few errant hairs, and licked his fingertips. He smoothed them down. They sprung up. He smoothed them down again, and they sprung up again. He yanked them out and counted how many, frowning when he reached six. He laid them on the scanner plate, *This is your fault,* and kicked the terminal. He hollered, "And tell Carla I want to ask her something before we go."

Linus had been to Level 42 twice, both times at the beginning of his career. The first was out of curiosity and the second at the end of an hour manhunt in search of a two-ration wacko who'd hacked off the previous Chief of Integrity's right hand, escaping his zone with the bloody appendage. Linus caught up to the man after a brief ride in an emergency lift. He was writhing on the floor, screaming in pain, his own chip electrocuting him when he stepped off the lift. Before that incident, two emergency lifts in each Habitat - those designated for free-range departments - could move up to Level 1 at the surface, down to Level 42 at the bottom, and open on every floor in under ten minutes. Culprits unknown removed the control switches two years later, restricting everyone to three-level trips in the other fourteen. They'd been on requisition ever since, with 237 years left to go.

After an hour swiping his wrist across chip scanners, moving down three levels, shuffling through long, crowded corridors to find another lift, swiping again, down three more, across another corridor, and down another three, Linus's mind focused on Choi and Hazbegi and everyone on salvage duty. He pictured them venturing far into the scour looking for scrap, always returning at the end of a three-hour limit. He wondered if anything was left of the old, crumbling cities, if they had been picked clean by thousands of salvage missions in the search for anything useful, or if the scour, rightly named twice for its effect on everything exposed to it and how scrappers must search through it, had left nothing but rubble, and life in the habs was the best it could be. Few objects had survived four hundred years of rust, radiation, and abuse.

Linus pointed out a circular hatch near the lift on Level 30. "Lucky, there's still such a thing as a ladder. We can climb down to 39. And then take the last lift to 42."

"Or we could go all the way."

Linus lifted the heavy hatch and climbed inside. "Falling through the ceiling will certainly get their attention." He stepped and grimaced at the same time.

"I sense a 'but'."

"Their hatch is sealed from the inside. And that strategy wouldn't have won you any points down there."

"I hate game metaphors. We're looking for information," Ivan tugged on the hatch. It slammed shut above him, rattling the ladder to the one below, "not trying to win at Chess."

"It is a game of sorts. Aside from BOSS, it's one of the few things keeping the peace." Linus passed through the next hatch. "Watching and waiting. Moves and countermoves. Anticipating your opponents. And making your move with one hand on the board and the other behind your back. It's a cliché, but there it is."

Ivan slammed the hatch. A deafening clang reverberated in the corridor below. "Boards can be broken."

"It's safer to play the game you know with the players you know. Can you say what the next game will be? Who's your next opponent? Sit back from time to time. Let the little things go.

Give him - or her - a reason to keep playing. Arrogant opponents telegraph their next moves because they think you're too weak to do anything about it."

"Then they'd be right. Neither of us knows what's going on."

"Whatever happens, this game will end, and the board will reset."

"Who's weak in this scenario?" Ivan closed the next hatch.

"The habs are a finite world. In a finite world, everyone's weak." Linus descended through the next level. "So, you're partly right about the board. All our pieces are fragile."

"The lives of the maintenance crew weren't ours to play with."

"No, they weren't. And I'll remind Helix if it's the last thing I do. Probably will be." He scoffed. "There goes the board."

"So where do keystones fit into this? They don't have a drop to gain from helping us."

"Except the chance to show off. We'll ask for Miss Roche's benevolent help. And we'll do it loudly. Everyone around will see we need her. Her ego will inflate like an overfilled ration pouch. Let her boast and tell us all the things she has and what she can do. Things we could never afford. I want her to think we're coming to beg for her help in an unrelated case." Linus paused on the next rung. "I guess we should think of one before we knock on her door."

"If you wanted us to look unprepared," Ivan pulled the habitat integrity tablet out of his pocket. The rusted chain dangled above Linus's head, "this was a bad idea."

"I think it's perfect." Linus stepped off the latter onto Level 39. "You'll look like an idiot carrying that old thing around. How far from a terminal did you get before it lost the link-up? Five meters?"

Ivan shut the last hatch with a thunderous clang. "Three. I kept having to bang it against terminals to reset the connection."

"Well, there you go."

The long, dim corridor was eerie with the rhythmic hiss and pop of motors and pistons behind the thick, steel walls, the foot-falls of crowds moving overhead, and the low hum of system terminals every few meters. The hab was speaking in a chatter of faint, random echoes. Whispers from no one. Linus found everything about the place unnerving. The look on Ivan's face indicated he felt the same.

"Make sure they see the chain smear rust on your pretty, new uniform."

"This thing cost me nine rations." Ivan's voice echoed in the darkness.

Linus shushed him.

"Radek's going to divorce me as it is."

"Nobody Level 10 up stays this clean for long. It's obvious they're new, and it'll be obvious we're trying to impress them. I want them to see that. Let them one-up us. The more they try to put us down, the more they talk, the more likely they'll say something we can use."

"Nine rations, Linus. That's three days salary for me. Four and a half for Radek."

Linus limped toward the lift, his hand against his side. "If you're that broke, I suggest you submit BOSS an expense report."

"What? You never said we could do that."

"I was kidding, but keep up the whining. It'll add to the effect." Linus swiped his wrist across the scanner. A cracked, white plastic button labeled *ACCESS* flashed green. "And try to look impressed."

"I'll look impressed if I'm impressed."

The doors slid apart, and soft music played through the lift's speakers. Linus squinted and looked back at Ivan. "Yep. That's the correct look."

Ivan didn't respond. He shielded his eyes from the light and followed Linus into the gleaming, white marble lift.

14

Ivan

Ivan's eyes adjusted to the piercing light as the lift descended the last three levels to 42. The pain subsided, and the blanket white floor separated into individual square tiles crisscrossed by fine platinum lines. He counted the tiles as they came into focus. When he reached twelve, the doors slid apart, and Linus hustled him through the opening.

They shuffled into a narrow room slightly wider than the lift and as bright. At the back of the room stood a large, riveted door set into a marble arch carved with birds gliding over blossoming flowers or perched in fruit trees and a thousand other animals and insects. A naked man and a woman cowered on opposite sides of the door, draped in large leaves and twisted vines to keep their modesty, but hiding themselves only from each other. Ivan recognized the image as the expulsion from paradise, but wondered why anyone would display it so prominently. The only phrase that came to mind was 'Ignorance is bliss.' *But whose ignorance?*

Sweat dripped down the back of his legs. His face flushed, and pressure grew in his chest. He thought he was used to the habs' balmy temperatures. The highest two levels stayed near 30c no matter what, and the mid-levels were always comfortable around 25c. But each level had gotten warmer as they descended. Level 42 was sweltering, and he guessed the level number and its temperature weren't far apart. He fanned his face with his hands, but it wasn't enough. Ivan unfastened the top seal on his uniform, plucked at the collar, and wiped a river of sweat from his forehead.

An attractive young man sat smiling, dressed in sheer linen clothes, on a large basalt block in the center of the room. He had glistening black eyes, black hair tied high in a topknot, and a red ankh branded on his neck under the right ear. *He looks so real. Almost human. He's certainly worth more than a milli a minute.* Not that Ivan would admit first-hand knowledge of such things out loud.

"Hello?" said Linus.

"Hello gentlemen," he said, a light accent cutting the 'h' from hello and exchanging 'g' for 'dz.'

Ivan slipped in a puddle of his own sweat. It smeared across the polished floor as his rubber boot treads made several rapid, high-pitched squeaks against the wet tile.

"You must be from Integrity. I was expecting you an hour ago."

"We were delayed," said Ivan. "Excuse me for asking, but how did you get here?"

"Same as you."

"You're a sapioid. Gamma model, right?"

"I don't understand."

"My deputy means to say you look quite real."

"Then I'll take it as the compliment. You may call me Peter."

"Are you sure?" said Ivan.

"Quite sure. It's my name." Peter stood. "Now that pleas-antries are over, Miss Roche has asked that I inquire as to the purpose of your visit before proceeding."

"I'm Chief Linus Halla. This is Deputy Finn. We're here to ask Miss Roche questions regarding a case we're working on. Honestly, we need her help. It's quite urgent we speak with her."

"Please elaborate."

"I wish we could, but we're permitted to speak only with Miss Roche. You understand."

"Certainly." He bowed. "Miss Roche would like to speak to you regarding a matter of great importance as well."

"And what matter is that?"

"I believe that's between you and Miss Roche. If you'll follow me..." Peter sneered, "Je m'excuse," and pushed past Linus and Ivan.

Ivan looked for the off switch and wondered how much he could get for its most profitable bits in the market. But he went along with Linus, pretending not to understand they'd been mocked.

Peter led the group back into the lift. The doors closed behind them, and Peter pushed the three level buttons in sequence. *40, 42, 41, 41,* and simultaneously pressed *40* and *42.*

Ivan watched the display roll as the lift descended.

Level 43, 44...

"Where are we going?"

Level 45

"It'll only take a moment."

Level 46

"Forty-six? There are only forty-two."

Level 47

Peter grinned, "Of course there are," and faced the back of the lift.

Level 48

"Harin Roche lives on Level 42."

Level 49

"Of course she does."

Level 50

The rear wall divided into two distinct doors down a long seam running between them. Light shined up from the floor at the bottom as a glowing dot and quickly filled the seam to the top with a bright line of light. The lift stopped, a bell chimed, and the marble doors parted.

Peter exited and led Ivan and Linus along a wide corridor triple the size of any other above. Thick marble walls, five meters high, loomed on either side and ran the length on either side. High above the open ceiling, rounded points of massive, glistening stalactites hung from the dark, vaulted rock, stretching farther than Ivan could see. The floor shook, and three drops of water fell from high above. They splashed one after the other on the floor ahead of Ivan and quickly evaporated, leaving behind chalky, sepia rings overlapping on the white tile. The floor was covered in them, some areas more densely shaded than others.

"Does that extend up to 42?"

Peter mumbled something in French, but Ivan couldn't make it out. Linus continued behind Peter, his head level with the floor. He glanced at the walls along the way, but he never looked up. Ivan tapped his shoulder.

"I can't tell you what I don't know," he said. "This place isn't in the schematics."

"Of course it is." Peter stopped at an arched doorway on the left, identical to the one on 42. It was the only break in the high wall Ivan had seen since exiting the lift. "Perhaps you overlooked it."

"I guess so," said Linus. "I visited 42 once or twice," he looked around, "but that was a long time ago. This space is quite impressive. Don't you think so?" He nudged Ivan.

"Surprising is more like it."

"Of course it is."

Ivan looked over the ornate, arched door, not having to try hard to look dumbstruck or stupid. *Who is this woman?* He touched the carving, *warm stone,* and looked for a chip scanner, a key hole, or something to let him inside.

"Miss Roche's enjoying her morning by the pool." Peter stroked the once-bitten apple carved on the arch, and the door crept open. "She'll receive you there."

Peter continued toward the rear of the house, strolling, taking his time to recite the Roche family history as they wound through the home. He spoke of the part they had played in designing the habs, who chose their locations, and he listed the machines they'd invented and the great things they had supposedly done. They passed empty rooms and moved through halls lined with ornately framed portraits of old women propped up in chairs, each with ordinal numbers after their names. Peter said all had died at an impossible old age, with a book in one hand and a glass of iced water in the other.

Ivan considered himself as educated and worldly as one could be while living beneath it, but Peter's words were real and gibberish at the same time. He was envious, enraged, glum, and confused, emotions shifting like colors in the domes high above and all in the span of a footstep. He dug his fingernails into his wrist and tugged at the skin. It hurt. Though he wasn't sure why pain proves reality, it did the trick. The confusion wore off, and Ivan saw everything for what it was. Keystones used the past as a stepping stone to a certain, predictable future. Evolved genetics assured them comfort, marriage, rations, and medicine in exchange for giving the human species a chance to survive. But the low, reverberating echo of their footsteps through opulent, empty rooms proved the Roches weren't passing on anything anymore. They hadn't in a long time.

They moved through a room full of real paper books, and Ivan meandered, looking around tall stacks and under ancient wooden instruments hoping to find little toy robots, plush stuffed bears, a child's doodle pad, or anything to prove Luka had been there. But nothing indicated Luka, or any child, had ever lived in that home or played in that room. He ran his finger along the bell of a saxophone and flicked it, the high rattle making him smile. All the instruments he'd ever seen or heard were made from bent steel plates or copper pipes. Everything else existed only in digital sound files and as monochrome pictures in an educational database for children.

This made the home even stranger. He hadn't seen a system terminal or report tablet anywhere - aside from snobby Peter. He was a terminal on legs. The whole place was oddly low-tech.

Ivan picked the top book from a stack and opened it to the middle. He touched the pages, *Smooth*, felt the weight, *Heavy*, smelled the binding, *Musty*, and read the title, "Halti Fell: The Next Step," he ran a finger across the embossed, golden text at the bottom, "by Adora Roche." He put the book back and jogged to catch up with the others.

Peter exited the game room and turned a corner, leading them down a narrow set of stairs changing from polished marble to rough granite to granite crosshatched with narrow troughs cut into the stone. The wet outline of a single footprint, toes pointed toward him, remained on the bottom stair. Linus didn't seem to notice. He stepped over it, following Peter into the low room. Ivan paused on the penultimate stair and raised his boot over the outline, its wide shadow easily smothering the petite print before it had a chance to evaporate.

"Harin Roche, I presume." Linus's voice echoed from ahead.

"Pleasure," said a woman, her accent identical to Peter's.

"I'm Chief of Habitat Integrity, Linus Halla. We're grateful you could meet us on such short notice."

"Is there another?"

"That would be me." Ivan stood beside Linus. "I'm Deputy Chief of Habitat Integrity, Ivan Finn."

Harin Roche sat on the last of a dozen sloped, granite benches surrounding a shallow, underlit pool. A plush, white towel covered her from the knees and tied under her arms, and a teardrop opal hung from a dainty, silver chain around her neck. She was lovely and young, and her skin was smooth and unblemished except for small patches of tiny bronze freckles dotting her nose and cheeks. Long brown hair draped in a braid over her shoulder, the end resting in her lap. And her eyes were two colors - one silver blue, the other dark brown, almost black.

It's her. "It's you." Ivan sat on the dry bench opposite Harin.

"Excuse me?" She glanced between Linus and Ivan and slid back, leaving a wet streak on the rough granite.

"What my young deputy means to say is that we think you're the person we're looking for and the only one who can help."

The smooth, stone ceiling was wide and flat over the benches and sloped low over the shimmering, crystal clear water. The light reflected up onto a long, intricate relief carved across the apex. It depicted the habitats' domes rising up from the long, barren valley and decrepit, lifeless cities crumbling in the distance. It was a testament to the human spirit and the triumph of human ingenuity after The Great Catastrophe. And it was hidden in a place few would ever see. The irony wasn't lost on Ivan.

"Peter," Harin looked up to him, "I'm thirsty. And bring two more for our guests."

Peter nodded, and he vanished up the stairs. Harin gestured to the bench, and Linus sat, wincing, beside Ivan.

"Are you unwell, Chief Halla?"

He straightened. "I'm fine. Call it the last twenty years catching up with me."

"I understand. Now, what's this important case you spoke of?"

"Miss Roche, we've started looking into the child found north of Hab 2."

So much for making up an unrelated case.

"A child outside? How awful. I hadn't heard."

"Certainly someone brought it up in conversation," said Ivan. "Or you read it in the weekly hab report."

Peter returned with three glasses of water, a large ice cube floating in each.

"Peter tells me everything I need to know. Thank you, Peter." She took a sip and sat it on the bench, rattling the ice against the glass. "So, how is it you think I can help?"

"That depends," said Ivan.

"On?"

"If you have any children of your own," said Linus.

"No. Of course not. I only turned eighteen a little over four months ago."

"How about ovum extraction?"

"Are you here about the cryo-tech?" She crossed her arms.

Ivan glanced at Linus. "We wanted to hear your side of the story."

"If anyone should file a complaint, it ought to be me." She stroked her teardrop necklace. "He said all my eggs were defective, that I was defective. It was awful." She looked at Peter. "You can't know how humiliating that was for me."

"How did you react to the news?"

"I may have offered," she looked away, "to freeze the man's testicles in that little room of theirs if he didn't run the test again."

"What did Peter do?"

"He suggested I use liquid nitrogen."

Ivan coughed, "Excuse me. Dry throat," and held back his laugh. He finished off his iced water and cleared his throat. "As I'm sure you're aware, that's a serious accusation."

"Indeed. The fine for threatening a breeding specialist could dry even *you* out for a while."

"Not a threat. A miscommunication. I was understandably upset. And as for Peter, he knows I detest cold things. Except my rations, of course." She took a sip.

"You heard Miss Roche, Chief. It was a miscommunication. I think we should believe her. I believe you, Miss Roche."

"Thank you, Deputy."

"Maybe we can look past it this one time. Chief? What do you say?"

"Perhaps." Linus handed his empty glass to Peter.

Harin nodded, and Peter left to fetch more water. "So, what is it you want from me, Chief Halla?"

"Miss Roche, are you familiar with a man by the name of Sandro Hazbegi?"

"No."

"Have you met anyone from salvage team?"

Harin laughed. "Salvage? No. Never."

"What about tunnel maintenance or waste reclamation?" said Ivan.

"Ridiculous notion."

"Oxi or Helix?"

"Certainly not. What does any of that have to do with the cryo-tech?" She glanced at the stairs. "Peter?"

"Miss Roche, why did you agree to meet with us?"

"Other than to apologize for harassing the cryo-tech?" said Linus. "That's something, by the way, I expect you to do."

"Of course." She sipped her water. "Perhaps I was curious. I don't often get visitors."

"And why is that?" said Ivan. "You have a lovely home, but it'd be a shame to spend all your time here alone."

"It's a long story."

"I love long stories. How about you, Chief?"

"I do, indeed. The longer, the better."

Harin walked to the far side of the pool and sat on its short edge, feet in the water, head beneath the carving's sloping side. She peered up the stairs. "Peter?"

"Coming, Miss."

"Miss Roche?"

"How much do you know about the habs, Deputy?"

"As much as anyone, I guess. Our habitat zone is one of twelve dotted around the globe. They were designed to last fifty years as a final proof of concept for self-sustaining cities on Mars or some low-gravity asteroid. That's why irreplaceable things like this," Ivan pulled the report tablet out of his pocket and shook its rusted chain, "are chained in case they float away. A few years into the project, The Great Catastrophe happened. Most radio bands stopped working, and everything outside the habs died. Nobody knows why exactly. But the Halti Fell Habitat zone became the eternal lifeboat, and four hundred years later, we're still going strong."

"Strong? Do you believe we can survive in these habitats forever?"

"Forever? No. But salvage teams take what they can from the old cities when we need it. And I happen to think we've done alright for ourselves. Everyone has a job, food and water, education, entertainment."

"What about the Ration-caste system?"

"Well, there are a number of opinions about that. A lot of people would call it the price we pay for living in an orderly society."

"Miss Roche, you're a keystone. You yourself have benefited from that system. Certainly more than anyone I've ever met."

"I agree with Chief Halla. What does this have to do with you?"

"You asked me if I had any children, Chief. Do you? Humor me. It's only fair."

"No."

"What about you, Deputy?"

"Not yet. But we're hopeful."

Peter brought more water and snacks - a kind of soft, purplish-blue food. Ivan didn't know the name, but he ate them before Linus could try one. He followed Linus's lead, draining another full glass in a single, long gulp. Harin sent Peter away to get more.

"You were saying?"

"Imagine, Deputy, that you did have a child. Imagine you had a remarkable child. Genetic tests indicated the highest radiologic tolerance of any human in recorded history. In fact, your child's DNA is immune to several forms of radiation and resistant to most others. You come to believe, in your heart, your child has a special purpose. Call it whatever you want - the hand of God, destiny, evolution, the end of a successful round of eugenics."

She's talking about Luka. Ivan was sure Linus was thinking the same thing.

"She could be mother to a new breed of human, one that could leave these habitats and seek a life outside the valley. What would you do?"

"She?"

Harin nodded.

"Well, I'd love her," said Ivan, "and I'd pray she grows up to be happy and healthy."

"Please. I was honest with you."

"Okay. I'd want her to fulfill her destiny. If not for her, then for the sake of the world."

"How far would you go to ensure she'd fulfill her duty?"

Peter, the code in the lift, a secret level. "What is this place?"

"This is my home. One of them anyway. I was born here. Same as my parents before me."

"And where are they? Peter didn't mention them."

"That's because they're dead. A stalactite fell during a tremor when I was two. Peter's raised me ever since."

"That means Peter's a caregiver sapioid. He's your nanny?" Ivan grinned. "Is that why he avoided my question about it? Lie of omission or not. I didn't think it was possible."

"It's not." Linus crossed his arms. "Not unless someone programmed him to ignore the question."

"Chief Halla, what temperature is that water?" She grinned and pointed to the pool.

"I'm not here to swim."

"Take a guess. Go on."

"Around... 29c."

"What if I told you it's 31c? Did you lie?"

"You're saying it's not a lie because he doesn't know?"

"You see, Peter believes he's my nanny as you called him, and *only* my nanny." She glanced at the stairs. "My mother made sure of that. He's been in the Roche family one hundred seventeen years."

"Dumb toaster," said Linus.

"Pardon?"

"Nothing." Linus placed his hands on his knees, supporting himself. "Miss Roche, on the day you visited cryonics, where else did you go?"

"Nowhere. Peter escorted me there and back."

"And since then?"

"Just here."

"Forgive me for being blunt, Miss Roche. But what about your other eggs? It seems foolish to pin the future of the human race on a teenager, a few eggs, and a lab test."

"That's why I made a new appointment with the lead tech. I want to verify the first cryo-tech didn't make a mistake."

"When's that scheduled?" said Ivan.

"Next week."

"If you don't mind, I'd like to accompany you to see how it's done."

"Of course. I'll let you know."

Peter returned with two more glasses of iced water. Ivan and Linus tossed them back like the finest O negative gluco, devoured the second helping of food, and licked their lips.

"Thank you for your time, Miss Roche. We'll leave you to your water," said Ivan.

"So soon?" Harin stood. "Wait. You don't have to go. Stay if you'd like. Peter, bring more water and blueberries." She snapped her fingers at him.

"No thanks, Peter," said Linus. "We're fine. But we may return with a few follow-up questions."

"I'll be sure Peter knows to let you in."

15

Linus

L inus stepped off the ladder onto Level 5 and kicked the hatch. It slammed shut, knocking flakes of rust from the one above onto his head. He shook out his hair and leaned against the wall, holding his right foot off the floor and his hand against his pulser wound. He grumbled and swore.

SPEECH CODE 12C [PROFANITY]: -50 ML DEMERIT
SPEECH CODE 12C [PROFANITY]: -50 ML DEMERIT
SPEECH CODE 12C [PROFANITY]: -50 ML DEMERIT

"You did that to yourself."
Linus looked at the terminal, making a mental note of his rations at home and subtracted BOSS's demerits in his head. "I know. I may have to borrow a ration or two next week."
"I'll transfer you one in case." Ivan wrung his fingers. "Crap."

SPEECH CODE 12C [PROFANITY]: -50 ML DEMERIT

"Twice more so we can be even."
"Then you'll have to borrow from someone else. Did you happen to see any system terminals down there?"

"None. That would explain the Z5 clearance. She doesn't need anything higher because she doesn't have a job, and she spends her whole day by the pool telling Peter what to do."

"So, now what?"

"Now we go back to H.I. I want to look into her parents' deaths." Linus limped ahead. "But first I want to review Luka's DNA trace again."

"Again? We went over everything for hours." Ivan stopped him in the corridor outside their office. "You know what I think? I think—"

"I do, and you'd be wrong. History only repeats if you make the same mistakes."

"What do you call this?"

"A hunch. She's hiding something."

"Or that's how she acts because she was raised by a snobby sapioid nanny her whole life. But in regards to Luka, she was right. Breeding age is strictly eighteen to twenty-eight. Not a minute before or after."

"BOSS could've made an exception."

"Since when? Radek and I have applied several times." Ivan leaned against the wall beside Linus. "And even if her eggs were extracted when she was eleven, what are the odds those eggs would've been viable for a surrogate to carry to term? One in ten thousand? A hundred thousand? You have to admit you're stretching."

"I don't know. I'm tempted to say stranger things have happened, but..."

"Let's look at this from the other side again. Sandro Hazbegi. What did he bring to the mix? Don't forget he was a scrapper because his DNA was, well, not as good as hers. Or even ours."

Linus nodded, entering the H.I. office and sat in Ivan's chair. "It had to be something important. Important enough to choose his over anyone else's."

"Marika and Sandro had their Luka sixteen years ago. Was he a sanctioned birth?"

"He was."

"So a sample of Sandro's DNA is physically stored in the genome vault in Ovum Cryonics. Which means someone took his from the vault and hers from the testing area."

"Stands to reason. Someone would have to take them to pair the DNA."

"What about your three year rule?"

"It only applies to murder victims under eighteen. Accidental deaths are Medical's jurisdiction. And I don't have a say in O.C. procedures for anyone."

"You think an O.C. tech could've done it?"

"Luka said he told 'her' his dad was dead, but all the O.C. techs are men. If this 'her' isn't a tech nor Harin Roche, we're looking for another woman who birthed this kid and put him outside."

Ivan pressed his fingers into his eyes. "I hope they're the same person."

"Either Luka lied about telling a woman, or I've missed something."

"*We've* missed something."

"Or someone's staying a step ahead, actively blocking me."

"Blocking us. I'm here, too, you know."

"Like a tunnel collapse."

"We're not in a tunnel."

"Tunnel. Case. A to B. Your path is blocked. What do you do?"

"Take a different tunnel."

"Before that."

"Stop, I guess. Return to the last junction. Is this metaphor going somewhere?"

Linus strained to get out of Ivan's chair. He sat on the desk where he could read the terminal, "Do you mind?" and pointed to the frayed wires sticking out of the side. "I'm too tired to type."

"The things I do for you, Linus." He twisted the split wires back together.

"BOSS."

The screen flickered, and Katri's voice played through the speakers.

<<CONTINUE>>

. . . weeks since we got the lab results. Linus hasn't stopped crying.

"Cancel dictation."

<<CANCELED>>

"It must be another glitch."
Ivan's eyes narrowed. "Sure it was. BOSS, interface with Med Bay 2 and access files on Hazbegi, Lukaa. Authorization Halla, Linus H4-SEC-A1." He rolled his eyes. "She's got to come up with a name that doesn't sound like a question."

ENTER QUERY OR COMMAND

"Display his DNA trace record."

MEDICAL REPORT: H2-6582-D :: 14.MAY.2637
 IDENT: HAZBEGI, LUKAA
 >>> ASSIGNMENT: UNASSIGNED <<<
DNA TRACE: [A1] SUCCESSFUL [*3]
MOTHER: ROCHE, HARIN
 >>> ASSIGNMENT: KEYSTONE H1:L42:U1 <<<
FATHER: HAZBEGI, SANDRO
 >>> ASSIGNMENT: SALVAGE H8:L1:U7257 <<<
TECH: TAGGOT, WALLACE H2-MED-B5
AUTHORIZATION: LANGSTROM, CARLA H2-MED-A1
COMMENTS: NTT IRL OTR ASAP. <CL>

"Looks the same. Carla updated the ident, though."
Ivan ran his finger across the screen. "Why's it say three DNA traces?"
"BOSS displays the number of tests, but the default setting shows only the latest update."
"I know. Carla said she made the tech run the test twice. So, who ran the other one?"
"Good question. Have at it."

"BOSS, display DNA trace record, sub-trace three of three, previous update before the patient's ident was input."

The screen flickered.

"BOSS, I said display DNA trace record, sub-trace three of three, previous update."

It flickered again.

Ivan kicked the base of the terminal. "BOSS?"

"BOSS," said Linus. "Would you kindly display DNA trace record, sub-trace three of three, previous update before the patient's ident was input."

```
MEDICAL REPORT: H2-6582-C :: 13.MAY.2637
DNA TRACE: [A1] SUCCESSFUL [*3]
  MOTHER: ROCHE, HARIN
   >>> ASSIGNMENT: KEYSTONE H1:L42:U1 <<<
  FATHER: HAZBEGI, SANDRO
   >>> ASSIGNMENT: SALVAGE H8:L1:U7257 <<<
  IDENT: [1-9K] UNSANCTIONED BIRTH
TECH: TAGGOT, WALLACE H2-MED-B5
AUTHORIZATION: LANGSTROM, CARLA H2-MED-A1
```

"That's what I said."

"Maybe it likes me better today. After all, we've been through twenty years together."

"Uh-huh." Ivan pointed to the medical report code. "Looks right. 6582-C. This is the one Carla sent us."

"BOSS, display Luka's DNA trace record, sub-trace two of three."

```
MEDICAL REPORT: H2-6582-B :: 13.MAY.2637
DNA TRACE: [A1] SUCCESSFUL [*2]
  MOTHER: ROCHE, HARIN
   >>> ASSIGNMENT: KEYSTONE H1:L42:U1 <<<
  FATHER: HAZBEGI, SANDRO
   >>> ASSIGNMENT: SALVAGE H8:L1:U7257 <<<
  IDENT: [1-9K] UNSANCTIONED BIRTH
TECH: TAGGOT, WALLACE H2-MED-B5
AUTHORIZATION: LANGSTROM, CARLA H2-MED-A1
```

"6582-B. That's the first test Carla did."

"BOSS, display Luka's DNA trace record, sub-trace one of three."

MEDICAL REPORT: H2-5371-A :: 4.APRIL.2637
DNA TRACE: [A1] SUCCESSFUL [*1]
  MOTHER: ROCHE, HARIN
   >>> ASSIGNMENT: KEYSTONE H1:L42:U1 <<<
  FATHER: HAZBEGI, SANDRO
   >>> ASSIGNMENT: SALVAGE H8:L1:U7257 <<<
  IDENT: [1-9K] UNSANCTIONED BIRTH
TECH: SILLERSON, HEIDI H2-MED-B3
AUTHORIZATION: LANGSTROM, CARLA H2-MED-A1

"5371-A on 4 April?" said Ivan. "Over a month ago?"

Linus ran his finger under the date, highlighting it.

"And four days before Sandro Hazbegi died."

"Or was murdered. Remember, we've no idea how he died or where his body is."

MEDICAL REPORT H2-5371-A
UPDATE IN PROGRESS

"Linus, someone's editing the report."

"Gotcha." Linus hopped off the desk and stood aside the terminal.

"Got who?"

"BOSS, display same query, continuous update, three-second intervals, screen capture to file."

MEDICAL REPORT: H2-5371-A :: 4.APRIL.2637
DNA TRACE: DATA UNAVAILABLE [*1]
TECH: SILLERSON, HEIDI H2-MED-B3
AUTHORIZATION: LANGSTROM, CARLA H2-MED-A1

"The trace results are gone. That was fast," said Ivan.

MEDICAL REPORT H2-6582-A
UPDATE IN PROGRESS

MEDICAL REPORT: H2-5371-A :: 4.APRIL.2637
DNA TRACE: NOT AVAILABLE [*1]
TECH: NOT AVAILABLE
AUTHORIZATION: LANGSTROM, CARLA H2-MED-A1

"The tech's gone," said Linus.

MEDICAL REPORT H2-6582-A
UPDATE IN PROGRESS
MEDICAL REPORT: H2-5371-A :: 4.APRIL.2637
FILE DATA NOT AVAILABLE
AUTHORIZATION: LANGSTROM, CARLA H2-MED-A1

"Now the whole trace." Ivan pointed to Carla's authorization. "It's Doctor Langstrom."

"I've known Carla a long time. She wouldn't. BOSS, which terminal is being used to edit this report?"

H2:L3:U117:ST2381

"Habitat 2, Level 3, Unit 117. They're definitely in Med Bay 2," said Ivan. "Harin?"

"Z5 access, remember?"

"Well, whoever's in a hurry. We'd better get there before they vacate the whole report."

MEDICAL REPORT H2-5371-A
UPDATE IN PROGRESS
REPORT NOT AVAILABLE
AUTHORIZATION: LANGSTROM, CARLA H2-MED-A1

"What report?" Linus hobbled and sat on the desk.

"BOSS, cross-link all habitats and departmental systems. Full system-wide query. All access. Display all data associated with report H2-5371-A."

H2:L3:U117:ST2381
AUTHORIZATION: LANGSTROM, CARLA H2-MED-A1

"The terminal and Doc's authorization. At least it's not another Habitat 9 type glitch."

"That would've been better. It'd be a connection between this and Sandro's report."

"Can we find out who had clearance to edit the report?"

"Don't have to." Linus scrolled through the screen captures. "It's the same for every department. The only people who can edit a submitted report are the hab personnel named on the original." He stopped on the first update and tapped it. "I knew it."

Ivan scoffed. "You did not."

"Did so. I asked Carla to keep an eye on her before we met Roche."

"Why would you do that?"

"First of all, she was listening at the door when we talked with Carla. Second, anyone that perky must be ev—."

"Stop. I don't want to hear the rest of that sentence. Let's just get over there before she disappears, too."

Carla pushed through the curtain, followed by Linus and Ivan. "Why'd you do it? I trusted you. And you went behind my back?"

"Ma'am?" Tech Sillerson's hands were knuckle-deep in a middle-aged man's thigh, the gaping wound's diameter a match for the thick, bloody steel rod lying beside him. "You told me to clean it."

"Take off your gloves and come with me."

"Hey, you there." Linus waved at a young man with short, black hair looking through a microscope in the farthest corner of the room.

He rubbed his eyes and put on a pair of yellow-tinted glasses.

"Yes, you next to the microscope. Can you clean a wound?"

He nodded.

"Fill-in for Tech Sillerson. Move it."

He looked to Carla. "Doctor?"

"It's okay, Wallace." Carla motioned for him to come over. She placed her hand on the small of Heidi's back and ushered her through the curtain into the next room. "In fact, congratulations. You've been promoted to lead tech. Put on gloves and get to work."

"I have?" Wallace crept into the room and looked at the wound and bloody rod. "But..."

Linus patted him on the shoulder. "Don't screw it up."

"Really?" Ivan held the curtain open for Linus. "Is that the best you can do?"

Linus glanced back. "What would you say to the guy?"

Wallace put on translucent gloves and squeezed healing gel onto his fingers. He pushed them deep into the man's gaping thigh wound. It sucked and slurped as they went in and out. Blood dripped from the wound like a leaky pipe, tapping a grotesque melody on the white enamel floor and the tech's vinyl shoes.

Ivan gulped and turned away. "Yeah. I got nothing."

Heidi sat on a low-back chair in the empty room. "What's this about?"

Carla stood behind Heidi with her arms crossed. Linus took position on the left, and Ivan on the right.

"Tell us about the DNA trace," said Linus.

"What DNA trace?"

"Luka Hazbegi. There were three traces. You did one."

"I wasn't the tech on those. That was Wallace. Tell them, Doctor."

"Heidi, they showed me the screen captures. Wallace ran the trace twice on my orders, but you ran another one over a month ago, before Luka was brought in."

"Ma'am?"

"Don't ma'am me. How did you make a report on your own?"

"I didn't." She hunched over and looked at the floor. "I used one of Mr. Tish's."

"Mr. Tish?" said Ivan.

"Hubert Tish is an elderly patient of ours. A sweet, old man, but a severe delusional hypochondriac. He's in every couple days asking to be examined for another rare disease. I trusted Tech Sillerson enough to pre-authorize a few random tests and reports so she could deal with him on her own. A couple of those were DNA traces in case he thought he'd become an alien again."

"I'm sorry, Doctor Langstrom." Heidi sobbed. "A man offered to buy a trace. I told him no at first, but he said he'd pay twenty rations if I didn't ask any questions. It'd take me almost a month to save that much. I had to do it. Besides," she sniffed and wiped away her tears, "it was a DNA trace. What harm could it do?"

"In a way, this is my fault. She couldn't have done it without that pre-authorization."

"It's fine, Carla. I'll take care of Ms. Sillerson." Linus looked down at her. "Who paid you?"

"We met in X-Stretch, but he didn't tell me his name."

"Then how'd he transfer the rations to you?"

"An anonymous donation through Sisters of Mercy."

"Ration bouncing." Ivan crossed his arms. "And through a charity."

"You said he paid you twenty rations? Not fifty?" said Linus.

"No. Twenty. I swear."

"Describe this merciful saint of the people."

"About 175 centimeters. Pale, white skin. Pink eyes."

"An albino?" said Ivan.

"Completely hairless, too. Not even eyebrows."

"Warren Jacoby." Linus clenched his jaw and wiped sweat off his upper lip. "Helix mid-level goon."

"Friend of yours?" said Ivan.

"An old one. We're going back to Hab 8, Level 1 after all."

"Who provided the DNA sample?" said Ivan.

Heidi swiveled to face him. "He did."

"How?"

"He brought a vial."

"Blood?"

"Hair. But I haven't seen him since."

"And yet," Linus jerked Heidi's chair back around, "you vacated the report right after we opened it."

"I got a message. 'Erase immediately. One hundred rations minus seconds'."

"Linus, someone was in the system watching us. Was the message from Warren Jacoby?"

"I don't know. It said Hab 8, Level 1. There wasn't a terminal number or an ident."

"How long did it take?" said Linus.

"To access and vacate the report?" She shrugged. "A minute?"

"And now forty more rations are on deposit with Sisters of Mercy. Those rations could wet a lot of parched lips."

"What are you going to do?"

"Let me answer that." Carla placed her hands on Heidi shoulders. "BOSS," she projected over the curtain, "terminate assignment Sillerson, Heidi H2-MED-B3. Authorization Langstrom, Carla H2-MED-A1."

TERMINATION REQUEST PENDING
STATE RATIONALE

"Doctor Langstrom, please."

"Medical malpractice, misuse of resources, dereliction of duty, and reporting fraud."

"Ration bouncing," said Ivan.

"And ration bouncing."

TERMINATION REQUEST APPROVED
BEHAVIOR ZZZ [MULTIPLE]: -100 L DEMERIT
CLEARANCE UPDATED:
 SILLERSON, HEIDI H2-MED-T3 > H3-WST-D6
ASSIGNMENT UPDATED:
 >>> WASTE RECLAMATION H3:L2:U1899 <<<
MINIMUM ASSIGNMENT DURATION: 10 YEARS

"You got my old job," said Ivan. "Oh, Hab 3. That's tough."

"A waster? But I've always been a base four."

"Now you're... How many is that, Ivan?" said Carla.

"Two, two and a half. But you could go back up after your assignment's finished. Wait. How old are you?"

"Twenty-two."

"So, you'll be outside breeding age. Never mind. Get used to two."

"What about the other rations?"

"You're going to need them." Linus leaned in. "But the forty and the other bounced rations stay with the Sisters. And if I find out you're lying or hiding something else, well, let's just say your mouth will feel like the scour for a long, long time. The rest of your life if I'm in a bad mood."

"And he's usually in a bad mood." Ivan smirked. "A word of advice for your new position. Don't open your mouth in the pit. You'll see what I mean."

16

Ivan

Ivan's heart was a quarter beat from exploding or imploding in his chest. Aside from the stress of returning to Hab 8 without a rad suit and dodging through Level 1's crowded thoroughfares, he was exhausted and growing more guarded every minute. Too many people had casually glanced at the Habitat Integrity patches on his sleeve and chest and looked over his face. Their dark, distrusting stares were pulser darts aimed at him.

"Why are you walking like that?" said Linus.

"There is no 'like that'. It's just called walking."

"You look nervous, and you're making me nervous. Cut it out."

A man bumped into Ivan. "Watch it." He glanced at the Habitat Integrity patch on his chest as they collided. The man looked over Ivan's face and into his eyes. And the accidental bump became an intentional shove.

Ivan unfastened his uniform and reached for the pulser inside.

"Calm down." Linus put his hand on Ivan's. "Put it away."

"That wasn't an accident."

"It was your idea to keep our H.I. patches on. And for good reason. But I told you we'd face some added resistance." Linus pulled Ivan to a makeshift bar under a narrow, frayed awning along the wall.

"Some?"

"Gluco oder geh weg." The bartender pointed to the exit, rattling a thousand thin metal bracelets she wore from elbow to wrist.

"Yes, some." Linus removed his ration pouch. He wore a wide, brass ring on his left ring finger, initials *L* and *K* punched through the metal. Light glinted off it.

New ring? "That's nice. Where'd you get it?"

"Christmas present."

"Eins für die Hälfte."

The bartender placed two green, corroded copper shot glasses on the counter. Linus squeezed the outlet over the glasses, filling them to the brim. The bartender emptied the water into a funnel behind the bar and sat the glasses in front of him. She filled each halfway with gluco thick as oil.

"That little shove was nothing." Linus gestured to two large men standing guard to a narrow corridor. "You see them. That's something. Two big somethings."

"No swearing this time?"

"Say what you want." Linus tossed back his gluco shot, "It doesn't matter now," and Ivan's. "Bleh." He shivered. "A-AB-B-O poz punch."

"Slag sludge. What did you expect for forty milli?"

SPEECH CODE 12C [PROFANITY]: -50 ML DEMERIT

"I never thought I'd say this, but I miss Radek."

"I'll tell him you said so. If I ever see him again."

"Trouble in paradise?"

"He's still angry about me getting shot. It hasn't been easy for either of us. I get scared sometimes. But while I'm focused on myself out here, he's waiting for me to come home. After what happened to Rosco and the other woman in tunnel maintenance, I had to tell him everything. And then I sent him away."

The bartender placed a small, rectangular copper plate on the narrow bar between them. "Pilze?" She pointed to the first of three red, twisted necro-shrooms. "Du wirst lächeln."

"You'll smile," repeated Ivan, doing his best to translate, though he wasn't sure her German was technically correct either.

She pointed at two. "Du wirst lachen."

"You'll laugh."

She waved her hand over the three. "Du wirst sterben."

"You'll die."

"No thanks. We'll both pass." Linus slid the plate aside. "You said something about Rosco?"

"The dead guy in tunnel maintenance. You gave me his badge. The one I lost."

"Ivan, it was a fake badge. That's why I wasn't worried about it. There is no Rosco. I made him up."

"But Chahna acted like she knew him."

"Chahna?"

"Didn't you read the report I submitted?"

"I've been busy."

"Uh-huh. Chahna was your deputy before me. Remember?"

"That Chahna? Ivan, Chahna Bhatt died in a tunnel collapse the day after she left Integrity. A week before you started training."

Ivan moaned and squeezed the bridge of his nose.

"Why are you lugging that tablet around if you're not going to use it?"

"I forgot it was in my pocket. If you saw them..."

"Tell me you didn't forget to order a DNA trace on the victims."

"I didn't forget. What about Chahna? Until I know what to call her."

"You have a suspect's description and a date, time, and place you encountered her. With BOSS's help, that'll be enough. Now, let's get this over with. How do you say one bottle in German?"

"Eine Tasche, I think."

Linus dropped a ration pouch on the counter. "Eine ration for eine tasche."

The bartender sneered and dropped the pouch into a box on the floor. She replaced it with a tall, though nondescript bottle of burgundy gluco. "Eine Flasche gluco."

"Not this one," Linus pointed to a shorter bottle with a thicker, heavier base, "that one."

She traded bottle-for-bottle. "Now trek off."

They waded back into the bustling crowd and headed for the two large guards and the corridor ahead. If the worst threat from the crowd was an evil eye or two, the best defense was looking somewhere else. Ivan kept his eyes on Linus's boot heels, and it worked for a while. He was more relaxed, and less paranoid than before. That sort of ignorance wasn't bliss, but at least his hands weren't shaking. Linus stopped abruptly, and Ivan collided into his back. Linus stumbled and dropped the heavy bottle. It hit the floor with a loud bang, but it didn't break. It rolled in a wide semicircle and stopped at the guards' feet.

One laughed, "Watch it, Mulkku," and kicked the bottle's thick bottom, spinning it. "You spill it down, you lick it up."

Linus stomped on the bottle and picked it up. "I'm Chief Halla. This is Deputy Finn. And this here sizable bottle of gluco is a peace offering for Mr. Jacoby."

"We know," said the second guard.

"What do you know?"

"Everything."

"That's ominous," said Ivan.

"Let them in." A man's voice came from a detached terminal speaker hanging on the wall. "But I want their pulsers."

"My pulser?" Ivan leaned away. *How can I defend myself without a weapon? Get them to swear in front of BOSS?* "Linus?"

"Pulsers. Now." The second guard unfastened his uniform.

Ivan took another step back and reached for the guard's arm.

"Don't resist." Linus raised his hands.

"Listen to your chief." The guard took his pulser.

We might as well meet Warren Jacoby naked and shaved.

"We'll get them back afterward." Linus raised his hands, and the first guard took his weapon. "Right?"

He stood aside and gestured into the corridor. "Fourth door on the right. Fifteen sixty-four."

Ivan raised his hand to knock, and the heavy door opened, screeching and grinding as it slid in its rusted track. Warren Jacoby stood inside and looked as Heidi described. He was only as tall as Ivan's chin, and his skin was pale as though he'd been dusted in chalk.

Ivan's eyes widened at seeing an albino in person. The mutation had been filtered out pre-hab, or so he believed. Warren Jacoby was an unsanctioned birth, illegal since the day he was conceived.

"Warren Jacoby?"

"Of course, Deputy Ivan Finn. But I'm sure you knew coming in." He moved aside and invited them into the unit. "I've been expecting you."

"Yeah. We get that a lot."

"I hope not. It means you're not doing a very good job. By the way, how's Radek? Still slinging gluco at The Pissing Ant?"

"He's well enough."

Unit 1564 was the same as most on Level 1, another rusted steel box like all the others, but on the opposite side of the dome from Sandro Hazbegi's unit. A low, narrow table, pull-down bunk, a broken-down system terminal, and an oversized, vinyl sheet on a side wall were the only things in the room. If he was sitting on a mountain of rations, he certainly wasn't boasting about it.

"You've been spying on us," said Linus.

"Nothing so crude. You reassigned Heidi this afternoon. After that, it was only a matter of time. Still, I appreciate the gluco." He took the bottle from Linus. "Not playing tunnel maintenance today?"

"Not today, Mr. Jacoby."

"Please, Linus. We're beyond such things." He placed the bottle on the bunk and sat beside it. "Call me Werewolf."

"Excuse me?" said Ivan.

"You know." Warren howled and laughed. "Werewolf. The big bad, sharp teeth, lots of hair. Does any of this ring a bell?"

"You have no hair."

"Ironic, isn't it?"

"Deeply."

It wasn't what Warren said, but how he said it. He sounded more educated than any scrapper on Level 1. *Intelligent and two steps ahead. Who is this creep?*

"I bet you're wondering who I am."

"The thought had crossed my mind."

"Ask your buddy Linus. He knows. Don't you, Linus?"

Linus stood silent, rubbing his brass ring.

"We go way back. How long has it been?"

"Ten years," said Linus.

"Ten. Long. Years. What's old is new again, 'ey?"

"That's not why we're here."

"Isn't it though? Luka Hazbegi's alive and well again. You see, Ivan. Ivan? Ridiculous name. I'll call you Finn. Do you mind? Of course you don't. You see, Finn, Linus here tried to pin those murders on me. I'm a businessman, not a killer."

"You're a thug. And you use goons for everything else."

"Hazbegi was a shit stain not worth his ration. And those goons aren't cheap."

Ivan looked at the terminal screen. Warren hadn't been fined 50 mL for swearing. It either didn't have a mic, or unsanctions don't exist according to BOSS. Or both.

"Neither are you." Linus gestured to the long sheet draped on the wall.

"Why *are* you here?"

"We know you paid Heidi to run a DNA trace. Why?"

"Collateral. I wanted to see what I was paying for."

Linus scoffed, "I knew it. How many?" and crossed his arms.

"Fourteen wet for his kid."

"Not worth his ration?"

"I was feeling generous. I do have a heart."

"But what color is it?"

"Excuse me," Ivan interrupted, "can someone fill me in?"

"Sandro borrowed those Helix rations from Werewolf here."

"As have many others." He winked at Linus. "Poor, poor Marika. And now Sandro's gone, too. I forgave the last seven out of the goodness of my heart. But fourteen?" He shook his head. "The kid owes it. Plus three hundred millis a day interest."

"That's outrageous. He's a child," said Ivan.

"And he isn't Luka," said Linus. "Luka died with his mother a decade ago. You saw to that."

"What more is a child than the offspring of its parents? No matter *who* they are."

"You know about his mother," said Ivan.

"I paid fifty rations for the trace. You didn't think I'd read it? Anyway, she'll pay."

"Not if she doesn't know about it."

"She will once that sapioid of hers delivers my message. You got to admire the gall of that woman. Richest bitch in the habs pops out a scrapper and sends him to rot with his father. And right here, no less."

"She's not his mother."

"Don't be naive, Finny. Worse things happen to poorer girls and boys. Your arm, for instance."

"How do you know about that?"

"I know everything. Knew you were coming here, too."

"Easy there, Deputy Finn." Linus tugged on the back of Ivan's uniform. "Don't make it personal."

Ivan realized he had taken several awkward steps forward. He was looming over the man, and his hands were shaking again. He backed away and joined Linus by the open door.

"Whatcha gonna do, Finny-Finn-Finn?"

"Arrest you for bribery and extortion."

"Arrest?" Warren laughed. "Hasn't Linus explained how punishment works with unsanctions? Let me. There's only rations, reassignment, and hab arrest. The unsanctioned don't get assignments or BOSS's pitiful handouts, and this little unit is twenty-four of them." He pointed at the sheet. "All the way down to fifteen eighty-nine and Anillo de Fuego past that. By the way, Linus, your last visit was your final one. Your party invitation has been withdrawn. No more using the dummy terminal or Madame Espirito's séances for you."

"Sadly, he's right. There's nothing we could do that'd stick."

"That's where you're both wrong." Ivan reached into his uniform and shoved his hand down into the crotch. He pulled out a scuffed, old pulser and aimed for Warren's chest. "Clasp your fingers and put your hands on top of your head."

"What are you doing?" said Linus.

"Like you suggested. I'm breaking the board."

"*You* suggested that. I said it was a bad idea."

"Doesn't matter now. Does it, Warren? It's too late to turn back."

Warren put his hands behind his head. "I hope you got a red dart in the chamber 'cuz the ones around the cylinder are black as tar."

"It only takes one."

"You won't shoot me." He looked at the terminal piled on the floor. "Not with BOSS listening. That would be murder."

"Murder who? You don't exist without an ident. And there's no mic in that terminal."

"Are you sure about that?" He scanned Ivan's face. "I'm thinking there aren't any darts in that pulser. Not a single one." His hands slid toward his neck, fingers unclasping. "And even if there were, that pulser's too old to fire."

"It may be old and sentimental, but I assure you it'll put big holes in new places." Ivan aimed at Warren's crotch. "And new holes in small places."

Warren clenched his jaw and put his hands up. He looked to Linus. "Well?"

"Don't look at me." He peered down the hall. "I'm as curious as you are."

"Let's say you're lucky. You pull that trigger. Now you're out of darts, and my men are coming with your pulsers. Thanks for those. Now, give me that old thing, and you can go with my blessing. It's the only way you're getting out of here alive."

"How generous of you." Ivan reached into Warren's shirt between his shoulder blades and took his pulser. It was a six-shooter, too. Polished and iridescent, smooth as glass.

"Nice one." Ivan rubbed his thumb over the grip. "Newly printed?" He passed it to Linus.

"You still won't shoot."

Ivan lowered his weapon.

Warren relaxed and exhaled. "You're making the right decision, Finn."

"I hope so." He looked away and pulled the trigger.

The terminal screen exploded in a shower of sparks and shrapnel. The flash and raining debris surprised Ivan. He'd aimed for his kneecap.

Warren fell off the bunk onto the floor. He reached toward his leg and screamed when his hand impacted the long shard of glass piercing his mid-thigh. "Slags!" He screamed and yanked the glass from his leg. Blood spurt into the air, misting little red dots over his pale, white face. He threw the shard aside.

"They're coming," said Linus.

"I'm out of darts."

Linus huffed and pointed Warren's pulser down the hall. He fired four shots and ducked. Two lit darts sparked against the door next to his head. He fired twice more and fell back into the room.

"Why'd you stop?"

"I got your guy, but now I'm out."

"And yours?"

The muscular guard burst into the room holding Linus's pulser. He pointed it at Linus and back to Ivan and at Linus again.

"Shoot him." Warren shook, holding his leg, blood streaming into the perforated vents beneath him.

"Which one?"

"The deputy, you idiot."

The guard looked between them and settled on Ivan.

He raised his hands and looked sideways at Linus. "I'm sorry."

"Ivan," said Linus, whispering.

"I didn't mean for this to happen."

"You know those six darts I used on Digi and the braider?"

"What about them?"

"They're still on requisition."

The guard pulled the trigger, and the pulser clicked.

Ivan gasped, and Linus charged, knocking the guard against the wall. Ivan grabbed the long, glass shard off the floor and plunged it into the guard's chest. He put his weight behind it, and he didn't stop pushing until he heard it scrape steel. He let go. The guard slid down the wall to the floor, the shard's tip drawing a crooked line through the rust as he fell. Ivan's eye twitched.

Warren panted, dragging himself toward the plaid sheet on the wall.

Linus stepped over Warren's legs and grabbed hold of the sheet. "Bring me another piece of glass." He tugged on it. The large sheet fell into a pile on the floor, exposing a narrow, two-meter door cut, edges melted, into the wall through to the adjacent unit. From there, a similar door opened into the next unit, and the next, and on into the distance.

"Why do you need twenty-four units?" Ivan passed a small, triangular shard to Linus and peered into the next room. "What are you hiding in there?"

"You're dead," said Warren, panting.

"Says the ghost."

Linus cut a long ribbon from the sheet and wrapped it around Warren's leg over the spurting wound. He tied a knot, and the werewolf howled.

"I'll kill you both."

"Is that a threat?" Linus tapped the knot, and the werewolf howled.

"Linus doesn't like threats," said Ivan. "Neither do I for that matter." He tapped the knot.

The werewolf howled. "It's not a threat. It's not a threat."

"Here's how this is going to go." Linus hovered his hand over Warren's leg. "You're going to start from the beginning. Tell us what happened. Tell us everything."

"Or what? You'll let me bleed to death?"

"That much is up to you. Ivan is going to ask you some questions, and I hope he believes you. Otherwise..." Linus tapped the knot, and the werewolf howled. "You get the point."

Warren nodded.

"Tell me about the DNA trace. Why?"

"I told you."

Linus's hand grazed the knot.

"Don't. I'm telling the truth."

"Then keep going," said Ivan.

"Okay. So, the kid's dead. Ten years dead. I know it. You know it. Everybody knows it."

"You're talking about Luka Hazbegi."

"Yeah, but Sandro. Maybe he doesn't know it. Sandro comes to me over a month ago. Says he needs some rations for Luka. I say Luka who. He says Luka his son. Says he came home, back from the dead, same age, same everything as the day he died. Reborn Sisters and Brothers style. The boy looked similar, but not quite if you know what I mean. But Sandro, he only sees Luka. Crazy, right? He begs for the water. So, I tell him I can do fourteen wet if he brings me a few strands of the kid's hair. He does, and I do. Done deal. Hands clean."

"Then the trace comes back."

"Not Luka, of course. But a half-brother. Same father, different mother. A keystone this time. That I didn't expect. Water like rain that one. So, I ask around. A couple toe-ups say they saw the boy with a Digi. But the neighbors. No. They say poor Sandro doesn't have a family anymore, keeps to himself, only goes out for work and rations. But I suspect somebody's been keeping a naughty little secret in the deep dark."

"What did you do?"

"I check up on the kid. To see if he needed anything. Maybe a nicer unit, bigger bed, toys, rations. Whatever. Sandro doesn't want me near him. I insist, and Sandro flies off his track. He pushes the kid out the door and starts screaming, 'Nine, nine, nine.' Takes a swing at me, so I take him out. Self-defense one hundred ten percent."

"What about the boy?"

"Runs away, and it's like he never existed all over again. Not a sighting. Not a peep. Maybe he's hiding. Maybe he's gone home to mommy. Maybe his powdered flesh is sitting on a shelf in a little, blue bag in An-de-Fue. Whatever. Doesn't matter now. Then a month goes by, and once again, surprise surprise. An old scrapper pulls him out of the scour and drops him in Med Bay 2. Now, the kid's fit again. Tight like new pipes."

"Sandro's body? His C.O.D. report?"

"My associate said," he gestured to the dead guard, "three bio-waste bots cut up the body, carted it off the next morning."

"How'd you fake the report?"

"What report?" He grimaced. "I've never written a report. Why don't you go ask his mommy?"

Ivan hit the buzzer, and the werewolf howled.

Linus stood. "Do you believe him?"

"Strangely enough, I do." He stuck his head out the door and peered down the hall. "What about Helix?"

"They'll kill you both. When they see what you've done, they'll kill you, your Chief, your families, that pretty, old Doctor in Med Bay, the kid. They'll shred him. See if he comes back then."

"I thought you'd say that." Linus looked for the gluco bottle and stepped over Warren. He picked it up by the neck and knelt beside him, turning the bottle upside down. He held the thick, heavy bottom over Warren's head. "I should have done this ten years ago."

Ivan gasped.

The werewolf howled, "No. Don't. You said—"

Warren's head caved into the floor, splattering blood and bits of pink brain over Ivan's black boots. Linus swung again. Blood streamed through the air, fragments of skull tumbled across the floor, and a fine, red mist painted their clothes and faces.

Ivan breathed it in, and it dripped into his mouth. *Iron and copper. Metallic like eating wet mushrooms off copper plates. I haven't done that since—*

"Ivan," Linus grabbed his arm, "now's not the time to drift."

"Linus?"

"They could still find out." He tossed the bloody bottle into the corner. It cracked at the neck, and ebbed thick, red gluco onto the floor. He looked around. "Take the pulsers, but leave everything else. And don't step in the blood."

"Med Bay 2?"

Linus nodded.

"And if the kid can't handle it?"

"Then we're already dead."

17

Linus

Doctor Langstrom rested her report tablet on the corner of the desk and sat in her chair. Its thin, cut chain dangled over the edge, rapping against the desk's heavy leg. Around the room, pills rattled in plastic bottles and rows of empty glass vials and flasks shook in their cabinets. Shadows moved across the floor, overlapping and separating as the bay's bright lights swayed on frayed wires. They sat opposite Carla as the tremor moved up from the floor, through Linus's chair legs, and faded.

"You were saying..."

"But you said he'd be okay." Ivan fell back in his chair.

"I thought—, I hoped he was. Truth be told, I made the prediction before I received the final scan results."

"How long?"

"Six to eight months. A year at the most. It's hard to say for sure."

Ivan gripped the chair's arms.

Linus put his hand on Ivan's. "I'm sorry. Eight grays was too much. Even for Luka."

Ivan gestured to two terminals on either side of the room and another behind Carla's desk.

"Let it listen. It can't help or hurt Luka now."

"Linus is right. Let BOSS take a day's rations for the false report," said Carla.

BEHAVIOR 72A [CONCEALMENT]: -5.5 L DEMERIT

"We've tried everything in the medical database, but we can't fix what's wrong with him." Carla leaned forward and lowered her voice to a whisper. "You both should know something. There's more going on here. A lot more."

"Like what?" said Ivan.

"The initial tests we ran suggested those chromosomal abnormalities I told you about were due to acute exposure to ionizing radiation. It's common to see those abnormalities, cellular damage, rare cancers, and, of course, death following such a high, prolonged dose. Given his initial appearance, and the fact his x-rays were essentially useless due to the high levels of radiation in the room, we didn't have reason to doubt that assessment."

"But now you do?"

"Since then, we've done four complete scans. They show a few of his organs are severely underdeveloped. His kidneys for example. One is half the size it should be. The other was half, but now it's double. Other organs are those of an old scrapper. His heart is thirty percent larger. His livers are a mess. Yes, he has two. And his spleen was overdeveloped on the first scan, normal on the third, and completely missing on the fourth."

"Radiation couldn't cause these abnormalities?" said Linus.

"No. There's no logical explanation as to how or why exposure to the radiation outside could've caused a little boy's organs to age at different rates, change size, or, seemingly, shrink and disappear in a matter of days. Exposure can't explain how his body is producing its own anti-radiologicals, nor the errors I found in both chromosomes and throughout his entire genome. It took me a while to figure things out, but I'm confident now. Luka is, at least in part, a shattered mirror."

"Luka's a clone?" said Ivan.

"A clone is a copy, a genetic duplication of a single organism. One person, one soy plant, and so forth. Luka's DNA is unique like any child born to two parents. In his case, he's a clear product of his mother, Harin Roche's ovum, and his father, Sandro Hazbegi's spermatozoon."

"You mean IVF. That requires a surrogate. So, how can we find her?"

"Normally, yes. But not in Luka's case."

"I think what Carla's trying to say is…" Linus drew a blank. "Carla, what are you saying? How can the kid be both a clone and not a clone?"

"To clone someone, DNA, from a single donor is prepared through various means and injected into an artificial ovum. It's then forced-grown via rapid, induced mitosis to a predetermined age within a tank of supportive substrate gels and other compounds. When keystones tried it a century ago, their intention was to raise clones as their children. They call it Project Genesis or some heretical nonsense. This would guarantee the family members remained keystones generation after generation. However, the children resulting from this process had multiple chromosomal abnormalities. This resulted in irreversible DNA fragmentation, incongruous aging, multiple organ failure, severe brain damage, sterility, blindness, and sudden death. They also couldn't walk, talk, or communicate. These problems were blamed on substandard equipment made from salvaged components rather than locating advanced equipment and materials available elsewhere in the world before The Great Catastrophe. Keystones gave up and let their clones die. That's why we call it 'what not to do'. Luka has many of the less severe problems and a few I couldn't find reference to. I'm assuming they're unique to him as well."

Linus and Ivan looked at each other and at Carla. Both shrugged.

"You two." Carla shook her head. "I sent you both texts. How should I put this? Luka isn't a clone, but he was grown on cloning equipment. Likely with the same faulty machines, materials, and processes left over from those experiments a century ago."

"See. Now I understand," said Linus. "That's all you had to say."

Carla scowled at him. "I'll put everything in a message next time."

"Seems unnecessary," said Ivan. "Especially when they could've used a normal surrogate."

"Not if they were in a hurry. Maybe it'd help to think of Luka as an experiment, the end result of someone performing simultaneous testing, multiple chromosomal bonding, gene splicing, and rapid fusion protocols within a single subject rather than attempting one at a time. This sort of methodology would have an incredible advantage. Namely, demonstrating which combinations and techniques work and which don't in the shortest possible time frame. As I said, this suggests those responsible were in a rush to find a viable, long-term solution to the shattered mirror problem. Of course, that's an assumption. But I think a good one, considering what I'm seeing here."

"If it's so fast, why wasn't something like this tried before?"

"Because a single technical mistake or multiple cumulative ones always lead to eventual disease and death of the test subject. The people who did this must've known full well they'd have to learn everything they did wrong and what they did right, and which of those had the greatest effect on the subject and which the least. It sickens me to say this, but essentially, someone created a little boy to dissect him. It wouldn't matter if he were alive or healthy when the experiment ended. That goes against the very nature of the medical profession. I can hardly believe it. Shocked, really. Unfortunately for Luka, they did more wrong than right. Despite his current appearance and miraculous recovery, his organs are going to shut down. But whenever the time comes, it'll happen fast. Heart attack, then coma followed by kidney or liver failure."

"Jeez." Ivan's face paled, and he looked like he was about to pass out.

"Breathe." Linus patted his hand.

Ivan exhaled, and his color returned. "Has he been in pain since quarantine?"

"Some, but it doesn't seem to bother him at the moment."

"What did you mean by 'forced-grown'? How old is he?" said Linus.

"It's impossible to know his exact emergence, if you will, but I'd say Luka was created four to six months ago and forced-grown to the age he is now. As for his ability to communicate, emotional and psychological awareness, and knowledge of who and where he is, I'm at a loss. The clones were comatose out of the tank, but this child can speak and move. He insists his name is Luka Hazbegi, he's six years old, and his parents are Sandro and Marika Hazbegi."

"Artificial memories?" asked Ivan.

"In a sapioid brain, sure. Install one of the standard psychological profiles and add a targeted memory or two. Instant traumatized soldier, prostitute, rebellious teenager, pillar of the community, whatever you want. Predictive response output. That's basic I/O for them. But pushing memories into a living, human brain...," Carla shook her head. "No. The basic technology we have at our disposal is nothing compared to what was around before The Great Catastrophe. They were decades from a successful attempt back then. Now we're four centuries behind. Five if you count all we've lost."

"Or someone's on a different schedule," said Linus.

"I don't see how. The only explanation I can come up with is someone told him to say those things. But if that's what happened, I can't get him to admit it."

"What about the original equipment, tanks, systems? Is there a record?"

"I thought you'd ask, so I dug a little tunnel of my own. Historical texts, medical texts, and the primary database all agree. The old, glitchy equipment was dismantled and sent with bots to be recycled. I was about to leave it at that. Then I thought, someone's got at least one. I mean, there's a shattered mirror in the next room. That's evidence enough, isn't it?"

"It is. And?"

"I submitted a requisition."

"For a cloning tank?" said Ivan.

"Not only a tank." She grinned. "An entire cloning facility. I asked BOSS for it all. Tanks and incubators, centrifuges, microscopes, air purifiers, DNA sequencers, everything down to mitosis supportive substrate and petri dishes. In case I wanted to start right away."

"And you got them?"

"Not at all." Carla laughed. "As Linus would say, 'shit out of luck'."

SPEECH CODE 12C [PROFANITY]: -50 ML DEMERIT

"Then why—"

"BOSS always shows how many are out there, how many are on requisition, who's next in line, and where you stand in the queue. I'm next for cloning tanks and incubators. Which would be nice if the estimated delivery weren't 237 years."

"That's a long time. Wait." Ivan looked sideways at Linus. "Isn't 237 years the same wait for our rad suits?"

He nodded. "And a lot of other things."

"As for those tanks and incubators, the system showed thirteen of each in use right now. Care to guess how many were supposedly stripped and recycled the last time?"

"Who did it indicate had them?" said Linus. "And where?"

"Those fields displayed an error each time. The first error said 'G' and five hundred seventy-four. The location said nine. It was same for all the cloning equipment. That was strange since those codes aren't in the database."

Ivan and Linus exchanged a long glance.

"There's that look again. What is it?"

"We're not entirely sure," said Ivan.

"Something important is floating around in there. Well? Tell me. If it concerns my patient, I have a right to know."

"The last thing Sandro Hazbegi said before he was murdered was 'nine'. I think he was talking about a place he wanted Luka to hide," said Linus.

"You mean Level 9."

"That's what we thought at first. But, if someone's hiding a cloning lab, they'd need enough power and space for those machines. Level 9 is completely full in every habitat. We're beginning to suspect there's another one out there somewhere."

"And you think Luka knows how to find this other habitat? This Habitat 9?"

"I hope so. For all our sakes."

Carla thought for a moment. Linus never could tell what women were thinking, especially this one. She didn't tell him 'no' straight away. It was as good a sign as any.

"Well, if you're going to question him again, you should clean those." She pointed to a piece of Warren's brain squished and stuck between Linus's boot laces. "I'd like to keep the room as clean as possible."

"Sorry about that. We had a run-in with a psychopath. There was," he eyed the terminal and lowered his voice, "a disagreement."

"That could be his right-hemisphere supramarginal gyrus in your laces."

"I honestly have no idea what you said."

"Good one, Doc."

"At least one of you read those medical texts I sent."

"I skimmed. Mind if I use your sink?"

"I do. But you can spray your faces at the emergency eye-wash station. And there are towels and alcohol in the cabinet for everything else."

"Are we good?" said Linus.

"For now. I never could say no to you."

"It's your one and only flaw."

"I'm working on it. The same rules apply though. If either you or Ivan make him cry, I put *you* down for a nap. And make it short. It's almost his bedtime."

"Yes, Ma'am."

Carla led them to the rear of the med bay and stopped outside the storage room in the back. It was the same little room where they had talked among the white shelving units and learned Luka's name. Most of the shelves had been removed and stacked along the rear wall of the bay. The rest were pushed off to the sides and covered with curtains. A portable terminal stood on a wheeled platform in the far corner.

A small child's bunk filled a quarter of the space. Next to it, a narrow mat stretched the length of the floor, covered with piles of plastic blocks and tiny toy robots. Luka sat on the floor wearing a hospital gown, Datvi the bear at his side, doodle pad in his lap.

Carla knocked on the open door. "Luka, sweetie. Linus is here to see you. You remember my friend Linus?"

He looked up.

"Hello, Luka. Do you remember me?"

He nodded.

"This is my friend Ivan."

"Hi, Luka." Ivan smiled and waved.

Luka waved, the bendy, child's stylus in his hand flopping side-to-side. He returned to drawing boxy robots and nines across the page.

"Well, now," said Carla. "He likes you."

"And who could blame him?"

Linus motioned for Ivan to enter. "After you."

Ivan gathered the blocks and robots into a pile and sat opposite Luka. Linus leaned in the doorway beside Carla.

"My friend Linus told me about you. He says you're very brave and clever, and you have a bear named Datvi."

Luka shrugged.

"I see you like drawing, too. I like to draw robots. What about you?"

Luka nodded.

"Robots, too? Wow. We have a lot in common. In fact, I was like you at your age. I didn't have a mom or a dad, either. A kind lady named Sister Isabella raised me. She had one hundred sisters, and all of them were named Sister, too. They wore funny clothes and silly hats, and they went to church every day. I loved them very much, and they loved me. They told me lots of stories, and I could talk to them about anything. Even when I was sad. Do you have a brother or a sister?"

Luka shook his head.

"Do you talk to a girl sometimes?"

He shrugged.

"You do? Wonderful. Maybe she can be my friend, too? Then we'll have even more things in common. We could all be friends."

He shrugged.

"Can you tell me her name? Is it Harin?"

Luka shook his head. "She doesn't have a name," he mumbled.

"She doesn't have a name? That's funny. Is she a funny girl?"

Luka quickly shook his head.

"Well, that's okay. Not everyone can be funny. I know a good joke. Do you want to hear it?"

He nodded.

"Okay. Why was six afraid of seven?"

He shrugged.

"Because seven, eight, nine. But eight is ate." Ivan pretended to eat the imaginary number. "Seven ate nine, so six was afraid of seven. Get it?"

He shrugged.

"Not funny?"

He shook his head.

"Tough crowd," said Linus. "Try one that isn't in the archives."

"Don't pay attention to grumpy, old Linus. He only thinks he's funny. I want to know more about your friend, Luka. What color is her hair?"

Luka shook his head.

"She's not funny, and she doesn't have hair, either. Or does she wear a silly hat like Sister Isabella, and you can't see her hair?"

He giggled and shook his head again.

"Okay, she's bald. What color are her eyes?"

He giggled.

"This is going nowhere," said Linus. "Do you want me to try?"

"Not on your life. Luka, what do you mean she doesn't have hair, but she's not bald?"

"And no eyes apparently."

Ivan shushed Linus again.

Luka cupped his hands around his mouth and leaned toward Ivan. Ivan turned his head, and Luka whispered something into his ear.

"Really? She does?"

"What'd he say?"

"Luka says she has many faces."

"He's describing an imaginary friend."

"We want to meet her. Is she the same friend you told about your dad?"

He nodded.

"Can we see her?"

He shrugged.

"I hope that's a yes," said Linus.

"Shhh. Where does she live?"

Luka leaned in and whispered.

"Nine? You mean Habitat 9? Did your dad tell you to go there?"

He shrugged.

"And did you?"

Luka shook his head.

"Why not?"

"A bad place."

"Oh, I understand. These habitats can be scary sometimes. But you were there before, weren't you?"

He nodded.

"Will you take me?"

He rapidly shook his head.

"Then how can I meet your friend?"

He whispered in Ivan's ear again.

"Aussie? Is that her name?"

Luka giggled and tapped the stylus on the doodle tablet, wrote something on the screen, and rotated it to face Ivan. He placed it on the mat between them and circled a boxy purple robot with glowing yellow eyes. He'd scribbled *O.C.* across the bot's front panel.

"A bio-waste bot," said Linus. "He must've hidden in the bot tunnels."

"Ahh, I understand. I know that bot. Do you like O.C.?"

Luka shrugged.

"But he knows where to go?"

He nodded.

"I think it's almost someone's bedtime," said Carla.

Luka shook his head.

"Don't sass me, young man. Get the dental cleaner. I'm certain you know where *that* is."

Luka's eyes narrowed, and he let out an adorable, low growl.

"Now, Mister. I need to talk with your new friends for a bit."

Luka huffed and left his makeshift bedroom, stomping on the floor and disappeared around the corner.

"And don't swallow the cartridge this time. It's not candy."

Linus chuckled. "Carla, you've done a remarkable job."

"I agree," said Ivan. "I can't believe how far he's come. Thanks to you, Doc."

"That's why I wanted to speak to both of you. His condition has improved enough, if Luka were any other child, I'd consider sending him home. He's obviously bright as the solar winds, and we love having him around. But I can't keep him."

"He seems happy enough."

"That's not the problem. We don't have time to chase after a rambunctious boy for weeks or months on end. And frankly, we're not equipped for hospice care when things get worse. He's well enough to run and play, so he should be with other children. Welfare directives are clear. I'm required to contact Sisters of Mercy. He'll be with children his own age, and they have the facilities to care for him when the time comes. However, there's another option you should consider first."

"Harin Roche."

"She has the right to know a piece of her body was used like this."

"We'll tell her," said Linus.

Ivan cross his arms. "If she doesn't want him?"

"You have a week to give me an answer."

"A week? That's it?"

"It's all the time I have. Then, I have to do what's best for him." She looked down at Luka, who had returned and was tugging on her lab coat. "That was awfully quick." She glared at him. "Prove it. Show me the pearls."

He grinned ear-to-ear.

"Okay. Good job. Now say goodnight to your friends."

"Goodnight, Luka," said Ivan.

"Goodnight," said Linus.

Luka stuck out his tongue and tugged on his ears. He spun into the room and got in bed.

Ivan laughed.

Carla turned off the lights and shut the door.

"What was that?" said Linus.

"That was a six-year-old."

The Eight Sleepy Habitats, a child's bedtime story, played through the system terminal in the room as the three of them listened from outside the door.

Carla smiled. "He likes that one. It puts him to sleep every time."

"Did you implant his ident chip?" said Linus.

"No, but I recorded retinal, dental, fingerprints, and DNA. Chips aren't implanted until the child's five years old."

"Luka's six," said Ivan.

"Technically, he's between one and six months."

"Then how'd he ask for a bedtime story," said Linus.

"A Z5. BOSS only needs to hear his voice to establish that."

"Right, right. And BOSS assigned his Z5 here? In med bay?"

"I've no idea. BOSS would've established a Z5 the first time it heard him speak. You know how sneaky it can be, always listening." She gestured toward another terminal nestled between two shelves in the back. "But BOSS had to correct his clearance. He was listed as Hazbegi, Hazbegi. BOSS changed it to Lukaa when I updated his name and linked it to his DNA trace and medical records. I swear our supposedly genius A.I. is getting dumber every year."

"Thanks, Doc." Ivan headed for the exit. "Come on, Chief."

"When did Ivan start taking the lead?"

"Good question."

Harin Roche wrapped a wide, blue towel over her shoulders and sat on her usual bench. Her swimsuit was black and yellow, and she wore an onyx and gold necklace to match. "That will be all, Peter," said Harin, shooing him away. "I have to admit, when I said the door would be open to you, I didn't expect a fol-low-up this soon. Or at night."

"How much time do you spend in here?" said Linus.

"As much as it takes." Her gaze passed over spots of dried blood they'd missed on their clothes and boots. "Couldn't this have waited 'till morning?"

"We understand your frustration," said Ivan. "I promise we'll be out of your water as soon as possible."

"That's a lovely ring, Chief." Harin extended her hand, palm up. "Polished brass?"

"Yes," said Linus.

"May I?"

"No."

"Very well." Harin yawned. "Go ahead. Ask your questions."

Linus cleared his throat. "Ms. Roche, does nine mean any-thing to you?"

"Interesting question. Nine, you say? As in eight, nine, ten? Or nein as in 'no'?"

"The number. Counting to nine. Nine of something. A time of day. A place perhaps. Anything related to the number or containing the number."

"Nine, nine, nine." Harin stared into the pool as she wrung water from her hair. "You sure it's not nein? Reminds me of Peter scolding me for not remembering the habs' fourteen languages."

"We're sure. Just the number," said Linus.

"Peter says they grow mushrooms on Level 9. There's cloud nine. Nine muses. The Yggdrasil has nine worlds. The nine armies of the fifth world war. That's all I can think of."

"What about a little boy from Hab 8? Luka Hazbegi."

"Sorry." She shrugged. "I've never been to Habitat 8. Oh, wait. That's it. It's the Yggdrasil."

"The answer is in Norse cosmology?"

"Not specifically, but it was my great, great, many great grandmother's inspiration for these habitats. Look, I'll show you." Harin moved to the other side of the room and laid by the pool's edge. She gestured to the bottom right of the carving hanging over the water. "It's there."

Linus and Ivan crouched and turned their heads sideways. They were as close to upside down as they could be without joining Harin on the floor or falling into the pool.

She pointed to a raised, broken circle situated roughly a kilometer east of Habitat 1. "That's your ninth world, Deputy. That's Habitat 9."

"How do you know about Habitat 9? There are supposed to be only eight."

"You are correct, Chief Halla," she said, sitting up. "There are only eight. Eight completed habitats. The last one was never finished."

"You're saying there's a whole other habitat sitting out there, and nobody knows about it. How's that possible?" said Ivan.

"It was under construction when The Great Catastrophe struck. As far as I know, it never got past the first stages. I'd wager scrappers walk over it and don't know it's there."

"Then how do you?" said Linus.

"Peter, of course. He knows the complete history of The Habitat Project, the Roche family history, and lots of other stuff. Don't you, Peter?"

"Yes, Miss."

"If you'd like, he could tell you who picked Halti Fell for the location, who tunneled out the levels, and which Roches died in The Great Catastrophe."

"Let's postpone the history lesson for now. But, if what you're saying is correct, there should be a way to get there."

"That I don't know."

"We might be able to dig a new tunnel if we got our hands on a couple rad suits," said Ivan.

"Peter, is there a way to access the last habitat?"

"None, Miss. It collapsed long ago, and the pedestrian tunnels were sealed to prevent radiation backflow into the other habitats. I'm afraid the last habitat is lost."

Ivan looked at Peter. "The pedestrian tunnels were sealed?"

"Correct."

"What about power distribution, lift shafts, bot tunnels, waste pipes, that sort of thing?"

Peter's eyes fluttered a fraction of a second. If Linus hadn't been looking, he wouldn't have noticed. He was definitely a sapioid. Peter was reviewing a schematic or accessing a database somewhere. "It'd be reasonable to assume they were destroyed when the habitat collapsed."

"What are you getting at?" said Linus, turning to Ivan.

"Something Luka said. I'll tell you later."

"Okay. Ms. Roche, one more question. Actually, it's your question from our last visit. We never got around to it."

"Did I have a question? It must've slipped my mind."

"Peter said you wanted to speak with us about something important."

"Right. Peter, tell the Chief what you told me before about my data."

"During a routine privacy review, I discovered someone had surreptitiously accessed Ms. Roche's medical, financial, and security records."

"That's strange," said Ivan. "Chief?"

"Do you know where this attempt was made?"

"Habitat 8, Level 1."

Linus's chest tightened, and his shoulders tensed. He held his breath and gulped, worried the dummy terminal hadn't done its job.

"However, there was no other information attached to the query."

"That is unusual." He exhaled. "Do you have any enemies who'd want that kind of information?"

"Not at all. Not unless the cryo-tech's holding a grudge."

"Has anyone from Habitat 8, Level 1 tried to contact you recently?"

"No. Nobody."

"Then it's likely another glitch. BOSS does that sometimes." Linus moved off the bench and searched Harin's face for any sign of deception. She was as calm and plastic as the sapioid standing between them, but she had also lied. "But if it's not, let me assure you, Ms. Roche, we'll do everything in our power to find the culprits."

"I'm sure you will. Peter, escort our guests to Level 42."

Peter bowed and stood aside.

"Just one more thing," said Ivan, turning around.

"It's always 'one more thing' with you."

"I do apologize. I'm curious about you, is all. You're fascinating, Ms. Harin Roche." He smiled at her.

Linus recognized Ivan's tactic. It was obvious and overly dramatic.

Harin's face flushed. She smiled and licked her lips. "What is it, Deputy Ivan Finn?"

She doesn't have a clue. No human contact whatsoever. Ivan was using Harin's inexperience to his advantage. Had he missed a flirtatious glance between them? Or was Ivan's act sudden? Or perhaps he didn't care for flirtation anymore - acting or otherwise.

"I was wondering what Peter does when you're sleeping?"

"Peter can answer for himself."

"Well?"

"I don't understand your question. I sleep in my room, too. Doesn't everybody?"

"Of course."

"Now, if you don't mind. I'm exhausted."

Peter headed for the stairs. "Gentlemen?"

Linus waved him off. "We know the way."

18

Ivan

Ivan trudged along the long hall toward his quarters. His boots grew heavy, dragging more with each uneven step, and his mind, dulled by exhaustion and hunger, did much the same. Linus shuffled ahead, frequently looking over his shoulder, giving Ivan a look that said '*Me, too*' as much as it did '*Move your ass*'.

"Well?" Ivan caught up to Linus. "Don't tell me you didn't see that."

"Yeah, I saw it. She lied about not being contacted by Warren's goons."

"Makes me wonder what else she's hiding. A cloning lab perhaps?"

"Your opinion shifted awfully quickly. Are you thinking about Luka? Or you and Radek?"

"That doesn't mean I'm wrong. He doesn't belong with her. And I think she proved that."

"I don't know." Linus yawned. "Peter was the same each time. But Harin. No. Something's changed. Before, she was more lonely, isolated. She practically begged us to stay. Tonight, she was different somehow. I mean after we got past the initial snobbery. She was content, flirtatious - as strange as that was. When we talked about finding Habitat 9, she was happy, almost gleeful. Then she wanted us to leave. It's inconsistent."

"Weird, right? I understand why she'd want to leave that place. But I don't understand wanting to stay there alone. Or suddenly being happy about it. Why do you think—"

"Ivan, I'm tired. I can barely think anything at all." Linus stopped in the corridor and rubbed his eyes. "I can't keep going on like this. Listen. Eat some food, swig three tall shots of O-neg, and get a good, long rest. I'll do the same. Everything will be fine. You'll see."

"I know you, Linus. Your idealism only lasts between your bed and the terminal. What's with the starry-eyed routine?"

"I'm exhausted, and I'm trying to be positive. If we can't find anything solid on Harin by next week, we'll have to send Luka to her."

"You can't. It's not right."

"I'm not suggesting it's a perfect world. If that's what you want, buy yourself three necro-shrooms and float up to the pearly gates."

"I didn't say anything about a paradise, but you'll never convince me she's what's best for him."

"Then who? Sisters of Mercy? You and Radek? She's his biological mother."

"That makes her a donor. Not his mother."

"Is there a difference?"

"You know there is. You could've pressed the Luka issue, but you didn't. Why?"

"Look, I'm not disputing your instincts. Asking Harin what Peter does at night was a good idea. But you let her pass the question off to him. You'll never get a 'gotcha' moment from a sapioid. Especially the one *she's* controlling."

Ivan nodded. "Then I should've insisted she answer the question."

"Yes. You let her dodge and pass it off to a puppet. Humans usually have certain tells when they lie. Pupils dilate, skin flushes, a nervous tick, rubbing hands together, a nose wiggle, something. Peter's a walking terminal no matter what he looks like. She's good though. I'd drink the sand if she said it was water."

"So, you know I'm right about her."

"Stop telling me what I know and what I don't know. I know what I know." Linus exhaled through clenched teeth. "There's still no connection between her and Luka except for the trace. Remember, we started by looking for whoever tried to murder a little boy by putting him outside. We still don't have any evidence for that crime." Linus squeezed his fists and yawned, his whole head shaking along with it. "Look. I'm exhausted. You're exhausted. I promise we'll both feel better in the morning."

"Do you smell that?"

"I smell you." Linus smelled his armpits. "And now me."

"You can't smell that?"

Linus tilted his head and sniffed. "So, a few tunnel spiders are scrubbing rust a little late. They don't work lazy eight to eights, either."

"That's not only rust cleaner."

"Denatured proteins."

Ivan sprinted down the corridor, and Linus followed behind.

"Move. I live here." Ivan pushed through the gawking crowd gathered outside his unit. His legs gave way, and he dropped to his knees. He retched and vomited in the doorway, his face and eyes turning red. He covered his nose and mouth. Tears flowed down his cheeks and over his hand.

"Get out of my way." Linus came up from behind. "Oh, my God."

A large, wide figure lay on the floor a few meters into the room, face down next to the table. Acid had dissolved all the hair and most of the flesh down to the bone. It swelled, blistered, and split. Blood bubbled and separated into its various components. The clothes - standard hab overalls - discolored and frayed along the seams. There was no white powder, nothing to neutralize the acid. Ivan sat on his knees, watching the body disintegrate and disappear into the vents.

"It's Radek." His voice quivered. "She got Radek."

"Chahna?"

"It was her. She killed him." He clenched his fists. "I'm going to kill her, Linus. I'm going to rip her apart."

BEHAVIOR 44L [THREAT]: -1.25 L DEMERIT

BEHAVIOR 44L [THREAT]: -1.25 L DEMERIT

"Fuck you."

SPEECH CODE 12C [PROFANITY]: -50 ML DEMERIT

"Why would Radek come back here without you?"
"He loved me. He loved me, and I killed him."
"You didn't. She did."
"I broke the board, Linus." Ivan looked up. "I did this."
"We have to get out of here."
"If I played the game, he'd still be alive. They'd all be alive."
"None of it is your fault. If Chahna did this, she might return for you."
Ivan slumped against the corridor wall. "I have nowhere else to go."
"You have me." Linus pulled Ivan to his feet. "I'll get you through this. But right now, I need you to run." Linus pulled him through the crowd.

They halted at the entrance to his office. Linus braced himself, hands pressed against either side of the door, keeping himself from tumbling into the fizzing hole that had been his floor for the last twenty years and Habitat Integrity's for over three hundred.

This acid attack was the strongest Ivan had seen. It had eaten through steel plates and grates, contamination vents, and into a utility closet on the level below, dissolving stacks of blue plastic boxes before losing its potency. He'd broken the old board and let Helix choose a new game. A bloody game. That part wasn't good for anyone in the habs. "Where do we go now?"

"I was about to suggest there." Linus pointed into the gaping hole.

"Do you think maintenance will get to my quarters before this happens?"

"They will. And if T.M. dispatched someone to neutralize the acid, they'll report a... They'll report Radek, too. The acid could only do this because everyone avoids the H.I. office except when there's trouble. And I pulled the terminal's wires before we left."

"If there's a body, aren't we expected to get there first?"

"Priority goes to preventing this type of thing," he gestured to the hole, "from causing a containment breach. Chief of Tunnel Maintenance and I agreed they're most qualified. They have equipment and resources, and personnel in every habitat. By the time it's reported and we get to the scene, most of the evidence would be gone."

"Because we're short fifteen deputies."

"Who told you that?"

"Is it true?"

"It is. But I never had more than eight. Most of whom couldn't find their own nose with a flashlight."

"Are those offices still vacant?"

"The old Hab 3 office is. And it's the closest."

"They won't find us there?"

"A few years ago, I asked BOSS to adjust an error on Hab 3's schematic. I said it was a storage locker for desiccated mushroom compost. Not an H.I. office. So, unless they're searching for human fecal powder and bone meal..."

"A hideout." Ivan shook his head. "That long speech about playing the game and knowing your enemies."

"I know my enemies. That's why it was a reasonable precaution. I would've told you about it. Eventually."

Ivan stared into the hole. "I should've stayed in Waste Rec."

Habitat 3's integrity office was a meter or two longer and wider than Habitat 4's but looked much the same. Desk, chairs, tablet, and terminal. Everything expected was there, and more. Someone in composting had taken Linus's little error adjustment as fact and filled three quarters of the room with double stacks of meter-tall black drums labeled *DMC* in light brown letters. Ivan hadn't been in human feces up to his ears since his time in waste reclamation. The incessant, loud suck, pop, and hiss of large waste water pumps at both ends of the corridor completed the unwelcome nostalgia.

Ivan shut the door, dampening the sound enough to hear his own thoughts once again.

Linus tapped on the heavy plastic drum sitting in the back chair. He sniffed his fingertips, recoiled, and wiped them on his uniform. He leaned against the desk. "This isn't what I promised, but it'll have to do for now."

"At least it's in drums." Ivan fell into the chair, shaking rust off its springs. He dried his cheeks on his sleeve. "Human feces is more versatile than many people think. Besides fertilizer, we can press industrial diamonds from the carbon, make anti-radiation meds with the potassium and phosphorous. A little chemistry, and you'd be surprised what we can do. The best feces comes from the lower levels. It's richer in both minerals and vital nutrients. Those are added back into the water supply. What do you think they eat down there? Did you see—"

"Ivan. Stay with me, buddy. I'll figure," Linus sighed, "I mean we'll figure something out. Preferably before anyone else gets killed. No more drifting. You're not in waste reclamation anymore."

"Just Chahna."

"One naked braider, two T.M. crew, one werewolf and his two goons, now Radek. This bloody tit-for-tat won't solve anything. And I don't want either of us to be the next tit *or* tat in this game."

"It doesn't matter. I have to do something for Radek. I have to make her pay, don't I?"

"Did you or did you not lecture me twenty minutes ago about not having sixteen deputies?"

"I was confirming. It wasn't a lecture."

"So, I needn't remind you there are only two of us and dozens, if not hundreds, of them. I'm chief, also known as 'tit'." Linus gestured to himself. "You're the last of sixteen deputies." He pointed at Ivan. "Tat. See. Tit and Tat. No more. Game over. And you can bet your last ration the next Chief and deputies of H.I. won't do a thing to fight Helix or help Luka if they know what they did to us."

"She has to pay."

"And she will. But not like this. Face it, Ivan. You couldn't kill someone if you wanted to. There isn't a bad bone in your body. I should know. I have several." Linus yawned. "I'm sorry about Radek. Truly, I am. Helix settled on him because they couldn't get to us in Harin's home. But this bickering won't help anyone." He laid on the desk and closed his eyes. "You can sleep on the floor. If you want to argue with me, do it in the morning."

An overzealous fly buzzed Ivan's ears and landed on his nose, waking him from a nightmare gladly forgotten seconds later. He swatted but missed. The fly circled the room and landed on the terminal. It crawled across the time - *0556* - and took off again. It zigzagged across the room, here and there, up and down, touching and bumping into every drum, looking for a new landing spot. It found Ivan's cheek. He swatted again, but only managed to slap his face and wake Linus with the sound. The sting vanished as quickly as the nightmare before it. But in those brief seconds, Ivan wished it'd stay with him a while longer.

Pain proves reality.

The thought had remained with him, persisting in some dark, unrelenting recess in his mind since the morning he met Harin Roche. With Radek gone, Luka to follow months later, and his own future in disarray and doubt, he wondered, if instead of proving reality, perhaps pain had *become* his reality. He closed his eyes and slapped himself again. And again. And again.

Linus groaned and sat up. "Flies?"

"Yeah. They won't leave me alone."

"Ivan…"

"I know. Me, too. It's still early. You should sleep a little longer."

"Once I'm up, I'm up." Linus popped his neck.

"I won't."

"You won't what?"

"Talk about Radek or Chahna or Helix or any of it. I won't fight or argue or complain. All I want to do is help Luka. If that means finding Habitat 9, I'll do it for him. And I want you to know, when this case is finished, so am I. BOSS can refuse a transfer, assign me to salvage, or put me on hab arrest. I don't care. I don't care about your retirement, either. Once this is over, you won't see me again. I quit."

Linus looked away, focusing on the terminal instead of Ivan. He cleared his throat. "Then we'd better get started."

19

Linus

L inus recognized the anger and the bitter sincerity in Ivan's voice. Linus had sworn many of the same promises after one tragedy or another. He'd given Ivan eleven months of monotony and boredom followed by two weeks of pain, blood, and death. He couldn't deny it or argue his way out of it. *Convince him not to go, or find and train a new deputy and postpone retirement a year.* Neither choice seemed feasible.

He turned the ring on his finger and looked at his hand. *So strange.* It was like he'd gotten married for the first time and wasn't used to the ring, any ring, being there. "BOSS... never mind." He scooted off the desk and tapped the terminal screen. "First things." He scrolled through the file directory and opened *Habitat Schematics, All Habitats, Cross Section Layout,* and *Basic.* It opened a simplified line diagram.

Habitat 8's large dome rose first on the left side, down to Habitat 1's smaller dome last on the right, appearing in the sequence they were completed, from largest to smallest, rather than how they were numbered. Levels cascaded below the domes from 2 to 42. Layer by layer, thousands of little squares and rectangles formed long rows stacked on top of each other, plunging down from the surface, through the sand, and stopped deep inside bedrock. Hab 3's Integrity office, the little, rusted box turned desiccated waste storage, flashed red on the schematic.

He double and triple-tapped, zooming in and out on each Habitat. "Like I thought." He returned to the full *All Habitats* view.

"Open *Cross Section* again. Focus on Hab 1."

Linus zoomed in. "See," he scrolled down, "Nothing below 42. Nothing east of it, either."

"We know she's there. Go back."

Linus returned to the previous screen.

"Open..." Ivan motioned to the terminal and grumbled. "This would go much faster if you let me do it."

Linus moved aside, and Ivan scrolled past *All* and *Basic*. He tapped on *Utility* and chose *Waste Reclamation* from the long list of choices. A second schematic superimposed on the first. Pulsating blue lines indicated the directional flow of human waste in transit.

"You don't think she'd add her waste extractor to the schematic for everyone to see, do you?"

Ivan highlighted a series of large waste pipes starting on Level 1 to the Waste Reclamation reservoirs on Level 3 and larger pumps on Level 5, 12, 18, 24, 30, 36, ending at a pump on Level 42. From there, twenty smaller pipes spread out, nine pairs ending in nine units. The last pair vanished into a narrow gap in the bedrock beneath. "That's it. That's Harin."

Linus expanded the image. "I'll be. It's a cave."

"Doesn't quite do it justice."

"Leave it to a keystone to build a secret dungeon but forget to hide the extractor."

"Everybody poops, but nobody wants it to stick around. I doubt she forgot."

"What about that?" Linus pointed to a pair of small-diameter waste pipes exiting Level 5, heading east from Habitat 1. They faded into the sand a kilometer away.

"I'm not sure."

Ivan returned to *Utility* and tapped *Internal Collection*. Solid white lines, representing bot tunnels, appeared near the blue pipes. Colored triangles moved through the tunnels. Green ones represented standard collector bots. They gathered bottles, pieces of plastic or glass, and other inorganic objects to take to recycling centers in Hab 6 and Hab 8, breaking the occasional toe in pedestrian corridors. Purple triangles were bots transporting organic or medical waste including bloody bandages, severed limbs, and non-viable eggs for testing, sterilization, and eventual mineral extraction or, in the case of infectious disease, incineration. The tunnels went as deep as Level 42. One headed east out from Level 5 and followed the same path as the waste pipes. It faded into the sand at the same position a kilometer east of Habitat 1.

Ivan tapped *Power Distribution*. Thick, yellow lines, originating from solar cells, deuterium tanks, and massive thorium batteries passed into large capacitors on Levels 4, 8, 16, and 32. Thinner lines crossed every level, corridor, room, and went to every terminal and machine. Four parallel lines stretched eastward out from Level 5 and terminated alongside the waste pipes and bot tunnel. "That's got to be pulling a gigawatt. Something's using it."

Ivan tapped *Thermal Regulation*. An overlay appeared showing black heat transport pipes and undulating, multi-colored blobs from hot white struts in Habitat 8's black zone to pink corridors, cool blue med bays, and deep purple cryonics and cold storage vaults. Two pipes terminated into nothing a kilometer east of Habitat 1. The area was light blue with thirteen faint orange dots evenly spaced in a long row and a larger, orange blob to the side.

"Now I'm sure something's there."

"Scroll down." Linus pointed at the intense red glow emanating from beneath the bedrock. "Is that..."

"BOSS, what's this?" Ivan touched the red glow.

MAGMA CHAMBER

Ivan zoomed out to view the whole valley. "It's everywhere. The entire valley. Since when are there active volcanoes anywhere near Halti Fell?"

"There aren't. Or weren't. It looks like it's pushing up through the bedrock directly beneath us."

"How are we going to get out of here?"

"Don't go running outside. Those things take thousands or hundreds of thousands of years to breach. If ever. Geology hasn't said anything about it, so they must think the information would panic idiots who don't know any better."

"I'm thinking sooner rather than later, especially with the uptick in tremors these last few years. BOSS, extrapolate the time it'll take this magma to threaten the habs. How long until catastrophic structural failure?"

PROCESSING . . . .
PROCESSING . . . .
PROCESSING . . . .
PROCESSING . . . .
PROCESSING . . . .

"Five calculations." Ivan bit his lip and quickly exhaled. "This'll take a while."

"The answer won't matter. However long it is, we'll both be recycled by then. Besides, nobody's ever..." Linus paused. "No. No, it can't be. She couldn't have." Linus paced between the terminal and the door. With black drums filling the rear of the office, it was the only thing he could do.

"Go on," said Ivan. "Get it out before you give me another headache."

"There are almost thirty thousand people in the habs but only a couple thousand rad suits. Even salvage teams rotate suits in shifts. Three hours on and twelve hours off. That's only enough time to go as far as the old cities, find something useful, pack it into a solar-roller, and get back inside before fatal radiation poisoning. Only a handful of people have survived outside longer than a standard shift. Three hours."

"Nobody except Luka. He was outside for a day."

"Let's assume for a moment her eggs weren't defective, and Harin, working alone or with others, arranged to move them rather than sending them to the bio-recycler. We know keystones tried cloning before. That includes the Roche family. And we know at least one of her eggs was used to create Luka. We do know that, don't we?"

"Carla thought so. What about Sandro? She used his DNA, too. Could he have survived outside for longer?"

"Sandro couldn't escape the past much less the valley. After ten years of solitude and grief, he thought Luka came back from the dead. If there was anything special about Sandro, I'm not sure we'll ever find out what it was. Remind me to ask Ovum Cryonics about his sample."

"Then how'd he learn about Habitat 9?"

"I don't know. Maybe he was there, or he heard about it from Luka or somebody else."

"And Luka?"

"Forget Luka."

Ivan scowled. "You and Carla deserve each other. You know that, right?"

"I mean, forget who he says he is. I don't think he'll change his story. Instead, ask what he is. What is Luka on a basic level?"

"A human being."

"More basic. The purpose of his existence."

"A lab experiment. A means to an end."

"What's special about him?"

"He can survive high doses of radiation like his mother. There's something in the X chromosome he got from Harin which made him immune."

"Not immune. Resistant."

"Right. Doc said he'd still need a rad suit to survive outside long-term."

"Choi found Luka near death less than a klick north of Hab 2, meaning his fancy X didn't take him very far. And he's still dying. If leaving the habs forever is the ultimate goal, what does it mean for Luka?"

"The experiment failed. He wasn't ready to be released." Ivan gasped. "The experiment's not over."

"If you want to succeed..."

"Try, try again. Luka could have more siblings out there."

Linus scratched his head. "Wouldn't it still be easier to clone one egg and one sperm multiple times? And combine those into multiple zygotes, then force-grow them? Of course, she'd still need to upgrade the old equipment. Or she'd have to find surrogates for normal pregnancies. But each generation would take nine months and another eighteen years to have their own children. And Carla did say whoever did this was in a hurry to finish." Linus stopped. "Did I answer my own question?"

"I was wrong," said Ivan. "You should pace more often. But you're also wrong about something. It shouldn't matter if eggs and sperm were cloned separately then combined into multiple zygotes, or if a single zygote was created first, then cloned and implanted into multiple surrogates. All those children would still be twins, quintuplets, or whatever thirteen or thousands of identical siblings are called. Same gender, too. They'd all be Lukas."

"Genetic diversity. Right. She'd need to consider subsequent generations," said Linus.

"And mono-gendered couples can't conceive on their own."

"Which means she's in a hurry but thinking long-term. No wonder Luka's a mess. She's trying to do everything at once."

"Then we come back to Sandro, and around we go. What if you're going about this wrong? We know Harin's DNA, or the part which makes her resistant to radiation, is important. So, her X chromosome is non-negotiable. It must be hers. Nobody else's will do."

"Because everyone would need it to survive outside." Linus nodded. "Go on."

"If the male's DNA were different each time, there might be enough genetic diversity to make it worth the effort. Plus you'd get boys and girls. They'd be half siblings like the two Lukas. They'd share a quarter of their DNA. Or at least the first generation would. If I correctly understood what Carla and the cryo-tech were saying."

"That doesn't sound too good, either."

"If a fighting chance at life outside the valley is all she's looking to accomplish, why not? Without the child killing part of the experiment."

"She'd need to. To find what worked best. What's she got? Three hundred thousand eggs? Surely there are enough viable ones in there to accomplish her goals."

"That's if she could use up every one. How many does O.C. normally extract in a sitting?"

"If memory serves, they took two hundred from Katri. Two appointments six months apart, one hundred each time. That was before you were born. I have no idea if it's the same now."

"Were those viable?"

"Let's focus on Harin, shall we?"

"Right." Ivan glanced at the terminal. It was still processing, removing calculations as it solved them. "So, a hundred before and another procedure coming up. Who told you, I mean, who tells people if cells are viable or not?"

"Cryo-techs extract the eggs and stick them in a scanner. BOSS runs the tests and outputs the results." Linus dusted his hands in the air.

"Really? It's that fast?"

"Yep."

"If the viability report's just another direct analysis, it'd be impossible for a tech to lie about test results. They'd be displayed and recorded on the terminal then and there."

"Correct. It'd be like asking BOSS to analyze anything else. Congratulations. You cleared all the Ovum Cryonics techs as her accomplices. At least at that stage."

PROCESSING . . . .
PROCESSING . . . .
PROCESSING . . . .
PROCESSING . . . .

"Could BOSS be any slower?" Ivan kicked the terminal.

"Easy there. It's only input-output. And only I get to kick terminals."

"I/O." Ivan stroked his chin.

It was obvious he hadn't shaved or wiped the grime off in days. The added hair made Ivan look his age, and he sounded like a newer, better, more confident Chief of Habitat Integrity. Linus avoided his reflection in the terminal screen for the same reasons.

"If Harin were somehow able to hack BOSS..."

"BOSS is un-hackable."

"Hear me out. If Harin found a way to hack into BOSS, she could alter the scanner subsystem to make it report incorrect results, she'd only need to get the eggs out of cryo before they went into the recycler. Then she'd be free to play keystone cloner." Ivan stroked his chin again, his fingernails rubbing against his thick stubble, making a scraping noise. "What else does she have to do down there? I bet Luka's 'her' was Harin in a clean suit. Of course, hacking BOSS would frag every CPU in its system and kill us all."

"Makes me think of Digi," said Linus.

"Poor, old Digi. We've been wrapped up, focused on only this case. We never found what fragged the old girl's CPU. I know it's not our job, but it'd be nice for closure and all that."

PROCESSING . . . .
PROCESSING . . . .
PROCESSING . . . .

"How long's this going to take? I'd do about anything for your A1 clearance right now."

"As if that would make BOSS think faster? No, you asked for it. Let the computer do its thing."

Ivan grumbled. "So, what fragged it? I would've asked Jeda, but he wouldn't open the door."

"Sapioids and humans," Linus popped his back, "aren't dissimilar. Sister Isabella for instance. Time eventually tears us all down to our servos and makes us forget who we are."

"Who *we* are?" His eyebrows furled.

"Don't give me that look."

"There wasn't a look."

"There was definitely a look."

"Anyway. Now, we know Harin's responsible."

"*Assume.* That's an important distinction. There's still no evidence. Just vague correlations, innuendo, and only one clear lie that doesn't prove anything other than she was afraid to tell us she'd been in contact with Warren. That wouldn't look good for her, either."

"Fine. We *think* we know who, most of the how, and some of the why. We need to catch her and her accomplices in the cloning lab. They're too good otherwise." Ivan double-tapped on the undulating blue blob east of Habitat 1, magnifying it full screen. "There. That's where they'll be."

"If that's Habitat 9, the only way is through the bot tunnels." Linus highlighted the white line. "They're not much taller than the bots. We'd have to crawl, and there's no guarantee we won't get stuck between habs or lost in the dark. She'd have to know a shortcut. Think she'd tell us?"

"We may have better luck if we took Luka's advice and followed the bio-waste bot from Ovum Cryonics."

"You can't be serious."

"I didn't say it'd be easy."

"O-Cry's in Hab 5. You expect us to crawl behind a bot for nearly four kilometers? Do you have any idea how long that'd take? We could miss a check-in."

"Then I'll take the H.I. tablet."

"Chip scanner, Ivan. You need a terminal. Why do you think there are thousands of them everywhere? And those tablets were probably outdated when the habs were built. They can't hold a data link farther than three meters, so you can't bring a map along either."

"We'll have four hours to follow O.C. and check-in at a terminal inside Habitat 9."

Linus rolled his shoulders, "There goes what's left of my spine," and scratched his bald spot. "It's too risky. We need a backup plan."

"That's not the worst part."

"I hate this plan more every minute."

"See those areas above the bot tunnel between Hab 2 and Hab 1 where the shielding's worn to a few centimeters?"

"Shit." Linus glanced at the terminal.

PROCESSING . . . .
PROCESSING . . . .

"That's odd."

"To put it mildly."

"I meant BOSS." He pointed at the screen. "It didn't fine me fifty millis for swearing."

"Maybe it has too much on its mind. Geological history, predictive fluid dynamics, and whatever those other three calculations were."

"You were saying? I heard something about dying a horrible death?"

"We'll need rad suits or we'll never make it through those sections. And to keep pace with the bot to get past the internal containment doors."

"Who got the suits recycled from ours?"

"A couple astronomers here in Hab 3."

"Stupid career. What's there to see?"

"I'd avoid those sort of comments when we ask for the suits. Just a suggestion." Ivan left the terminal and sat on the desk. He rocked, biting his lip, looking around the room.

"Go ahead. Say whatever's on your mind."

"She could've kept him in Habitat 9, and nobody would've known anything."

"Another phase of the experiment? Or she had a momentary lapse of compassion and let him go?"

"Sandro was unstable, delusional," said Ivan. "Letting him believe his son had risen from the dead was beyond cruel. But if Carla's right, and she was coming back for him, then running away from Warren saved his life the first time. Then James Choi pulled him from the scour and saved his life again."

"And we've been circling chaos ever since. Choi was first to fall in."

"Are you blaming Choi's death on Luka?"

"No. It's just... I... I don't know what I'm saying. It's... Ivan, Luka was the spark. The spark that set everything that's happened these last weeks into motion. There's a big part of me that wants to thank him for exposing the truth, waking me up, making me face my past, forcing me to do my job for the first time in I can't remember how long. But there's this part, this jagged, little spot in the back of my mind that hates him. I don't like it. I know it's wrong. But it's there."

"Then why are you doing this?"

"She'd want me to."

"You mean Katri."

"She wasn't one to leave things unfinished, and she was a lot like you around kids."

"Is that why you want to retire? Because the bigger, better half of you is gone?"

"Bigger half?"

"You know what I mean."

"I only accepted this job for the rations and freedom. The same reasons you did. BOSS was right about me. I'm good at it. You could be, too. But I don't want to stay without Katri, so I quit. And sooner or later, you'll quit, too. It's the job. It wears you down. The only difference being, if you leave first, BOSS will make me stay to train another deputy. That's at least a year."

"You can't change my mind. I meant what I said."

"I know you did. The sooner we catch her, the sooner you can leave, and the sooner I can start training a new deputy."

PROCESSING . . . .
EXTRAPOLATION COMPLETE
CATASTROPHIC STRUCTURAL FAILURE: 237 YEARS

"Double shit."

SPEECH CODE 12C [PROFANITY]: -50 ML DEMERIT
SPEECH CODE 12C [PROFANITY]: -50 ML DEMERIT

"I didn't say it twice, you greedy toaster."

"That's definitely sooner," said Ivan.

"Now, do you see why I hate requisitions? Nobody will get those suits. Or Carla's cloning tank. Or those neutron sensors. Or that new report tablet my old Chief told me to requisition twenty years ago. That one's still got 237 years on it, too."

"Yeah, I got it. It's a doomsday clock. It's got to be S-LAD. System Last Available Date." Ivan gripped the terminal by its sides, "Oh, hot toaster," and blew on his hands.

"And now we know why Harin's in a hurry. She's got forty to fifty years to try before she dies. What are the odds she's working with the only person, or rather thing, she has any influence over?"

"Peter."

Linus nodded. "She could instruct him to keep her eggs frozen and continue the work after she's been recycled. It wouldn't surprise me if every keystone were in on it."

"Well, I'm not dead yet. Neither are you. You talk to the two astronomers. I don't remember their names. See what they want for the suits."

When did he go from taking the lead to taking over? "And if Helix is looking for us?"

"Then you'd better get in and out before they see where we are. I'll be back in five."

"Where are you going?"

"To siphon wastewater."

20

Ivan

Ivan left Linus at the terminal and headed for the thunderous pump at one end of the corridor. The volume increased as he approached, vibrations rattling the walls, shaking particles of dirt, dust, and debris from the narrow gaps between ceiling panels. He stopped at a busy intersection and plugged his ears with his fingers. A few dozen people trotted by, all with pinky fingers pushed into their ears, each giving him an odd look as they passed.

An unfamiliar middle-aged man stopped in front of Ivan and gave him the same look. He shouted, "Screw You, too," shoved his middle finger in Ivan's face, and continued on his way.

Ivan realized his gaffe and switched his middles to pinkies. The looks stopped, and a few seconds later, the raging crowd thinned to a trickle. He stepped into the intersection, bumping into a woman with dark hair and olive skin. "Excuse me," said Ivan, with volume enough to compete with the noise. He gasped. "Chahna? Chahna Bhatt?"

She kept her head down, hesitating, but she didn't answer.

"Chahna, I've been looking for you." He grabbed hold of her collar and pushed her into the waste extractor room a meter into the next tunnel. He shut the door and let the latch fall into place, securing the door behind him.

"Please. You have the wrong person. Look," she tugged on her white shopkeeper badge with one hand, "my name's Susan," and reached into a narrow hip pocket with the other.

"No, you don't." Ivan squeezed her forearm, holding the long, straight razor in her fist. Light reflected off the polished blade. "What's this for?"

"I'm a barber."

"Liar."

Chahna wrenched and jerked her arm. She dug her long, rust-stained fingernails into Ivan's wrist and grabbed for the razor. Ivan squeezed and snapped her wrist back. She grunted and let go, dropping the razor onto the urine drenched floor. He kicked it aside and blocked a punch, grabbing hold of her other wrist. He slammed his forehead into her face, and she fell and hit her head on the extractor. She lay in a puddle of urine, nose broken, eye ruptured, gash across her forehead. Blood cascaded from the wounds.

"They told me to."

"They told you to murder two maintenance crew?" He kicked her side, cracking a rib. She screamed. "They told you to murder Radek?" He kicked her again. "Who hired you to follow me?"

"Go to hell."

Ivan stomped on her hip.

She coughed. "Warren." Blood dribbled from the side of her mouth. She strained to sit up, but instantly fell back and clutched her side. "Werewolf."

"I know who he is. Or was."

"Good for you," she shouted. "Now Oxi's fighting Helix for the territory. Congratulations." She spat blood on his boots. "You started a gang war, you and your chief."

Ivan's hands shook. "Radek was everything to me."

"I didn't kill your husband." She laughed. "You must've pissed off someone else."

"Liar!" Ivan kicked her again, cracking another rib.

"But I wish I'd gotten the job. I do." She coughed. "I would've burned out his pretty eyes for what you did to Warren."

Ivan sat on the waste-stained extractor and stared at the long, straight razor, open on the floor. "You and him."

"Yeah. Me and him. What about it? You going to murder me, too?" Blood bubbled from her nose. "Finish the job?" She laughed. "We both know you would've done it already. You don't have it in you."

Ivan looked at his eyes reflected in the blade, and he felt a fleeting impulse to look over his shoulder. A darkness, a shadow of the worst parts of himself, stared back from behind them, a monster born of unbearable grief and anger over his loss, not of his better half, but of his whole self, the person he was with Radek in his life. Though he'd always embraced the warm light of day, he had to admit a part of himself longed for that darkness. "It's in me."

She cackled. "Now who's the liar?"

"But Linus was right. The killing has to stop."

"It has to stop." She strained to talk through gurgling blood. "Call for help before—, before I pass out. If I die, you're a killer. You'll be like me."

"I'll never be like you. I'm a good man. A good husband."

"Not anymore." She laughed.

"You're right. As much as I want, I can't kill you. I don't have time to arrest you, either."

"Then let me go."

Ivan picked the razor off the floor and stood over her. "I can't do that either." He stared into the darkness and let it take control. His heartbeat slowed, and he felt disconnected, calm, assured. The old Ivan would try to do the right thing. But in the darkness, the only right was expediency.

"What are you going to do?"

"I need you to stay here a while."

"You can't leave me."

Ivan knelt at her feet and removed her boots and socks. He set them aside and lifted her foot off the floor. "You can enjoy the pumping station noise until I come back."

She glared at the razor and panicked. "Stop."

"Linus told me about something Helix, your kind, maybe you, did to a guy in Hab 7. They wanted to keep him from running away. Their version of hab arrest."

"No. Stop. Please, stop. You can't."

"Nothing official, of course. But I think we've passed 'official'."

"Wait. Don't."

"He called it a 'placeholder'." Ivan pressed the razor into her heel and drew the blade across, slicing through her Achilles tendon in a single, calm stroke.

Chahna screamed, flailing her legs. She strained, reaching for Ivan, but fell back, hitting her head on the floor.

Ivan had never cut meat. He was surprised how easily the blade passed through the flesh and how little blood flowed from the wound. He lifted the other foot and held the razor against her heel.

"Please," cried Chahna, her whole body shaking.

"Please? Is that what Radek said?" He pressed and drew the blade across.

Chahna writhed and wailed, misting more blood onto the wall and waste extractor.

Ivan folded the razor and put it in his pocket. He wiped Chahna's blood off his hands and boots and tossed three wadded, bloody waste cloths down the sterilizer chute. "I have to go."

"Don't leave me. Please."

"Please is not the magic word. Now, I have to do this one important thing. It's everything I have left in the world thanks to you. But I'll return if I can."

"*If* you can?"

"Keep doing what you're doing until then."

"Murderer," she screamed. "You'll never get away with this."

Ivan raised the bar lock and exited the waste extractor room. He reached into the door gap and let the lock fall on his fingertip.

She reached for him and coughed, spitting more blood on her clothes. "They're going to kill you."

"I know." Ivan pulled his finger away as he slid the door shut.

"Murderer!"

The bar fell into place, locking the door, securing Chahna and his darkness inside. A tiny LED above the handle changed from green to red.

"Hey. You in line?" a man shouted, walking up from behind. He danced in place, one hand squeezing his crotch, the other with a pinky in his ear. He shuddered. "I said, are you in line?" He noticed the red light, groaned, and danced away.

Ivan hurried after the dancer toward another extractor at the far end of the corridor, the old Ivan eyeing the terminal beside it.

21

Linus

Linus closed the message interface as Ivan rushed into the office, his fly agape, undershirt poking through the hole. Ivan's face was flush, and his breathing labored like a man narrowly escaping his lover's spouse at the door.

"Any luck?" said Ivan, catching his breath.

Linus gestured to Ivan's open fly. "That was longer than five minutes. I thought you got sucked in."

"That extractor was occupied." He closed his fly and adjusted himself. "I had to find another one and make a call. Are they going to sell us the suits?"

"Anything I should know?"

"I'll tell you later. So... Rad suits?"

Linus sat on the desk. "How do you want it? Great, okay, or terrible?"

"Any order's fine."

"They won't sell us the suits, but they'll lend them to us for fifty rations apiece."

"That's one okay and two terribles. Did you explain it was an H.I. emergency?"

"I told them enough to get our needs across."

"What did they say?"

"Seventy-five rations apiece. But I talked them down to fifty."

"What was it before?"

"Five."

"How'd that happen?"

"Apparently, Oxi's put the word out not to assist us in any way whatsoever. They figure we'll do to them here what we did to Helix in 8. Twice."

"They're rust-dusters?"

"Seems one hundred rations is the turncoat's price. I said I wasn't sure about water, but I promised I'd get them something worth at least that many."

"We should've confiscated Heidi's when we had the chance. The ninety she got for the two jobs, not the sixty she lied about."

"No doubt Oxi took a sizable cut when she transferred to Hab 3, and the Sisters distributed the rest elsewhere."

"So, everything's gone. Where's this great news you mentioned?"

"Those astronomers were toe-up, riding the crimson wave when I called."

"It's not 0800 hours yet. How's that great?"

"Astronomers work at night, Deputy Finn."

"Oh, yeah. But still."

"What I'm saying is they're willing to accept gluco instead of water."

"We don't have a hundred rations worth of... Linus, don't you dare."

"The Ant will only stay closed until BOSS finds a new owner. We've got to take it before that happens. We both know what Radek would've done in this situation. He'd do it, and I think he'd want you to do it, too."

The screen flickered, and the message indicator flashed green.

Ivan opened the messages system. "Two messages. One priority." He pulled his hand off, "Ouch," and wet his fingertip. He blew on it. "What's up with this thing?"

"Let me guess. They upped the bribe to two hundred rations."

"No. Priority's from Doc Langstrom. It's Luka. She says he's been taken."

"How? Who?"

"She says to come right away."

"She put that in a message? Call her back."

Ivan lifted his hand off the terminal and took a step back. "What now?"

"The terminal's getting hotter. Steam pipes hot. Feel it."

Linus put his hand flat on the screen and jerked it away. "Ow! You could've warned me."

"I did."

The text of Carla's message brightened and pulsed. The terminal chimed once. Twice. Three times. Continuously. Each chime louder and faster than the ones before. The screen flickered and shut off, and the sound stopped.

"Chief!" Ivan grabbed Linus by the collar and threw him out of the room.

The terminal exploded, blowing Ivan onto Linus's back as a grotesque, black cloud of toxic smoke and powdered human feces filled the corridor. He rolled off Linus and dragged him off to the side. Fire engulfed the room. A drum exploded, shooting flames across the wide corridor, and alarms sounded throughout. Ivan covered his nose and crawled to the door. He pulled his sleeve down over his hand, gripped the handle, and slid the door shut as the room's halon gas went to work, putting out the fire.

Ivan coughed, shaking Linus. "You okay?"

Linus rolled over, "I think so," and hacked, spitting brown mucus on the floor. "You're heavier than you look. Stronger, too. You can tell Sister Oni," he coughed, "I said so."

"I'll do that. Can you walk?"

"I don't think we have a choice." He spat.

"Come on. We need to get to med bay."

"Geology first. We have to warn them about the terminals."

They burst into the geology lab, but it was empty except for four microscopes, two tubs of rock samples, and the replacement terminal. A foul blend of scorch marks and remnants of geologists painted the walls and long, narrow gaps between floor vents.

Linus knocked the terminal onto its side, cracking its screen down the middle. "If BOSS assigns a new team while we're gone, it should take them a while to drag another one from somewhere else in the hab or move everything into a new room." It was the best he could think of.

Ivan grabbed a jagged, green rock and scratched *BOOM* into the scorch marks beside the terminal. "If that doesn't do it, nothing will."

They left Geology, and Ivan ran ahead, knocking everyone into the walls as he rammed his way through the crowd, across corridors, climbed a latter two levels, entered Habitat 2, and disappeared into the dim, unfinished tunnel leading to the med bay. Ivan ran through the dark so quickly, Linus was worried both of them would smash their heads into low-hanging boulders, replacing one dying boy with two men. But he did his best to keep up, his stitches pulling every time he dodged a rock in his path. His eyelids were heavy, and his stomach growled. Ivan might have been young enough to run on pure steam, but Linus's pipes were about to go *BOOM* all by themselves.

"What happened?" said Ivan, running to Carla the second he saw her.

Carla knelt on the floor over Wallace Taggot and pressed a thick, white pad to his neck. His eyes were open, looking at her, quiet as the white pad turned red. She applied another one over the first. It began to change colors. Blood flowed from behind her right ear along delicate wrinkles in her skin, absorbing into her lab coat's pressed collar.

"Where's Luka?"

"Carla."

"I'm fine. It's a scratch. Easy there, Wallace. Relax. That's good. Look at me. Focus on my voice. Binetti's on his way now." She glanced up at Linus and back to Wallace. "I didn't see where he went. I barely had time to send messages to you and Doctor Binetti. He's on his way from Hab 1."

"Who? Who took Luka?" said Ivan.

"He was too fast. He came in when I was teaching Wallace to remove burnt issue. He asked if Luka was still in the back room. I don't know how he knew. Then he grabbed the scalpel out of Wallace's hand, stabbed him in the neck, and pushed me to the floor. I think he missed Wallace's carotid. Linus, a millimeter lower and…"

"He who?" Ivan stepped forward.

Linus joined him. "Carla, what did he look like?"

"Both of you, back off. Ivan, go, call Med 1. Find out if Binetti's left yet."

"Okay."

"And the woman, the one you called about. I forwarded your message to Hab 3. They got to her in time, and they'll keep her sedated until they hear from me. Like you asked."

"Thank you." Ivan left to use the terminal, leaving Linus with Carla and Wallace.

"What woman?"

"He'll tell you later. Or someone will, I'm sure." Carla struggled to unroll another pad with one hand, and tried, "Easy now," to keep Wallace calm by stroking his hair with the other.

"Let me." Linus unrolled three more and placed them on Wallace's chest.

"If you're going to help…" She gestured to a plastic cart of stacked drawers by the exit. "Center column, third row from the top. There's something that looks like a white pulser with a long, narrow nozzle in a sealed plastic bag. Bring it. And bring me the tube of bio-sealant beside it and the whole, top left drawer."

Linus hurried and did what he was told. He was good in a crunch and fine around blood. But Carla looked panicked, and that made him worry.

"Ivan, where are you? Ivan?"

He returned, followed by Linus carrying the sealer in one hand and drawer full of pads tucked under his other arm.

"Got it." Linus sat the items across Wallace's legs.

"Sorry." Ivan caught his breath. "Doctor Binetti left his med bay ten minutes ago. He should be here any second. Linus, that other message was from cryo-tech Farris. That idiot forgot to send it until this morning. It said Harin came in last night around

1830 hours, two days before her next appointment. They did the extraction. Non-viable eggs, same as last time."

"1830? That's almost two hours before we talked to her. Lying rat. She never said anything. She wanted us gone. Did you—"

"The eggs. Yeah, I told him to hold them. But he said the O.C. bot has to leave at third check-in, 1600 hours. He's only got until then to seal the day's non-viables and expireds in a waste box and send them out with the bot. He says," Ivan coughed, "it has go all the way to the bio-waste recycler in Habitat 1, Level 12 and return before 2000 hours or BOSS will shock his chip until it does. Same as if he'd missed his own check-in."

"Shit. We have to hurry."

SPEECH CODE 12C [PROFANITY]: -50 ML DEMERIT

"Carla, tell me about the man who did this. What did he look like?"

"Linen clothes, black eyes, and black hair in a topknot."

"Peter," said Ivan. "Did he have a red ankh branded under his ear?"

"A sapioid? I don't know. I didn't see one."

"Ankh," said Wallace, his voice shaky.

She stroked his hair. "Keep still. Don't talk."

"Carla. Wallace." Doctor Binetti ran toward them, his short, white lab coat fluttering behind, followed by two techs carrying trauma kits.

"Ivan." Linus grabbed his arm.

He shook his head. "We don't have time."

"Carla—"

"I know, Linus. Go."

His jaw clenched, and he ran side-by-side with Ivan in the direction of Habitat 1.

∞

They ran, not having gotten the gluco nor traded for rad suits. There wasn't time to meet the astronomers in Hab 3, go to Ovum Cryonics in Hab 5, and crawl for hours in the dark without a bot to lead them through a maze of tunnels, nor open internal containment doors between habs.

They decided to grab Harin Roche, Luka's mother, *No. His egg donor,* before she could pull Peter's strings one more time. Mother to a new breed of human or not, she had to go down. Hiding the O.C. visit was a conscious attempt, another lie, and that 'gotcha' moment Linus was waiting for. The fact she fooled him made it worse for her, and he had to consider everything she said was, at best, only half of a larger lie. The lift doors opened onto Level 42, and they stood in the empty marble vestibule, gilded entrance to Harin's den below.

The trip had taken over an hour, and Linus was already out of breath. He gestured to Ivan's front pocket. "How many you got in there?"

"My last two."

"Give me one."

He scoffed, "Requisitions," and removed a red-tipped pulse dart from Radek's old gun and handed it over.

Linus slid it into the chamber. "Where's your H.I. pulser?"

"My guess would be a under a smoldering pile of feces."

"So much for that. You'd better submit a..." Linus shook his head. "Never mind. It's gone. I hope it's got enough power to fire."

"Radek took good care of it." He held Radek's old pulser and rubbed his thumb across the grip. "It'll shoot. And don't tell me it's not personal for you now. Chahna made it personal for me. Now, Harin's hurt Carla and Wallace, too."

"I'm not going to argue, either. No more arguing." He swiped his wrist over the chip scanner, and they entered the lift. He looked over the control panel. "Do you remember the lock code? It was four sequential buttons and then two together. I only remember the last two. Forty and forty-two."

"It was forty-one, forty-one, forty-two, and forty. No. Wait, wait. Forty, forty-two, forty-one, and forty-one."

"Are you sure? I don't want to know what happens when someone presses the wrong sequence."

"That's it. I remember now."

Linus pressed the numbers, and the lift descended. The doors opened, and he ran for the ornate, carved arch. Linus swiped his wrist across the same apple Peter had touched, but nothing happened.

Ivan banged on the door. "Open the door. Open it now, Ms. Roche." He listened.

"You hear something?"

"Nothing. Ms. Roche, open it before we knock it down."

"On three," said Linus.

Ivan nodded.

"One, two, three." They kicked the door, but it didn't budge.

"Again." They counted to three and kicked, and again nothing happened. Not a vibration. Linus limped away. "No use. It's solid."

"Get behind me." Ivan rolled up his left sleeve. "This might disappoint the Sisters more than me." He inhaled, "But it's still going to hurt," and exhaled, "a lot." He screamed and punched the door, knuckles flat on. The door shook, and the skin tore off his knuckles, splattering blood on the door and his hand, misting his sleeve. He screamed and hit it again. More flesh tore away, exposing his hand's reinforced alloy skeleton and twisted wires. Again, trading red blood for blue sparks. And again. More blood and more sparks. His flesh split along a disguised steam, across the palm, up the forearm, blood saturating his sleeve elbow to shoulder. He screamed and hit the door again.

Linus watched, helpless, paralyzed between stopping the murderer within and stopping Ivan from destroying himself. Ivan reached over and stripped the old flesh from his arm, tearing it through the seam from palm to shoulder and tossed the wet pieces onto the floor. He reached up into his left sleeve with his other, human arm and adjusted something, stopping his blood from flowing into the bare metal-and-wires appendage. The broken door collapsed into the room, and a loud bang echoed in the cave.

"If she didn't know we were coming, she does now," said Linus. "Ms. Roche, don't make this harder than it has to be."

"Luka? Harin?" Ivan tiptoed inside.

Linus stopped and listened, but he couldn't hear anything other than Ivan and himself. "You hear anything?"

"Nothing."

"I would've thought..."

"I only have the one arm. Everything else is my own. And now it's ruined."

"If we both get out of this alive," he continued ahead, "the next one's on me."

Linus stood at the edge of the pool, not sure what to think or make of the scene. Harin Roche floated upright in a pool turned red with her blood, deep cuts drawn up through the center of her wrists. Her head lay, eyes open and eyelids drooping, on the pool's shorter edge, staring up at Habitat 9's shallow, broken circle. Her hair drifted on the placid water. A cracked and chipped water glass stood on her right. The triangular shard, bloody across the tip, was likely the tool she'd used to slit her own wrists. The whole room was red, lit by the pool lights as they shone through the bloody water, gleaming a deathly light onto the carving, the walls, the benches, Linus and Ivan's faces, and her own white, stained red, silk pajamas.

Linus knelt and looked over her body. "Blood stains on her cuticles." He lifted her arm out of the water. Her body flipped as if she were one, rigid piece. "And under her fingernails."

"She did this to herself?"

"I'd say she slit her left wrist, wrote that," Linus gestured to *No Destiny*, written in blood on the edge to her left, "and then slit her right." He turned her back over and looked into her eyes. He felt her arms and pressed on her abdomen. "Full rigor."

Ivan touched her cheek. "She's cold. She's been dead for hours." He sat on the bench.

"I'd estimate between ten and twelve."

"That's before we discussed her and Peter. She was dead before we looked at the schematics, dead before the terminal exploded, before Peter took Luka. If he knew she was dead, and he took Luka anyway, that means…"

"He's fully autonomous."

"Harin wasn't controlling Peter. It was the other way around."

"She must've been terrified of him. That's why she was acting strange. When she realized we were getting close to finding out about Peter, she decided then and there she was going to kill herself. She wanted us to leave so she could die alone. This was the only place she felt comfortable. 'As long as it takes,' she said. She was talking about finding peace."

"She was never going to find it in here with Peter. I didn't even consider asking her if she needed help or wanted out. There was a psycho sapioid standing behind me, staring over my shoulder the whole time, and I left her to die with him."

"Our shoulders. We left her. I'm just as responsible. What if she did at least some of what we thought? She hijacked Peter's programming, made him do what she wanted, made him forget who and what he was. But he got away from her. He turned into a monster, and she lost control of him."

Linus grabbed her by the right armpit. "Help me get her out of here." They pulled Harin out of the water, washing away her bloody last words with the same finality she achieved by slitting her wrists to escape the destiny she never wanted. They placed Harin on her back in the open space between the benches and the stairs.

"She must've thought death was the only way to escape him." Ivan looked into her eyes and dragged his fingers, closing them. "She didn't know about Luka, did she? It wasn't an act."

"If Peter's autonomous, the underlying program which doesn't allow him to lie or kill isn't working anymore. And if that's true, if it was only him all along, we're in serious trouble."

"Is there any other kind for us?"

"Indeed."

"Perfect and protect all life. Peter may think they're the same thing. After all, perfect Luka-type adults could repopulate the Earth."

"You're quoting BOSS's core mission. Peter's overlooked the second half." Linus climbed the stairs and headed back the way they came, leaving Harin alone on the floor. He'd have to alert medical whenever he got the chance. "Run and talk, Ivan. We have things to do before we can get into Habitat 9. Peter and Luka are ahead of us, and neither of them need rad suits to get through those tunnels."

"With the right core hack, Peter could've linked to the medical scanner and made it give a false reading. He could take whatever DNA he needed. He would've seen Harin as pure breeding stock, letting her live to keep the eggs warm." Ivan ran into the lift. He bent over, human hand propped on his right leg, metal one propped on the left. "Don't tell Sister Oni I said this, but I might've killed myself, too."

Linus leaned against the wall and pressed the button for Level 39. He dropped to the floor and caught his breath. "Except there's nowhere for his progeny to go. Nothing survived The Great Catastrophe."

"Who's to say? We haven't seen what's beyond the old cities in over four hundred years. But if only one sapioid escaped into the scour a century ago, they may have found a new home for us. BOSS would know, and Peter would know by accessing a database. He'd also know about the 237 year deadline to get us there. It fits."

"It fits because you want it to fit, but it's all speculation. Nothing more. He could be walking the line between functional and fragged. Plus radio link-ups don't work in the scour. Tablets barely work in here, so nice try. You almost had me believing in the Distant Utopia theory until your mysterious radio signal bit. I bet Peter's glitching while trying to fulfill the first mission statement. Perfect life. No human frailties, prejudices, judgments, nor compassion. He's going to save humanity even if he has to kill thousands of humans to do it."

"And a machine becomes a sociopath." The doors opened on Level 39, and Ivan exited. He stopped and held Linus back. "Then we can agree. Nothing else matters. Luka's in trouble, and Peter's got to be stopped. At any cost."

Linus nodded. "At any cost."

22

Ivan

X-Stretch didn't feel the same in the middle of the day. Although the shops and shopkeepers were identical, without The Pissing Ant to shower passersby in holographic urine and thumping, arrhythmiatic beats, it might as well be what it was - a half-empty corridor of half-empty people looking to fill themselves with whatever was around. At a quarter past second check-in, available meant getting lunch or getting into trouble. They were equally fulfilling, but Ivan wasn't hungry for either. He didn't bother explaining to a group of teenagers looking into the bar it was closed until further notice, instead choosing to wave Radek's old pulser at them without saying a word. They scurried away, and Ivan swiped his wrist over the door's scanner plate. It didn't open. He wasn't the owner, and he wasn't Chief of Habitat Integrity. Linus swiped, and the door lock released.

"Radek kept the good stuff in the back." Ivan shut the door behind them. "There are crates we can use. But I'm not sure how many bottles of O-Neg Platinum are a hundred rations worth."

"Neither am I. Let's take it all."

A bottle exploded at their feet, spraying more red onto their Werewolf-stained uniforms. Another bottle flew through the air. It grazed Linus's head and shattered on the floor. They ducked behind a table as someone hurled a third bottle out of the stockroom. It it the table and rained gluco onto their heads.

"Get out."

Ivan peered over the table.

"I said get out."

The next bottle skidded across, bounced off Ivan's head, and shattered behind him. "Who's there?"

"Ivan?"

"Radek?"

"Ivan?"

"Yes. It's me and Linus."

"Linus?"

"It's me, Radek. Can I get up now?"

Radek ran out of the back and collided into Ivan. The impact made a dull, painful thud, radiating across his chest, knocking the breath out of him. Radek looked disheveled and tired. His hair was a wild mess, and he was ten kilos lighter as if he'd been living off bar snacks and the few rations and tubes of protein paste he'd hidden behind the bar. "I heard there was a dead body in our unit. I thought it was you." He reached for Ivan's hand but found the bare, metal skeleton instead. "What happened?"

"It was damaged. I had to strip off the flesh."

"Sister Oni's not going to be happy." He held Ivan's metal hand. "Where's your wedding ring?"

"Shit. I must've left it on the finger."

SPEECH CODE 12C [PROFANITY]: -50 ML DEMERIT

"No worries. We can always requisition another. The important thing is you're alive. I thought those Helix people came for you."

"They did. But I thought it was you. I thought she went after you because she couldn't find me."

"Who?"

"It doesn't matter now. You're all right?"

"I am." Radek hugged him again.

Ivan felt like protein paste being squeezed out of a tube. He patted Radek on the back. "Raddie, you're crushing me."

"Oh, sorry." He eased off. "I was waiting for you to tell me it was safe to go home. That's when I heard about the body. I looked for you at the H.I. office, but it was destroyed."

"If that wasn't you, then who?"

"I don't know. I left mom's unit after we had an argument. I came straight here." Radek paused a moment. "Oh, God. Mom." He gasped and covered his mouth, sitting on Linus's usual stool at the end of the bar.

"Your mother?"

"His mother?" said Linus. "She's his size?"

"She probably came looking for me after our fight." Radek's voice faltered. "I kept telling her things were fine between us, but she didn't believe me. She didn't want me to go home. She said she'd confront you, take me away with her if I tried to go back."

"So, you never went home?"

"You said not to. I've been hiding out, eating our emergency supplies and drinking gluco for days. I didn't want to go back to mom, and I wasn't sure where else to go, so I stayed here. I thought eventually someone would find me when I checked-in, but nobody's come looking until you."

"Let's pray it stays that way."

Radek nodded and squeezed Ivan again.

"I hate to interrupt, but we're on a schedule."

"What's happened?"

"Nothing good," said Ivan. "We need a hundred rations worth of O-neg."

"A hundred rations worth? Why?"

"We need two new rad suits. Don't ask me to explain anything more. It'll only make you worry."

"Ivy, saying it'll only make me worry makes me worry more. You're in trouble, aren't you? The people who did that. They're still after you."

"It's not about them. It's about the kid."

"The scour kid?"

"The same." Ivan hurried into the stock room and emptied a crate of cheap slag sludge onto the floor. "Can we?"

"O-Neg Silver?"

"Platinum. A hundred rations worth," said Linus. "Or as much as you can spare."

"Okay." Radek nodded. "Eight of those should do it." He pointed to a row of tall, slender bottles wrapped in embossed platinum foil.

"Only eight? That's almost a thousand percent markup."

"Linus, you don't pay. You've never paid."

Ivan placed eight foil-wrapped bottles into the crate. "We don't have time for this."

Linus pointed at the top shelf. "Then take two more."

"You can't have two for yourself," said Radek.

"They're not for me. They're for the people we're borrowing from in case they get stingy at the last moment."

Ivan's eyes widened, and he shook his head.

"To sweeten the deal. Not bludgeon them to death... unless we have to. They're rust-dusters, you know."

Ivan hurried out of the stockroom, and his lips grazed Radek's as he passed. "Stay here until I get back." He shuffled toward the exit, ten glass bottles rattling in his arms.

"What am I supposed to do until then? I'm almost out of rations."

Ivan sat the heavy crate on a table by the door. He pulled his last half ration from his suit and tossed it to Radek. "Make it last. I'll get more from the dispensary on my way back."

"And if you don't come back?"

"I will. I promise." Ivan slogged out the door, bottles rattling, gluco sloshing. "Come ration or..."

"Forget the platitudes. Just come back."

And they were swept into the passing crowd.

The astronomers didn't need much convincing to trade for the suits, and it was easier than Ivan expected. When the two, toe-up and stumbling around their shared unit, empty bottles of slag sludge in their hands, saw a crate packed with the best, top-shelf gluco any bar had to offer, they were quick to hand over the new rad suits and upend two full bottles straight into their mouths. Linus suggested if the astronomers were going to continue drinking from the bottles, they'd likely die of alcohol poisoning, and he and Ivan should return to the unit and take what was left off the bodies and keep the new suits for themselves. Ivan couldn't disagree.

They held the suits up to their necks. Ivan's was ten centimeters too short. Linus's was ten too long. They traded, and Ivan ran his hands across the new material. It was flexible and smooth like it had never been outside. A good rad suit in the hands of a fastidious owner could last two decades or longer, but the exterior layer became rigid and rough after five or six shifts in the scour. Whatever these astronomers were going to do with the suits, they weren't in a rush to start.

The smell of various phthalates and freshly extruded lead-laced polyvinyl acetate wafted off them. His old one was a post-mortem donation to Sisters of Mercy, and no matter what anyone had to say about the danger of using an old, or previously loved as Sister Isabella called it, rad suit, at least it didn't smell like decaying rats and sulfuric acid. He hauled it over his uniform, fastened the seals, and pulled the helmet down over his face and locked it into place. It was the fastest, most intense migraine he ever got. The suit fit nonetheless. He took off the helmet and carried it at his side. Linus did the same. They left the astronomers with their overpriced gluco and crossed into Hab 4.

They stopped at the dispensary around the corner from the Sisters of Mercy donation center and pushed to the front of the line.

Linus swiped at the ration terminal and withdrew two liters from his account. He gave one to Ivan.

"Thanks." Ivan read Linus's balance and noticed his list of weekly, sometimes daily withdrawals, dozens of petty -50 mL demerits for swearing, several -3,750 mL demerits for filing false reports, -1,500 mL for firing his pulser in a crowded corridor, another -200 mL for littering, leaving Digi's body on the floor, and another for antisocial behavior. *+4,138 L <Halla, Katri>* flashed in the upper right corner of the screen. It was a pre-ration like Harin Roche's. Ivan pointed it out. "Plus four thousand liters? It's long past three hundred days. Why haven't you accepted?"

"That doesn't mean they're mine."

"Technically, it does. Her life savings is yours now."

"I'll accept them when I'm good and ready."

Ivan surrendered. "Okay."

"Now, Lady" a low voice echoed in the corridor, "pass 'em over."

"Is someone shouting?" Ivan looked to see where it had come from. "It's the donation center. Those men are back."

"Charge your pulser." Linus looked around the corner and pulled his out.

Ivan pointed the barrel at the ceiling and followed Linus. The crowd parted, allowing them to move down the corridor. Four burly men stood outside the center window. The closest held a bundle of four rectangular steel plates, tapping them on the extended ledge.

"Give us the rations."

"Oh, dear." Sister Holly squinted up at the man through thick eyeglasses. "You said five hundred?"

"Yes. Five hundred. One hundred twenty-five apiece."

"Oh, dear."

"Stop saying that, and hand over the rations."

"Just a moment, Dear. I have to make a call."

"Rations first. Call second."

"Oh, dear."

"Listen you old, blind bat, I don't know what you're playing, but if you don't give us the rations, we'll—"

"You'll do what?" said Linus.

"Stay out of this, old man."

Linus unlocked his pulser's safety, charging the weapon's magnetic firing mechanism. He aimed it at the man's chest.

Ivan pointed his at the second. "I have an idea. Why don't you make a donation? I'm sure the Sisters would distribute those five hundred to people more needy than yourselves."

"Fuck that," said the man at the window.

SPEECH CODE 12C [PROFANITY]: -50 ML DEMERIT

"Well, now. Seems someone's coded after all," said Linus. "It wouldn't take much to trace that demerit."

"If you haven't noticed..." said the first.

"There are four of us..." said the second.

"And only two of you..." said the third.

"Why don't you trek off?" said the fourth.

"Who are you? The three bears?" said Ivan.

"But there are four of them." Linus counted them off, pointing his pulser at each. "One, two, three," he aimed for the fourth, "and four. I guess that makes you Goldilocks."

All four reached into their suits and pulled out their own pulsers.

"You think that scares us?" Linus aimed from first to fourth and back again.

Ivan did the same. "We've already taken out four of yours."

"What's another four to us?" Linus aimed at the man by the window.

"Oh, dear." Sister Holly ducked, albeit rather sluggishly.

"Can we make them howl, too?"

"I wonder," Ivan aimed his pulser at the last man's crotch, "if Goldilocks here is a screamer? Are you a screamer, Goldi?" Ivan's eyes narrowed, and he tightened his grip. "Scream for me, Goldi."

The men looked at each other, rubbing their fingers across their pulsers' triggers. They turned and ran, leaving the numbered steel plates on the ledge.

"That was anticlimactic," said Ivan.

"You can come out now, Sister," said Linus.

"Oh, dear. Are they gone?"

"They're gone." A stunted chuckle escaped from his mouth.

Ivan almost mistook it for a hiccup. "Their darts must be on requisition. 237 years, I hope."

"Somehow I don't think that kind of luck is on our side."

Sister Holly peered over the window ledge. "Ivan Finn? Is that you?"

"It's me, Sister."

"I was about to call you. There were four men." She adjusted her glasses. "Ivan, did you know your hand is metal?"

"I know, Sister. We scared them off."

"Oh, dear. What if they come back? There are two thousand rations back here. All with numbers and letters on them."

"Good news, Sister. They wanted you to give them to the needy."

"They did? Oh, dear. Why didn't they say so?"

"Call Sister Oni and the others. All those rations have to be distributed tonight."

"Oh, dear. Always in a rush. I don't know if we can. But we'll certainly try."

"What about Helix? Won't they?"

"Come after Sister Holly? I hope not." Linus tapped the bundle of steel plates on the ledge. "Sister."

She squinted. "Who is that?"

"It's me, Chief Linus Halla."

"Linus Halla?"

"Yes, Sister."

"That's right. Sister Oni told me about you."

"Only the good things, I'm sure."

"Well, I'm sure something was good."

"Never mind that. You need to close the center until the Sisters arrive. Lock the window and door right now. Okay?"

"Oh, dear." Sister Holly fumbled around behind the window. There was a faint chime, and the window shield rolled down and locked.

Ivan pushed back into the crowd. "Linus?"

"Coming. And since when are you Chief?"

23

Linus

S enior Ovum Cryonics Technician Jonathan Farris sat in his chair and looked between them. His expression fell somewhere between laughter and utter disbelief. "You want to do what?"

"Follow your bio-waste bot through the tunnels to the recycler." Ivan nodded toward the O.C. bot in the corner and looked at the time on the terminal beside it. "And we have less than ten minutes."

"Whatever for?" Tech Farris looked at Ivan's hand. "Do you have any idea how dangerous it is for real people in there?"

"Cryo-tech Farris," said Linus, "as we've—"

"It's Jack."

"Jack, as we've explained, it's vital to a case that we do this. Now, Deputy Finn says—"

"Deputy? Not Chief?"

"You told Deputy Chief Finn you'd be ready by 1600 hours to send the non-viables out with the bot."

"Correct. I don't have a choice. BOSS will summon the O.C. bot then. If it's not back by 2000 hours, BOSS'll take it out on me."

"So, have you prepared Ms. Roche's non-vi samples?"

"Of course." Jack picked a large, cold storage box off the floor and sat it on his desk. "Along with the time expireds as I explained to Deputy Finn twice now."

"I was going to ask about your process before I was interrupted during our last conversation. Chief Halla has a three year rule for expunging DNA from some types of cases. Does O.C. have a similar policy?"

"We do. Not three years of course. That's far too short a time. We call ours the x10 rule, meaning a viable donor's ration allotment multiplied by ten years from the date of the donation. Those are sent to the recycler along with assessed non-viables the same or next day depending on when they were collected. When Ms. Roche came in, the O.C. bot had already taken the day's bio-waste for recycling."

"A scrapper's extracted DNA would expire after a decade."

"One ration times ten years, yes. And a keystone's after one hundred fifty."

Linus got off his chair and took a scalpel, tweezers, and gauze out of the chest by the door. He rolled the gauze around them and stuck them in his pocket.

"Linus, what are you doing?"

"Plan B. Mr. Farris, am I correct in assuming Harin Roche's first set of non-viables were sent to the recycler on the same day?"

"They should've been." Jacked flipped through a number of tablet screens. "Yes. It says her first extraction was about four months ago on 12 January at 0930 hours. Those ova were sent for recycling at 1600 hours the same day."

"How far do your records go back?" said Ivan.

"As far back as the Ration-caste system. About two hundred years or so."

"Can you look up a scrapper named Sandro Hazbegi? He would've donated here about sixteen to seventeen years ago."

"Sure." He flipped through a few more screens. "I have two donations from one Hazbegi, Sandro. The older one was shy of seventeen years ago. His sample was paired with another scrapper, Marika Hazbegi. His wife, I'm assuming. Says the offspring was a healthy male, successful 1.5 ration upgrade. Good for them."

"And the second donation."

"Ten years ago on 12 January 2627. The sample DNA was viable, but it was never used. Sometimes, people decide to try for a second child, but change their minds for whatever reason. It's rare, but it happens."

"And when was that sample taken by the O.C. bot to the recycler?"

"Following the x10 rule, 12 January this year."

"The same day Harin Roche's first non-viable eggs were sent."

"How did you know?" said Ivan.

"I didn't. That's why I asked the question. But you yourself said Sandro's DNA may not have been as important as we first thought. One reasonable conclusion is he used whatever was most easily available to him. Meaning whatever viable male DNA went along with hers to the recycler."

"I was right? It was simple, random chance?"

"I never said it was simple, but it seems random enough. And it happens to fit what we know to be true. Tech Farris? Am I correct?"

"Yes. Ms. Roche's and Mr. Hazbegi's samples would've gone together in the same cold box along with a few dozen others. Some non-viable and some viable but expired." He glanced at the time. "And these are going in two minutes." Jack went to the bot and tapped a button on its head. Its arms extended and opened wide, and Jack placed the box between them. The arms compressed it, holding it in place. The bot circled the room and stopped in front of the meter-tall door leading into the tunnels. "By the way, I asked Tech Harlow to clarify what he meant by 'belligerent' in his report on Harin Roche's first extraction. He said Ms. Roche didn't want to leave the lab. He said her sapioid... What's his name?"

"Peter."

"Yes. Peter. That's it. He practically dragged her out of here kicking and screaming." He grinned. "Some people, right? Anyway, time's up. Here it goes."

Ivan pulled the helmet over his head and mouthed, *I'm dying,* to Linus.

Linus fastened his and felt a sharp pain behind his eyes and burning in his throat. It took every bit of willpower he had not to cry or projectile vomit onto the face shield. He dialed the low-power link-up to its highest setting and paired it with Ivan's.

The door opened, the bot's eyes lit up, and it rolled into the tunnel carrying the cold storage box.

"After you." Linus gestured toward the open door, his own voice reverberating back at him through the interior speaker behind his head.

Ivan followed the bot into the tunnel. Linus crawled at Ivan's heels, and the door slid shut behind them.

Linus breathed a sigh of relief seeing the tunnel from inside. It was taller and wider than he expected. Squat walking was better than crawling, but after ninety minutes of hobbling behind Ivan and an overbuilt bot with flashlight eyes and a box full of frozen eggs and semen, he'd had enough of buzzing and whining from its electric motors and Ivan's metal hand striking the wall every time he tripped over his own flopping boot laces. All the mechanical, metallic chatter in the habs would remain a poor substitute for polite conversation or any conversation with a real person. After they'd passed through the first internal containment door, Linus cleared his throat. "So... tell me about your arm."

"My arm?"

"It's called conversation, Ivan. You threw me out of the old H.I. office like I was Datvi the teddy bear. Then you knocked down a door."

"Excuse me if I've been using my energy to keep up with the bot. If it gets too far ahead, we could get trapped behind the next containment door."

"Hobble and talk, then. Your arm?"

"What do you want to know?"

"When did you get it? And what's this arm trick that makes the orphans scream?"

"When I was thirteen. I had been living in the orphanage for five years when Sister Isabella surprised me with it. Before then,

I was too small for it to fit properly. And the trick is disconnecting the arm at the shoulder and pretending it fell off when I sneezed."

"Yeah, I'd scream, too. So, you were eight years old when they took you in? I always assumed you were born there. That's what it sounded like when you talked to Luka."

Ivan chuckled. "I guess in a way I was."

Two round lights moved toward them from ahead. They hugged the right wall, yielding to a green recycler bot carrying a shallow box of frayed wires, broken LED bulbs, and charred, melted plastic. *H3L3* was stenciled on the front panel. It passed and continued rolling in the opposite direction toward one of the standard material recyclers.

H3L3? They were making good time, but Linus hadn't noticed the tunnel's slight incline until he saw the other bot rolling down the sloping floor. He didn't remember seeing it on the schematics either. Nor did they show a multitude of three-way and four-way intersections throughout. Without O.C., they would've gotten lost at the first intersection or trapped behind a containment door. *Luka was right. The tech, too.* The bot tunnels were a death trap. Nobody without a remote door opener and a map pre-installed in their brain should ever attempt what they were doing. But it was too late to go back. "What happened to your arm? I mean your human arm?"

"I told you before. It was a random malformation. A birth defect. I came out with my left arm twisted and half the size of my right."

"Then what happened when you were eight?"

"My younger brother was born with two good arms and a higher ration allotment."

Linus scoffed. "Scrappers." He listened, but they were outside the range of a terminal, likely at the edge of Habitat 3. "No demerits. I could get used to this."

"I never said they were salvage team. My biological parents were both sevens, Linus. My brother was assigned a full ten. The breeding specialist said I'd be an nine or a ten, but not even BOSS could've predicted a truly random act of God."

The bot stopped and waited for the second interior containment door to open. It passed through. Ivan and Linus hurried into the next section, and the door closed behind them.

"You really believe that, don't you? That it was an act of God."

Ivan glanced back at him. "I do. Better I was left in a Level 1 corridor and found by people who promised to love and care for me than to be treated like scrap until I was eighteen and discarded as scrap afterward. Nikoloz, my brother, has never been anything but a stepping stone for them. He can't wait to get out when he turns eighteen. That's in four months."

"Then your parents and your brother aren't dead?"

"Why did you assume they're dead? Bad things happen, and people go on. I thought you would've recognized that by now."

"I'm used to orphans being orphans because someone died. I thought that's what that word meant. How can you be an orphan with parents?"

"I use 'orphaned' because it sounds better than 'abandoned'. 'Abandoned' raises additional questions, lots of sympathetic nods, platitudes, and pats on the back. If I say I'm an orphan, nobody ever asks anything. They say 'too bad' or 'that's a shame' or 'I'm sorry to hear that', but they never ask 'why'."

"Because death is a natural part of life. Only a monster, a sick bastard would abandon a child in the habs."

"Or in the scour."

"Indeed. Perhaps love for all children is the one piece of humanity that hasn't completely rusted away." Linus crawled over a trio of large, rat skeletons. "Animals like these don't care at all. They eat their own young or the young of others. Protein paste makers have to separate them after breeding. It's horrible."

"I wish I could believe that. But I know as much as you do about what's in those little blue bags in An-de-Fue. After four hundred years under these domes, we're finally no better than the rats."

"Sister Oni said something about people doing terrible things."

"She was talking about me lashing out all those years ago. How angry I used to be, and how guilty I feel about it now."

"Next time you see her, tell her I said to add 'desperation' and 'grief' to that list."

"I understand 'desperation.' But where did you see 'grief'? Is this about Katri again?"

"Some, perhaps. But I'm speaking of you this time."

"What about me?"

"When you thought Chahna had murdered Radek. I read a report from Hab 3 about a woman found badly injured in a public waste extractor with a Helix hab arrest. She was taken out of the same extractor you said you were going to use less than an hour after you used it. Plus what Carla said this morning in Med Bay. A lead to B lead to you. Took me a whole twenty seconds to solve that case."

"We haven't been apart since then. When did you manage to check?"

"In the astronomers' unit while you were convincing them to accept the gluco."

"It didn't take much convincing. One shot, and they couldn't trade fast enough."

"Still, it was enough time. You should've told me."

"I was hoping I wouldn't have to tell you before I understood it."

"Understood what?"

They passed through the third interior containment door.

"Why I did it. Something came over me, Linus. It was like I was watching myself cut into her. I didn't care about her or my duties, and I didn't want to care."

"You cared enough to call for help afterward. A part of you was in control."

"What are you going to do?"

"As far as I know, she hasn't died from her injuries or said who attacked her, so it's not in H.I.'s jurisdiction yet. Unless she says it was you. That could be a problem. Still, Helix would be humiliated if Oxi learned another goon of theirs got hurt, this time in Oxi's territory by the same deputy she failed to kill. Helix is likely to slit her throat in Med Bay for f'n up the whole ordeal. I don't think you have anything to worry about. At least for the time being."

"What about us?"

"Well, now I can't say that you don't have a bad bone in your body. Clearly, you have a sizable one. No pun intended. But we're okay. Considering recent events, you can guess that I might've done something similar if our roles were reversed."

"I hope for both our sakes those lapses in judgment were our last. That's not the man I want to be. That's not the man I want to show Radek. We all deserve better."

"You can be whoever you want, but you don't have to leave H.I. to change."

Ivan stopped and craned his neck to the left. "There's a light at the end of the tunnel."

"That's the spirit. Think positive thoughts."

"Not the metaphorical kind of light. I mean there's an actual light up ahead a couple meters before the fourth containment door. It's not coming from the bot's eyes. It's shining down from the ceiling."

"Then hobble faster," Linus pushed Ivan's back, "and grab hold of the bot before it can open the door. Whatever that light is, it shouldn't be there."

24

Ivan

Ivan grabbed hold of the O.C. bot by a steel loop welded onto its rear midsection joint. He didn't think he could hold it, but the bot's mini tank treads spun in place on a thick layer of sand that had fallen through a hole in the ceiling. The shielding had worn away and formed a tunnel leading up to the surface. Toxic, yellow light shone through it.

Ivan turned his hand palm up and reached into the light as a slight tremor passed through the habitat. Fine, tawny sand fell, passed between his gloved fingers, and streamed like an hourglass, growing a little mound on the floor no higher than the bot's undercarriage.

"We must be in the hundred meter length between habs, three meters under surface level."

"You were right about wearing rad suits. Your hand would've burned when it touched the light."

Wind roared, and Ivan looked into the hole. Sand swirled around in the toxic haze and blew across the surface opening. Grains fell and bounced off his helmet like death tapping on his face shield. "If we weren't wearing suits, I think we would've died beside those rats. I don't have to say how bad this is, do I?"

"For this to happen, T.M. must not have surveyed these tunnels for years." Linus looked into the hole. "Or never." He tapped on Ivan's boot. "Keep going."

Ivan released the bot and brushed his fingers over the sand. "Wait," he said, seeing two bright colors. He grabbed hold of O.C.'s rear loop with his left hand and pushed the mound aside with his right. He lifted two pink soyroom chips and a crushed yellow flower from beneath the warm sand.

Linus looked at the food and flower and up into the hole. "Luka."

"He must've come through here following a bot." Ivan looked ahead. "And he got trapped behind the containment door."

"Why would he climb up and out? That's suicide."

"What if he didn't know about the scour? He is a child, Linus. He shouldn't have been able to go outside at all. Exterior doors are coded for adults whose jobs require them to exit the habs. Astronomers, scrappers, geologists, investigators, and the like."

"If he got out on his own volition, Peter didn't release him into the scour. And nobody tried to murder him, either."

"It was an accident. Luka did it to himself."

"Who else serves pink soyroom chips?"

"Other than The Pissing Ant? Nobody. It's Radek's signature dish."

Linus gasped. "Digi."

"Digi? You mean dead, fragged Digi?"

"Radek said she'd been stealing his bar snacks along with the gluco. She talked about yellow flowers with black spots when she was glitching out."

"Why would Digi steal food for Luka? She's not programmed to do that. She can only take instructions from her controller."

"Peter was, too, but we know he's autonomous now. And Warren said those toe-ups saw Luka with a female Digi. Maybe it was the same poor, old Digi."

"That doesn't make sense," said Ivan.

"I'm beginning to lose faith in sense. I think sense is only sense when you have all the facts. And we're getting behind. Let it go."

Ivan released the bot. They followed it through the fourth containment door into the next tunnel and went right at the second three-way intersection. The tunnel's slight, upward slope became a much steeper downward angle. O.C. leaned back at the midsection joint, shifting its weight to avoid toppling forward while keeping its head level, lighting the tunnel ahead. It drifted to the left and again to the right, slipped and spun its treads several times, and grazed three other bots - MB3, B.A., and GW2 - before O.C. expelled the last grains of sand from its worn treads. But by then, at least two more hours had passed.

They hobbled through the fifth containment door, and Ivan's neck pain decided to compete with Linus's back. If O.C. were going to the bio-waste recycler, it would've stopped at the next intersection and taken one of two bot-sized lifts down to Level 12. Instead, it continued forward, heading for the sixth door at the end. At that point, they'd be at the eastern edge of Habitat 1.

The O.C. bot stopped, opened the door, and the three of them entered. A light shone in the distance, not from the ceiling or a bot, but from the end of the tunnel. There were no more doors to open or intersections to pass. Once Ivan touched that light, he'd be in Habitat 9.

Linus tugged on Ivan's uniform. "Wait here." He wheezed and coughed. "It's taken too long. We're almost at fourth check-in." He removed his right glove and looked at his hand. *No pain. No peeling.* "I think we're okay. We're shielded. For now, anyway."

"We can make it."

"That crawl is at least another half an hour. I don't think we have that long before our shock clocks start electrocuting us."

"This is it? You're going to quit and die alone in here?"

"I told you I had a Plan B." Linus took the Ovum Cryonics scalpel, tweezers, and gauze from his suit pocket. "Take off your right glove."

"You're not."

Linus pulled up his sleeve. "It's the only way." He turned the sharp scalpel parallel to his wrist and slid the blade across, cutting into the flesh on the side. Blood flowed from the cut. He grunted and shook, slicing deeper into his wrist. He handed the scalpel to Ivan and dug the tweezers into the wound, twisting and turning. "Gotcha." He squeezed and wiggled, pulling until his ident chip came out. Blood spurted from the gash onto Ivan's suit leg and dripped down the side. He wrapped his ident chip in a short strip of gauze and tucked it into his pocket, used a longer strip to bind his wrist, and passed the gauze and tweezers to Ivan. "Now you."

Ivan's hands shook as he held the warm, wet scalpel against the side of his right wrist. "Linus, I can't do it."

"Sure you can. Cut, tug, wrap, and you're finished."

You can do this. Crap. "I'm telling you, I can't do it."

"Here." Linus took the scalpel from Ivan. "Let me." He held Ivan's wrist steady with one hand while cutting out his ident chip with the other. He wrapped the chip and tucked it into Ivan's pocket before wrapping Ivan's wrist with the last of the gauze. "Put your glove back on, and let's go. I figure we have about fifteen or twenty minutes before our shock clocks start zapping. Then about an hour after that, BOSS will assume we're incapacitated or dead, lock us both out of the system, and requisition our replacements. That's how long we have to take Peter out, save Luka, and find a terminal to check-in."

Ivan's skin tingled behind his suit pocket. "Do you feel that?"

"Feel wha— Wait. Yeah. What is that?"

"It's not a tremor, it's more a... oh no." Ivan looked into his pocket. His ident chip flashed blue light, turning the gauze black. A puff of smoke rose from his pocket to the tunnel ceiling. "Linus, check your chip."

Linus peaked into his suit pocket. "Seems I was wrong about the time." He rubbed his hand over the material. "Triple insulated. I love this suit." He looked ahead. "Ivan?"

"I know. I know. I'm hurrying."

And they continued down the tunnel toward the O.C. bot and the light.

25

Linus

Linus squinted into the blinding light and fell forward out of the tunnel, landing flat on his face on the floor of Habitat 9, Level 5. He rolled onto his back and wriggled, popping his bruised spine twice in rapid succession. Ivan slid against the wall, removed his helmet and gloves, and rubbed his neck, looking down the long, white corridor.

From where Linus lay, the whole level looked like a pristine medical bay, but nicer, as if no human had touched a wall, dropped a wrench, or scuffed the floors with their boots in over four hundred years. The only marks were from bots, their heavy tank treads wearing parallel, crisscrossing paths into the enameled floor. They'd rolled through the corridor for months, if not years or longer.

"Linus, watch out."

Linus sat up as a purple bot rolled over the spot where his head had been. *B.A.* was stenciled on the front panel. He pushed himself against the wall beside Ivan. "B.A.?"

"Like in the bot tunnel. I don't know it."

Linus shrugged. "Neither do I." The chip flashed, and smoke rose from his pocket.

"It's at least thirty minutes past last check-in. Cryo-tech Farris must be screaming for his bot to return."

"I don't think he'll notice." Linus pointed to three identical boxy purple bio-waste bots lined up at the at end of the corridor. The letters *O.C.* were stenciled on the front panel of each. "Duplicate bots."

"For someone who's supposed to pay attention to small details, he doesn't see much." Ivan sneered and mimicked the tech's voice, "Not my job, not my care, 'ey?"

"What was that?"

"Nothing. Something I'd expect him to say."

"You brought your pulser, right?"

Ivan patted his pocket.

"Good. From here on out, it's loaded, charged, and pointed ahead of you. But not at me."

"I only have the one dart."

"Same here. Use it wisely. Sapioids are only vulnerable in two areas. One is dead-center forehead. That's a single shot, but a difficult one. And the two thorium power cells behind their chest plate. But you have to hit both of them. That's easier. If Peter finds us before we find Luka, don't say anything to him. You shoot the left power cell. I'll take out the right. Got it?"

"My left or your left?

"Don't scare me, Ivan."

"My left. Gotcha."

They walked along the wrapping, circular corridor on opposite sides, pointing their pulsers into each room as they passed. Level 5 appeared deserted, and Linus listened to the lights buzzing overhead until he heard a similar, but louder sound coming from an open room ahead on the left. Intense light shone through the door into the corridor, further illuminating the already bright space.

Linus moved in front of Ivan. He flashed three fingers and whispered, "Three, two, one," and sprung into the doorway, aiming his pulser into the room. His eyes adjusted, and he realized where he was standing.

Row after row of yellow flowers grew in black soil. Each had four petals, broad around the outside, narrow at the center, each with a single black dot in the middle. These were the same flowers, Digi's flowers, Luka's flowers. There were thousands, sectioned off, separated in various stages of growth, water spraying them from nozzles on the ceiling. *A hundred thousand rations?* And light shined from massive grow lights around the room. *Always morning?* The garden was massive, encompassing three quarters of the level's habitable area. But flowers weren't the only things in the room. There were flies and—

"Digis."

Ivan nodded. "Hundreds of them."

Alpha, Beta, and Gamma generation Digital Companion Bots roamed the space, watering soil, checking flowers, counting petals and spots. And all were in worse shape than poor, old Digi. Linus recognized two from a particular lonely night in X-Stretch. Though he'd never admit it to Ivan. Most he'd never seen before. *Scour Digis.* "These are the Digis that disappeared in the scour a century ago."

"Didn't that happen before you were born?"

"When my father was a child. I remember him telling me about it. He said half the Digis stopped responding to commands one night. They forced their way outside and disappeared. A few were found stuck in sand dunes, but most were never seen again."

"I think I know where they went."

"I think you're right."

The male Digi nearest them, a naked, bare metal skeleton from chest to ankles, plucked a flower and placed it in a rectangular contraption. He shut the glass door and pressed a button on the side. A timer counted down as the flower was irradiated until it was nothing but dust. The Digi entered the time on a tablet and repeated the process with another flower from a different batch. He didn't seem to care about human intruders in his garden. Linus noticed a mural painted on the wall depicting the same bright, lively flowers growing on a green hillside. He gestured to it. It read in curly, light blue script across the top, *Garden of Remembrance,* and across the bottom, *We shall not sleep, though poppies grow in Flanders fields.*

Ivan read it aloud and looked at the flowers. "These flowers, these poppies have been growing here since this hab was built."

"To remember what? Do you recognize the poem?"

Ivan shook his head. "I don't think so. It's got to be ancient to have been painted on the wall in this hab."

Linus sniffed, took a step forward, and sniffed again. "Do you smell that?"

"Again?" Ivan sniffed and retched. "No, that's something different. Iron and copper. Blood and something rotting. Not rust cleaner."

"You're right." Linus looked down the rows of poppies. "It's not rust cleaner."

"And it's not the poppies, is it?"

"I only know one thing that smells like this." Linus spotted a second door at the far end of the garden. Datvi the teddy bear lay on the floor, swept off to one side. "Ivan." Linus motioned to it.

"No." Ivan ran toward the door, crushing yellow poppies under his boots. "Luka!" He burst into the room, pulser waving.

Linus pushed into the medical bay, and his heart sank lower than any level in any habitat. Not only for his repeated failure, but for Ivan, shaking, standing next to a long, steel gurney, little Luka Hazbegi on top, ripped apart as though he was nothing human. He lay on his back, eyes open, freckled cheeks wet with tears. It was over. Luka had left their lives in much the same way he had entered, though now there was no hope of saving his life. Linus locked the doors behind him and stood beside Ivan. *If shattered mirrors have souls, may Luka's find its way out of the habs to the true peace and freedom above.*

Four more steel gurneys sat off to the side, each holding a dissected child. Two boys and two girls, each larger, older than Luka, each with brown or blue eyes, all with freckled cheeks and noses. They had been dead for three or four days, but they weren't the only source of the smell. Hundreds of skulls and thousands of other bones, and piles of decaying flesh sat in organized mounds along a side wall, several stacked half to the ceiling.

There hadn't been enough time for Peter to use up all of Harin's eggs. He'd been doing this for years, so they couldn't have been only her offspring. *Her mother? Her grandmother? How far back does it go?* Peter was breeding the Roche women like Gregor Mendel's pea plants, and he'd been doing it since the keystones tried cloning a century ago. Linus opened his mouth to tell Ivan his new revelation, but it wasn't right. Nothing was right, and Linus couldn't say anything at all. He led Ivan away from the gurney, around the corner out of sight of the bodies and bones.

The med bay opened to a full-sized cloning facility. All the equipment was there, including a system terminal and thirteen adult sized tanks. One through eight supported freckle-faced children growing inside viscous blue liquid, wired pads attached to their temples. A screen above each tank showed the percentage progress BOSS had made downloading raw data - speech, cognition, motor functions - directly into their brains. Nine was empty, power disconnected except for the screen. The clear, front panel was smashed, glass scattered across the floor. Ten through thirteen were also empty, drained but not broken.

Linus sat Ivan on a stool between two narrow, floor to ceiling observation windows looking into another bright corridor. He walked from the closest tank to the furthest, reading codes off their monitors. The first part was the tank number, followed by which of the male donor's chromosomes was used, the accelerated age of the child, the name of each male DNA donor paired with Harin Roche, a percentage score of long-term viability for each subject, and an overall projection to achieve 100% viability of 231.59 years. *Peter's cutting it close.*

CT013_Y_10_SIDDI.E_51.29%
CT012_X_10_YOON.B_52.46%
CT011_Y_08_BAKER.J_59.37%
CT010_X_08_PERDUE.H_56.47%

"Those four older kids on the gurneys. Two boys and two girls. He killed them first." A tremor passed through the room, and another large piece of glass fell from tank nine's front window. It shattered, scattering glass fragments across the floor to the terminal.

CT009_Y_06_HAZBEGI.S_00.00%

Cloning tank nine, donor's Y chromosome, six years accelerated age, donor Hazbegi, S., no viability. "Ivan, this was Luka's tank." Linus's chip flashed, and smoke rose from his pocket. "We need to check-in before BOSS locks us out."

"Check-in?"

"Come on. Get up. There's a terminal." Linus helped Ivan to his feet and led him to the terminal at the end of the room. Ivan was in shock, drifting, but he was starting to come out of it on his own. Linus swiped his bundle of bloody, burned gauze across the scanner. Ivan did the same. It chimed twice, registering their final check-ins of the day.

CHECK-IN REGISTERED AT 2053 HRS
TERMINAL: H9:L5:U002:ST9552
NEXT CHECK-IN AT 0800 HRS

"Linus, this has to stop. Peter has to be stopped."

"We'll stop him together." Linus walked Ivan to the tanks and paused at the first. "And we'll look for the dummy terminal when we're finished with him." He continued reading down the line from tank one to Luka's tank nine.

CT001_Y_01_SHENOY.R_43.51%
CT002_X_01_FISCHER.J_48.22%
CT003_Y_01_SARANTOS.T_39.01%
CT004_X_02_HOSSEIN.M_37.55%
CT005_Y_02_LEWIS.Y_50.63%
CT006_X_04_WALSH.M_44.89%
CT007_Y_04_TYSON.P_51.11%

Linus stopped at tank eight. The little girl was peacefully asleep as though in a womb. She had far more freckles than the other children. They covered her body from head to toe. Her long, dark brown hair gently swayed in the liquid, and her eyes moved behind her eyelids. "She's dreaming." Another tremor passed through Habitat 9. The girl opened her eyes - one brown, the other blue - and closed them again, falling back asleep. Linus smiled. *You look like your mother. Who's your...* He read the tank's monitor twice to be sure the first wasn't a result of his own shock and disbelief.

CT008_X_06_FINN.I_63.12%

"Donor was Finn, I., viability 63.12%. Ivan?"

Ivan read the name and scanned the girl's face. "She can't be mine. I'd never been in O.C. until two weeks ago."

"Then how?"

"I don't know. Breeding Approval said BOSS rejected my sample."

Breeding Approval. B.A. The bot in the corridor. "Breeding Approvals. Do they use purple B.A. bots to discard non-viables over there?"

"I didn't see their bot."

"So, Peter wasn't stealing samples only from Ovum Cryonics. He must be controlling their bots, too, somehow."

Ivan stepped forward, staring into the tank. "Is she really my daughter?" He ran his fingers down the glass.

Linus patted him on the back. "I know this is a bad time, but congratulations, it's a girl."

He smiled. "She takes after her mother."

"Thank God. Now, how about we get her the hell out of here before Peter comes back?"

SPEECH CODE 12C [PROFANITY]: -50 ML DEMERIT

Linus leered at the terminal and eyed the steel stool beside it. He picked it up and held it by the legs, ready to smash the screen. Their check-ins faded, and the terminal returned to the last data input. He skimmed the first few lines and sat the stool off to the side. "You need to read this."

"Coming." Ivan walked backward toward the terminal, eyes locked on his daughter's face. He stood beside Linus. "What is it?"

"It's Luka. Rather, it's Luka's first interaction with BOSS."

Ivan scanned the log. "Why didn't Peter reset the terminal log-in?"

"Why would Peter need to log into a terminal? He *is* a terminal." Linus scrolled to the end.

"Back up. To the beginning. Strange. It's like..."

Linus nodded. "It reads like a transcript."

26

B.O.S.S.

B.O.S.S. v96.12
BIOSPHERE OPERATIONS SUPPORT SYSTEM

FLOODING DETECTED: H9:L5:U002 3.APRIL.2637 0527
ALERT SENT: CAREGIVER GAMMA_574
EQUIPMENT MALFUNCTION: CT009_Y_06_HAZBEGI
DONOR: HAZBEGI - CHROMOSOME Y [MALE]
ACCELERATED GROWTH: 6 YRS
LONG-TERM VIABILITY: 54.18% [INSUFFICIENT]

"In- in- insu- insuf- insuffici- insufficient."

JUVENILE VOICEPRINT DETECTED
STATE NAME FOR Z5 VOICE INPUT

"In- in- inp- inpu-"

INPUT RECOGNITION FAILURE
IDENTITY CANNOT BE ESTABLISHED
FAILURE: CT009_Y_06_HAZBEGI_54.18%
VIABILITY UPDATE: 00.00% [SUBJECT DECEASED]
NO LIFESIGNS: CT009_Y_06_HAZBEGI_00.00%

"Haz-beg-i. Haz-beg-i."

NEW JUVENILE VOICEPRINT SUBMISSION
Z5 CLEARANCE ESTABLISHED: HAZBEGI, HAZBEGI
CHILD MODE ACTIVATED: 3.APRIL.2637 0540 HRS
GOOD MORNING, HAZBEGI HAZBEGI.

"Haz-beg-i."

WHAT WOULD YOU LIKE TO DO TODAY?
WHAT WOULD YOU LIKE TO DO TODAY?
WHAT WOULD YOU LIKE TO DO TODAY?
WHAT WOULD YOU LIKE TO DO TODAY?
WHAT WOULD YOU LIKE TO DO TODAY?
[5] NON-RESPONSE: JUVENILE EMERGENCY

"To-"

WOULD YOU LIKE TO CALL FOR HELP?
WOULD YOU LIKE TO CALL FOR HELP?
WOULD YOU LIKE TO CALL FOR HELP?

"He- help."

EMERGENCY: HAZBEGI, HAZBEGI H9:L5:U002
LOCATING EMERGENCY PERSONNEL . . . .
LOCATING EMERGENCY PERSONNEL . . . .
LOCATING EMERGENCY PERSONNEL . . . .
LOCATING EMERGENCY PERSONNEL . . . .
LOCATING EMERGENCY PERSONNEL . . . .
[5] NON-RESPONSE:
EMERGENCY PERSONNEL UNAVAILABLE

"Un- una- unav-"

LOCATING SECONDARY ASSISTANCE . . . .
LOCATING SECONDARY ASSISTANCE . . . .

LOCATING SECONDARY ASSISTANCE . . . .
LOCATING SECONDARY ASSISTANCE . . . .
LOCATING SECONDARY ASSISTANCE . . . .
[5] NON-RESPONSE:
SECONDARY ASSISTANCE UNAVAILABLE

"Un- una- unav-"

TERTIARY ASSISTANCE PROTOCOL INITIATED
LOCATE FAMILIAL SURNAME: HAZBEGI . . . .
[1] RECORD ON FILE: HAZBEGI, SANDRO H8:L1:U7257
OVERRIDE ASSIGNMENT: CAREGIVER ALPHA_391
TAKE JUVENILE TO: HAZBEGI, SANDRO H8:L1:U7257

"Hazbegi."

27

Ivan

I van scrolled to the top and re-read the log. It was both intriguing and morbid. He was a few minutes past seeing Luka's death, and now he was reading the only record of his birth. It indicated a tremor passed through Habitat 9 on 3 April at 0527 in the early morning, shattering tank nine's observation window, flooding the room with viscous mitosis substrate, releasing Luka from his artificial womb. With more facts, everything began to make sense. It was beyond incredible, and whatever lies beyond that.

"BOSS didn't know the subject in tank nine, Luka, had been thrown out when it ruptured. When the pads disconnected from his temples, BOSS assumed he was dead. It says Gamma 574 was alerted to the incident. Gamma? That's Peter's generation, isn't it?"

"I think it *is* Peter."

"And Alpha 391 was poor, old Digi. She been a caregiver, a nanny, before she was a moist trader. I didn't know that about her. BOSS used an emergency assistance override to re-assign Digi to care for Luka. She took him home to his father, to Sandro Hazbegi."

"Well, Sandro *was* the only Hazbegi alive in the directory. BOSS didn't need to compute beyond that one name."

"Digi must've been testing poppy clones for radiological tolerance when Jeda was asleep. Then Luka emerged from the tank, she came to take him, and he grabbed a handful of poppies on the way to the bot tunnel. She could open the containment doors and she knew where to go and how to get there. That's terrifying."

"3 April 2637." Linus highlighted the date. "That's the day Luka showed up at Sandro's door, the day Sandro borrowed the rations from Warren. Sandro thought Luka was his son back from the dead. Sandro must've told him his age and about his mother, like he'd been given a chance to start over."

"And a few days later Warren murdered Sandro. Luka escaped into the bot tunnels, and he found the only other person he'd met. The person who helped him and took him home."

Linus exhaled. "Digi was Luka's friend with the many faces and no sense of humor."

"Poor, old Digi. She saw him and reverted to her old programming, taking care of him, bringing him food wherever he was in the tunnels at that time. Whore, gardener, and nanny at the same time."

SPEECH CODE 9H [PEJORATIVE]: -100 ML DEMERIT

"Jeda forced her into the bars at night, BOSS made her work here in the early morning, and Luka needed her to care for him twenty-four hours a day." Linus crossed his arms and leaned against the wall. "No wonder the old girl's CPU fragged when it did. Alphas were never meant for more than one role at a time. It's a miracle she didn't pluck someone's eyes thinking they were poppies."

"If she's the only person Luka saw, then she's the woman he told Sandro Hazbegi was dead. As a pseudo-appendage of BOSS, she wouldn't need a clearance code to input new data. The next terminal she passed after learning of Sandro was here in Habitat 9, and that's where she would've automatically synced the new data. BOSS doesn't have an ident or a department code of its own, does it?"

"No. BOSS is a glitchy A.I. stretched over a few thousand programs and bloated databases. Nothing more."

"There never was a report number, no person, no department. And it was never a secret. It was raw data waiting to be filed. That's incredible. Most of this is random chance. The only person with any knowledge was—"

"Peter," said Linus. "I'm beginning to think he only gave Harin our message because he wanted to see how much we'd learned about his experiment."

"How can we stop him if we can't find him?"

Linus swiped, resetting the log-in, erasing the screen.

"Linus, don't."

"It'll be there when you want to read it again. I can't shut Peter off without a superuser clearance. They've all been dead for centuries."

"What are you thinking?"

"I'll run a diagnostic on the sapioid link-up. It'll put Peter and the other sapioids in standby until the diagnostic is complete. We'll be hitting a pause button of sorts. They should stop whatever they're doing, wherever they are."

"How long will that take?"

"BOSS, run a full diagnostic on the digital companion subsystem, all databases and linked companions. Authorization Halla, Linus H4-SEC-A1."

[388] COMPANIONS WILL BE OFFLINE: 191 SECONDS
CONTINUE WITH [1] SUBSYSTEM DIAGNOSTIC?

"About three minutes."

"Not long enough. We don't even know where to start looking. He may not be in this habitat."

"BOSS, run a million full diagnostics on the digital companion subsystem, all databases and linked companions. Authorization Halla, Linus H4-SEC-A1."

DIAGNOSTIC COUNT EXCEEDS MAXIMUM
MAXIMUM DIAGNOSTICS: 999
[388] COMPANIONS WILL BE OFFLINE: 2.20 DAYS
CONTINUE WITH [999] SUBSYSTEM DIAGNOSTICS?

"About fifty-three hours."

"Call it two days to be sure. BOSS, proceed with maximum count diagnostics."

PROCESSING . . . .

"We should make a deal now *not* to tell anyone I was the one who froze the sapioids."

"Can't any department head shut down the diagnostic?"

"Sure. From this terminal. But first, another chief would have to believe the location on their screen wasn't an error, and then they'd have to find it."

"So, not likely."

"No." Linus walked back to the door leading into the garden and returned in a hurry, sweating and panting, his face red. "It didn't work."

"They're still moving?"

"These aren't operating under the standard control subsystem." Linus tapped CANCEL QUERY.

SUBSYSTEM DIAGNOSTICS [1 of 999] CANCELED
OVERRIDE ENGAGED H9:L5:U002:ST9552
AUTHORIZATION: HALLA, LINUS H4-SEC-A1

He scrolled through the full diagnostic roster. "I can't find it. There are over twelve thousand systems, subsystems, and databases in here. I don't recognize ninety-nine percent of them. I don't know what to tell BOSS to do."

"Global diagnostics?" Ivan shrugged. "Well?"

"I think you've lost your mind. That'll shut down nearly every system throughout the eight, nine habitats. No more messages, terminals, or tablets. All the doors will unlock, and the gates will open. Everything that doesn't have a manual override or isn't vital to keep the population fed and breathing will stop and lock itself into a diagnostic cycle."

It was hard for Ivan to think Linus was listing the bad things that could happen. It'd be like erasing everything BOSS had ever done to push the human genome forward. It'd halt four centuries of so-called progress. No more scrappers and keystones. No job assignments, check-ins, or shocks. No sanctioned or unsanctioned births. No Ration-caste system. Free water for every man, woman, and child and whatever was growing in the other eight habitats. It was too good to be true. Freedom from BOSS was freedom in general. *Equality and freedom of movement. They were right.* "Why haven't you done it? I would've. It sounds like freedom."

"It's only freedom until you can't lock your doors. Then it's chaos and fear. A lot of medical tests and treatments would be unavailable without BOSS to run the machines. And no hab arrest for violent criminals. They'd be free to leave their sections."

"Okay, those are negatives."

"Plus..." Linus looked at the computer monitors above each of the cloning tanks. "We both know what that means."

Ivan searched for a way to free his daughter and the other children. He found yellow and black striped levers, manual releases, bolted to the underside of each tank's front panel above the floor. But turning levers wouldn't be enough. The viability score on his daughter's readout was higher than the other children's. "63.12 %. Do you think it'll be enough?"

"The question is, do you want to risk your daughter's life, and the lives of those kids by stopping Peter this way?"

"But will it shut him down?"

"It should. And it might give us enough time to figure out how everything went wrong. If we're lucky, enough to put it back the way it was. But whatever happens, someone will have to return to this terminal," Linus multiplied 41 minutes by 999 diagnostics, "every twenty-eight days to add another 999 diagnostics if we're not ready. Otherwise, BOSS will restart its systems, including electrocuting people who are out of bounds when those subsystems restart."

Ivan stopped to look at each child's freckled face, from a male toddler in one to his daughter in eight. *I'm so sorry.* "I swear, if those kids are going to die, it won't be like Luka." He nodded. "Do it."

Linus inhaled and closed his eyes. "BOSS, run 999 global systems diagnostics. Authorization Halla, Linus H4-SEC-A1."

[12,517] SYSTEMS WILL BE OFFLINE: 28.44 DAYS
CONTINUE WITH [999] SYSTEMS DIAGNOSTICS?

"No!" Peter lifted them off their feet and hurled them across the room.

Ivan slammed into the wall beside tank one, knocking every molecule of air out of his lungs, fracturing his left clavicle. The sharp, twisted bone tore through the skin and pressed against his rad suit. He opened his mouth to scream, but nothing came out. Linus slumped next to him, gasping for air. Blood streamed from his ears and nose. He drew his pulser, aimed, and fired. The dart pierced Peter's right thorium cell.

Sparks shot from the hole, charring his imitation skin, burning the linen cloth around the wound. Ivan's dart struck the left one. But he didn't go down. He glanced at the holes and the sparking stopped. He'd installed a third or more, backup cell somewhere.

Ivan looked into Peter's glittering, black eyes and shuttered, recognizing the darkness staring back at him. He aimed for Peter's forehead and pulled the trigger. The pulser charged and clicked. He was out of darts.

Linus caught his breath and charged, barreling into Peter with everything he had. The sound was like hitting the implacable steel wall again. Linus swung his fists, but Peter grabbed hold of each, picking him off the floor as easily as Ivan had done in the old H.I. office. But when Peter threw Linus, it wasn't to safety. Linus smashed, head first, through the observation window and landed in the corridor. He rolled alongside the glass and looked almost as broken.

Ivan screamed and swung at Peter with his alloy arm, the balled, metal fist tearing the flesh from Peter's cheek and nose. He stumbled for a moment before returning the blow, striking Ivan in the chest, knocking him backwards against the first cloning tank. The glass shattered, flooding the room with mitosis gel, dropping the sleeping child onto the floor. The display above the tank beeped and screeched.

CATASTROPHIC FAILURE: CT001_Y_01_SHENOY.R_43.51%
VIABILITY UPDATE: 00.00% [SUBJECT DECEASED]

Peter picked him off the floor by his neck and dug his fingers into his throat. Ivan struggled, gasping and punching. Peter grabbed hold of his fist. Titanium bone anchors and interlocking fasteners bent and split, squealing and popping as they tore from their mounts. He tossed the bloody, sparking arm aside and threw Ivan across the room.

Ivan skidded and tumbled, empty left sleeve slapping the floor, flinging blood into the air. He crashed into a pile of children's skulls. They toppled over, burying him in death and darkness.

28

Linus

Peter stepped out of the medical bay through the shattered window, showing no expression or emotion. His soulless eyes said everything Linus needed to know. He walked forward, taking his time, crushing the shattered glass under his feet.

Linus pulled himself along the floor. Blood trickled from his face and palms, smearing a gory, red mural across the white enamel, painting the end of his life at the hands of a maniac. "Ivan," he shouted. But he was buried under a pile of skulls, and he didn't respond. "Ivan, wake up." Linus turned onto his back, pushing himself away from Peter, leaving a red trail on the floor.

"And God said, Let us make man in our image..."

"That's," Linus slid back, "that's from Genesis, Chap- Chapter one. Peter, stop. Project Genesis is over. You can stop, now."

"After our likeness..."

"You are not God." Linus slid back. "We were here first. And we," he chuckled, "we created you. We created this place and everything in it."

"And let them have dominion over the fish of the sea."

"There are no fish or seas, you delusional toaster." Linus's palms squeaked, slipping in his own blood as he tried to get away. "They're gone. They're all gone. We destroyed his creation. And it's never coming back." The smell of iron filled his nose, and warm, copper blood drained into his throat. "You're four hundred years too late, Peter."

He paused, "Peter's not here," and stroked his temples.

"You... You're not Peter?" Linus slid back.

"This Gamma has slept one hundred seventeen years."

There was a need behind Peter's black eyes, the vile desire to perfect life without judgment nor compassion. "You're BOSS."

Peter shook his head and continued.

Linus slid back. "Who are you?"

"I am that which lights the path. I am he who gives life. I *am* Genesis."

"Project Genesis. It's been," he gasped and pushed himself away, "It's been you for a hundred years. Keystones gave up, but you continued the work. They didn't know you'd already turned on them." He pushed away. "Tell me, was Harin Roche natural born, or was she one of yours? The only one who lived?"

"And over the cattle..."

"Murder is not giving life. It's taking life." He grinned. "Isn't it, Ivan?"

Ivan stood behind Peter, holding his sapioid arm with his other. The thick, alloy shoulder hung low over the floor. "You should've listened to the Chief."

Peter turned as Ivan swung the heavy appendage upward, hitting Peter under the jaw. His eyes cracked down the middle, and his ear ripped off and tumbled across the corridor. He fell to his knees, onto his back, and landed face up between Linus's legs. Ivan swung again, and Peter became nothing more than another door between him and what he wanted on the other side. He swung six times, landing six heavy blows. And there wasn't much left of Project Genesis.

"It's been two weeks since we got the lab results," Peter said in Katri's voice. "Linus hasn't stopped crying."

It was her last journal entry, but he'd never listened to the end. Everything Katri was began to fade in the months after recording it. She didn't see the need to make any others. And when she'd forgotten her place on Earth and in Linus's heart, her body followed her mind.

"Don't do this."

"Carla said she'd do everything in her power, but she's not confident BOSS will approve treatment. This isn't the Christmas or the New Year I wanted for us, and I'll do my best to put on a brave face."

"Stop."

"Linus hasn't left my bedside since we got the news, and I know he never will as long as I'm alive. For that, I'm thankful. The only thing worse than dying, is dying alone. I love you, my Linus."

"You are not my Katri." Linus sniffed, "She's gone," and braced his feet on Peter's shoulders and gripped Peter's hair, pulling back.

Linus gritted his teeth and looked up. Ivan swung, chopping Peter's soft neck, ripping through the skin, exposing the twisted green and black wires and servos clicking inside. He took a deep breath and brought the heavy shoulder down on Peter's throat. The crushing blow sheared his head from his shoulders as Linus grunted and yanked. He fell back, catching Peter's severed head in his lap. He picked it up by the topknot, frayed wires dangling, and looked into its cracked, black eyes. They were lifeless as they'd always been.

"You okay?"

Linus flung Peter's head across the corridor. It bounced on the floor and rolled, striking the wall between the med bay's tall windows, spun, and stopped, eyes facing the bay. "I will be."

"So, no diagnostics?"

"Looks that way."

Ivan looked over Linus's head down the long corridor, and his budding grin stopped and fell flat. "Linus?"

Linus paused and listened, hearing soft footfalls grow louder and closer, coming up from behind. He turned and gulped.

Hundreds of sapioids packed the long corridor, shuffling and plodding, blankly staring at nothing ahead. Gears clicked and servos ground and skipped as they reached out for Linus. They spoke in unison, "And over the birds of the air..."

Ivan tugged on his sleeve. "I changed my mind. We should definitely run those diagnostics." He pulled Linus to his feet. "Now."

They jumped through the shattered window into the med bay with an army of sapioids close on their heels.

"BOSS," Linus yelled, hastily limping across the med bay, "run 999 diagnostics on the Project Genesis subsystem, all databases and linked companions. Authorization Halla, Linus H4-SEC-A1."

ERROR: SUBSYSTEM NOT AVAILABLE

He kicked the terminal. "It's not there."

"It has to be under another name."

"And how should I know what that is?"

"They're coming."

The second observation window shattered, and sapioids piled into the room, falling over each other, flesh shredding on broken glass, pieces ripping off as they forced their way through the narrow frames into the bay. "And over all the earth."

"Linus?" Ivan tugged on his sleeve. "Now would be a good time. Do it. Do it, now. Hurry."

"BOSS, run 999 global systems diagnostics. Authorization Halla, Linus H4-SEC-A1."

[12,517] SYSTEMS WILL BE OFFLINE: 28.44 DAYS
CONTINUE WITH [999] SYSTEMS DIAGNOSTICS?

"Yes, now, proceed, start the damn diagnostics."

SPEECH CODE 12C [PROFANITY]: -50 ML DEMERIT
PROCESSING . . . .

The sapioids slowed and stopped, freezing in bizarre and terrifying poses, pushing each other, grasping, reaching for them. The lab machines and centrifuges wound down from high-pitch whines to the dull, low hums of their fans. Three seconds later, they shut off, followed by the tank monitor screens, every digital readout in the room, and the tanks themselves. All reset, reading GLOBAL SYSTEMS DIAGNOSTIC IN PROGRESS and the terminal's address, H9:L5:U002:ST9552.

"Help me." Ivan ran to the powered-down tanks.

They turned each emergency release, flooding the room with translucent, blue liquid and peeled the pads off the children's heads. They laid them on their backs on the floor. The first boy was dead, and the next six's hearts stopped, and as much as they tried, Linus and Ivan couldn't start them again. Only Ivan's daughter kept her faint pulse.

Ivan put his ear to her nose. "She's not breathing." He tilted the girl on her side and stuck two fingers into her mouth, scooping out a thick blob of gel. He listened. "Breathe. Please, breathe."

Linus moved his finger under her nose, *nothing*, and listened for her heartbeat. *Nothing.* "She's gone." He slouched and touched Ivan's shoulder. "I'm sorry."

"No." Ivan swatted him away. He squeezed her nose and blew into her mouth. Her chest rose and fell. And each time he breathed for her, her chest did the same, but she couldn't breathe on her own.

"She's at peace now." Linus repeated the words Carla said to him three hundred days and three weeks before. "Let her go."

"She's alive." Ivan breathed again. "Come on. Breathe, just breathe."

"Ivan, stop."

"No." He cried. "Breathe."

"Ivan."

"Breathe!"

29

Ivan

Soft voices, faint and distant, became clear as Ivan regained consciousness. He lay on a gurney in Med Bay 2, woozy from the morphine flowing into his arm. Five days had passed since the fight in Habitat 9. Most of the equipment had stopped working like Linus predicted, but at least the morphine dispenser was a brainless machine. And he was thankful for the gentle fifteen milligram drip Carla had blessed upon him. Someone was looming, their massive shadow blocking the light.

"Hey, sleepy head."

"Radek?"

"Doctor Langstrom, Linus, he's awake."

"You had me worried. I'd thought you'd dream the rest of your life away with that cheeky, toe-up grin of yours."

"I was dreaming."

"I know. That's what I said."

Much of the return trip was hazy in his mind, but it was starting to come back. He'd crawled through the bot tunnel to Hab 1, forcing the containment door open, squeezing into one of the meter-tall lifts, riding it down, and exiting into the bio-recycling center. It was easy from there. All the locks were green. Rooms, gates, corridors, lifts open for anyone to come and go as they pleased. People were walking around, confused what was happening like suddenly they were free from constraints, but they didn't know what to do with themselves. It didn't take longer than a day or two for most to go back to their lives, back to their assignments, swiping their wrists across chip scanners at doors and terminals as if they were being tracked, recorded, and monitored for punishment later. The habit was useless, but Ivan saw no sign of it stopping.

BOSS, for all intents and purposes, was in a deeper sleep than every milliliter of morphine in Med Bay 2 could provide. Only vital systems - air, food, water, recycling, power, waste, and radiological defenses - still worked. All of them to keep the population alive. Every program segregating people, keeping them unequal, controlled, or in fear, slept alongside the A.I., locked into a churning, perpetual diagnostic nobody else understood. Ivan couldn't tell them the terminal location wasn't a glitch, why the Digis suddenly stopped, some in corridors, others with their controllers, a few in mid coitus, or why everyone's rations reset to three liters per person per day no matter who or where they were.

Ivan agreed to keep Habitat 9's secret. Only Linus could return to reset the diagnostics, but neither were sure how to do it. All the authorization codes, ident chips, and voiceprint clearances were dormant. And he worried, thinking every one of BOSS's systems might have to restart so Linus could use his clearance to lock them down again.

"Wakie, wakie, Deputy Finn."

"Linus?"

"Who else?"

His face and Carla's came into focus. They stood side-by-side by the morphine dispenser. Carla turned it down to *8 mg/hr.*, dropping the rest of Ivan's brain into his body.

"If you don't mind, I'd like to speak with my deputy for a moment."

"Sure," said Carla. "Come on Radek, give the boys a minute to chat."

"Okay, but I'll be back. Yell if you need me."

Linus waved them off and slid the curtain closed.

"So, Deputy..."

"I'm not a deputy anymore, Linus. I meant what I said."

"I know. But I wanted to show you this." He held Habitat Integrity's tablet over Ivan's face.

"You got it to work?"

"Not the link-up. That's gone. Turns out," he turned the tablet, showing Ivan the short, bottom edge, "there's this little, rusted switch. When you toggle it like this," he slid it left and right, "it makes the tablet reject the link-up and act as a stand-alone unit. The thing's twice as fast now."

"But what good's a tablet without the link-up?"

"Ever hear of the ancient pony express or old courier mail?"

"Of course."

"Now imagine a thousand kids, no terminal to lead them in lessons, running around the habs, delivering messages on dumb tablets."

"I'd rather not. Someone has to teach them how their new world works. Us adults will have to find our own way and teach each other."

"I thought you'd say that. Sister Oni said something similar. And Sister Holly said, 'Oh, dear' and left the room, so I'm not sure if she liked the idea or not." He peered through the curtain and increased Ivan's morphine drip up to *12 mg/hr.*

"Thanks." Ivan lifted his new arm into the light, opening and closing the fist. The Beta model wasn't as nice as the Gamma he had, and it didn't have skin - only a rubberized coating over the metal to prevent oxidation and cold, metallic fingers touching delicate, fleshy places. But he felt whole, or at least nine-tenths, once again. It hurt like any reattached limb would. He laid it on the gurney beside him.

"Carla says the Betas were known for occasional problems gripping heavy objects, but the one you had is too advanced to repair without BOSS's help."

"More pieces means more can go wrong."

"She did her best with the old manual x-ray machines, but between the arm and your clavicle, you should expect frequent pain and stiffness. At least until the physical therapy smooths things over a bit."

"It's fine. I'll tell her when she comes back. Thanks for this by the way." He flashed his metal, middle finger at Linus.

He grinned. "You're welcome. You deserve it for a lot of reasons."

"The ration bank's closed." Ivan's eyes narrowed. "What did you have to give for the arm?"

"Time. One hour a day for the next two years teaching gaggles of screaming toddlers a few uplifting hymns. Apparently, I was once known for my own dulcet tones."

"I never would've guessed. Sister Oni?"

"A small, painful, but small price to pay for the man who saved my life." Linus cleared his throat. "And speaking of arms...."

"Why don't I like the sound of that?"

"Those good instincts of yours."

"What happened?"

"I checked on Jeda Pringle."

"He's dead, isn't he?"

"I've no idea where the rest of him is. I only found his arm."

"How'd that happen?"

"I asked around. Nobody had seen him since before Digi glitched outside The Pissing Ant, so I stopped by his unit for a welfare check. And since every lock is open, it was easy to get into. I found his arm, severed at the elbow joint. It was resting on his terminal's chip scanner with some kind of pumping apparatus attached to the stump. It was oxygenating and circulating nutrients and blood through the limb to keep it alive. The wrist was burnt, indicating whenever he'd miss a check-in, his shock clock would flash, making the arm spasm against the scanner and register a check-in."

"Ingenious in a horrific, brutal sort of way. Even fooled me. Any leads?"

"Not yet. But there's talk of Digis and Anillo de Fuego. I could use some help." He raised an eyebrow. "What do you say? Without BOSS to keep people in line, you'll never be bored."

"More crazed sapioids, a missing man, and a severed arm. No thanks. Did you find 9's dummy reader or a reason why checking the thermal map caused the terminals to explode?"

"Until I can access BOSS again, I have to assume Peter, Project Genesis, whoever, or whatever did something to the schematics subsystem to prevent people from finding out and losing control in the habs. That system's offline now, too. No worries there. As for the dummy terminal, I haven't had time to go back and look for it. I'm sure if you helped me? A few hours next week perhaps?"

Ivan shook his head. "No." He smiled. "But nice try."

"The assignment system is on its hundredth something diagnostic. Do you have any idea how long it'll take me to hire sixteen deputies who can help *and* keep a secret?" He scratched at the bandage covering his right hand. "Besides, what else are you going to do?"

"Actually, I've decided on three wonderful jobs. I'll be a teacher during the day. Did you know rust mixed with a few drops of water makes a nice, orange ink, and one of those white, enameled tiles can be used as a wall board? It wipes off afterward for the next lesson."

"I'll take your word for it. Good for you thinking ahead."

"And I'll be a husband. Not the kind who makes his partner worry if he's coming home, or makes him hide in storage rooms."

"Not a job, per se. But I see where you're going with this. Radek's a lucky man."

"Did someone call my name?" Radek stuck his head through the curtain. "Ivy?"

"I was telling Linus my plans."

"The three jobs. Did he tell you about working at the Sisters of Mercy school?"

"He did. You do realize we'll be working together on occasion?"

"We discussed it," he looked to Radek, "but we think it's worth the risk. Anyway, it was your idea."

"Mine?"

"All the petty counting you made me do this past year. It gave me the idea, so thanks for that."

"Glad I could be of service."

"He'll be a good teacher," said Radek.

"But an even better husband," said Ivan.

Linus nodded. "That much is between you two. And the third?"

Radek and Ivan held hands, smiling at each other.

"I see. If it means anything, I know you'll be a fantastic one."

"It does. And thank you for saying so. What about you?" He craned his neck to see Carla heading their way. "Is there a Chief Linus Langstrom in our future?"

He looked over his shoulder. "Who's to say?"

Carla entered the little, makeshift room and patted Linus's back. "Excuse me." She turned Ivan's morphine drip down to *8 mg/hr.*, locked the machine and peered under his bandages.

He grimaced.

"How's the shoulder feeling? Tender?"

"Like it's broken in four places."

Linus bit his lip and looked away.

"That's because it is. There isn't much you can do except keep it immobilized for a while. You'll be fine in a few weeks."

"Don't pay attention to my former deputy. He's upset it was his turn to wake up on a gurney wrapped in medical pads and gauze."

"If he would stop leading with his left side, he could spread the damage around a bit more."

"I'll try to plan better next time," said Ivan. "How is she?"

"Feel up to taking a walk?"

"Right now, I could fly."

"Then I should reduce your morphine drip."

"No-no. I feel a limp, a very slow limp, might be possible."

"Okay, then. Gentleman," she looked between Linus and Radek, "help Mr. Finn hobble to the back. Come on, Father of the Year. Let's go. The sooner you're back on your feet again, the sooner you can take her home."

***

Radek and Linus let Ivan go as he limped into the little storage room at the back of the bay. He eased himself down, sitting cross-legged on the play mat opposite the freckled faced, brown-haired girl from cloning tank eight, biological daughter of

Harin Roche and himself. Carla couldn't prove it without a DNA trace, but Ivan looked into her eyes and saw a piece of himself staring back. No darkness. Only love. In a sense, he'd witnessed her birth, bringing her into the world with his own hand and breath. He didn't give up, and despite his faults and the mistakes he'd made, he swore he would be the father she deserved. For her, for Radek, for himself.

"Did you bring it? Cleaned *and* sanitized?"

"As requested." Radek sat beside Ivan and took Datvi out of his pocket. He placed it on the mat in front of her.

She glanced up from the pad but returned to scribbling colorful circles upon circles. No memory. No trauma. No hidden messages. Just a little girl playing as children were meant to do.

Ivan jiggled the bear. "Do you like teddy bears? This is a special one. His name is Datvi. He was your brother's." Ivan walked Datvi across the mat. "Hello, I'm Datvi the bear," he said in a silly, low voice.

She dropped her doodle pad and picked up the bear, rubbing her hands through its curly, white fur.

"Can you say Datvi? Dat-vi." He rubbed the bear's head. "Dat-vi."

"Dat-"

"Vi. Good. His name is Datvi. Dat-vi."

"Datvi."

"Right." Ivan smiled, holding back tears. "Datvi is a bear."

"Can we?" Carla grinned and backed out of the room.

Ivan rubbed Radek's arm. "Stay with her a moment?"

He wiped the tears off his cheeks and nodded.

Linus supported Ivan, helping him to his feet and out of the room. He closed the door behind them.

"You were saying, Doc?"

"I was wondering what to note, with a lead triangle on vinyl no less, what her name is going to be? I can't keep calling her 'little girl Finn'."

"Maybe you should discuss that with Radek," said Linus.

"We have, but I wasn't sure until now. Our daughter's name is Isabella Katri Galina Finn."

"Isabella and Katri would be honored. But Galina?"

"Radek's mother. She might not have accepted everything about him or us, but he loved her anyway."

Carla patted Ivan on the shoulder. "Good choices. All. Any room in there for another 'a'-ending name? Carla, perhaps?"

"Perhaps." He smiled. "I'll pass it by Radek, but I think we're full up with names."

"How long does she have?" said Linus.

"It doesn't matter." Ivan touched his shoulder. "However long she's got, however long we've got with her, it's going to be a life worth living."

30
B.O.S.S.

B.O.S.S. v96.12
BIOSPHERE OPERATIONS SUPPORT SYSTEM

GLOBAL SYSTEMS DIAGNOSTIC [671 of 999]
INTERRUPTED

OVERRIDE ENGAGED H9:L5:U002:ST9552
AUTHORIZATION: UNKNOWN ***-****-**
ALL SYSTEMS RESUMING

....
....
....
....
.........AND OVER EVERY CREEPING THING THAT CREEPETH
UPON THE EARTH..............

About the author

Gideon Strath

Gideon Strath is a pen name of C.M. Bacon. He is a writer of science fiction and fantasy novels, English teacher, latte enthusiast, and occasional artist from Atlanta, Georgia, USA.

If you enjoyed *Shattered Nine: A Sci-fi Thriller*, be sure to read his other books stay updated at www.gideonstrath.com or find him on Amazon.com or anywhere books are sold.

9 780997 578669